I0732272

Transit
Lounge

Transit Lounge

JCL Purchase

Press

Published by 99% Press,
an imprint of Lasavia Publishing Ltd.
Auckland, New Zealand
www.lasaviapublishing.com

Copyright © JCL Purchase, 2022
Cover Image: *In the Midst of Life*, Copyright © Keith Morant 2022
Author photo: Marc Herbulot
Design: Daniela Gast

This book is copyright. Apart from any fair dealing for the purpose of
private study, research, criticism or reviews, as permitted under the Copyright Act, no part may be reproduced by any process
without the permission of the publishers.

ISBN: 978-1-99-116054-6

This book is dedicated to the misfits and mavericks,

moon dancers and crazy fakers,

star gazers and troublemakers,

dream chasers,

has-beens and no-hopers,

the go-for-brokers,

the desolation rowers,

the hooked-for-good lifers,

the riddle decipherers.

This book is dedicated to you.

Life is lived in the in-between
In transit
Between coming and going
Between staying and moving on
Between here and there

—   Wayne Visser, *Life in Transit*

Life is what happens to you while you're busy making other plans.

— John Lennon, *Beautiful Boy (Darling Boy)*

Time does not give one much leeway: it thrusts us forward from behind, blows us through the narrow tunnel of the present into the future. But space is broad, teeming with possibilities, positions, intersections, passages, detours, U-turns, dead-ends, one-way streets. Too many possibilities, indeed.

— Susan Sontag, *Under the Sign of Saturn: Essays*

The anti-myths of gravity and of belonging bear the same name: flight. *Migration, n., moving, for instance in flight or in transit, from one place to another.* To fly and to flee: both are ways of seeking freedom.

—   Salman Rushdie, *Home*

Contents

Love Me Tender

When Elmore arrived at the stage entrance of the Classic Supper Club at precisely six o'clock of an evening, Charlie, the elegantly attired doorman/security guard, would hold the door wide for him, ushering him inside with a bow. The two men would exchange a few hurried pleasantries, before Elmore disappeared down the maze of dark corridors comprising the rear of house.

Elmore liked to acknowledge what he called 'the little people' who managed his life by giving them the time of day. He needed to pause on the threshold anyway, to allow his eyes to adjust to the gloom. Stopping to chat provided a moment for El to brace himself between his two separate lives — private and public — before making his way to his dressing room to prepare for his show. Charlie basked in the brief attention Elmore bestowed on him; one of the perks of his job was being personally acquainted with the stars who performed at the Classic.

Elmore's private life was a different matter; something he kept somewhat under wraps. An aging cross-dresser, he lived at the top of Queen Street in an expensive apartment which was hardly big enough to swing a cat in, near K Road where he frequented gay bars and nightclubs in the wee hours. He had spent his early childhood in this part of the city, so it was 'home'. He needed to mount shows on a fairly regular basis to fund his profligate lifestyle, even though he often wished he could afford to give up being a performance artist. Having a public persona is not all it's cracked up to be, and certainly not as glamorous as some might think. Especially when you're getting on in years.

But appearing in the odd show satisfied public demand, for which Elmore was grateful, considering his age. He felt an obligation to his fans. He believed it the duty of those in the arts and entertainment industries in a country like New Zealand, where the pool of talent was large but audiences were small, to remind one's fans, regularly, they hadn't been forgotten — that you still appreciated them, that you were still willing and able to deliver the goods.

When Elmore reached his dressing room, his preparations for that night's show began in earnest. He was always in a state of high panic before a performance, dreading the long hours in hair and makeup followed by the demands of the show itself, after which he'd still have to get through the posturing, petty small talk and late-night socialising required by various high-profile visitors, sycophants, faux friends and the press, which his fame demanded. Routine was the antidote to his nervous agitation. Routine helped him *manage*.

As he hit the ancient light switches just inside the door, the dungeon-like room sprang to life, capturing his reflection in the light-bulb-surrounded mirror which dominated the far wall. When El caught a glimpse of himself in it, he knew the show would go on. If only *he* could go on. He'd ask his reflection whether he was up to it, whether he could still cut the mustard. Through long habit his eyes would fall on the black-and-white, ornately-framed photograph of his dear mother standing in pride of place on the bench, and he'd remind himself that this aspect of his life was non-negotiable. He did what he did for *her*.

He sighed, resigning himself to his situation, and locked the door behind him. He didn't appreciate being interrupted while he was psyching himself up for the show. He threw his bag on the couch, hung his jacket behind the door, and started working one by one through his list of ritual preparations.

First, he made himself a plunger of fresh Arabica coffee. Mum had said life was too short to drink bad coffee. She'd also said life was too short to stuff a mushroom — a contradiction, in the sense that both activities required careful preparation. *Why*, he often wondered, *is one worth doing and the other not?* He'd gradually come to understand, however, that his mother's wisdom was unquestionable. Mushrooms are a delight to eat on their own; there is no need to stuff them. Whereas cheap coffee is not only undrinkable; when acquainted with the real thing, it's unthinkable.

When his brew was ready he'd pour it into a large mug, stir in four teaspoons of sugar, and take a few large swigs. Then he'd prepare two lines of coke on the magnifying hand mirror on the dressing table, snorting them with a twenty dollar note. As his synapses fired, his state of panic and feelings of inadequacy would increase exponentially, relative to the sight in his reflection of the coarse hairs sprouting from his nasal cavities, the silver regrowth at his parting, and the unruly grey gristle that threatened to overpopulate his sideburns. *Thank God for tweezers and stage make-up*, he thought.

During the next fifteen minutes or so, while he savoured his coffee, he would recite various long-practised positive affirmations, subjecting himself to some gung-ho self-talk. Then he'd mentally run through his song list, and check his gear and props were in order.

At six thirty, Jane — his dresser and make-up artist — arrived. He knew her knock; they had a secret code. Elmore called her Sweet Jane because she did what was required to a high standard, doubled as his drug dealer, and kept her mouth shut. Elmore wasn't in the best of health. The middle-aged spread that hugged his hips and girth necessitated a full-torso girdle, elasticised trousers, extra width in the design of his jacket, and Diabetes 2 medication to boot. At five ten he was above average height in the world of men, but too short to convincingly play the icon he did, so he needed to wear built up shoes.

According to the show's director, for the purposes of verisimilitude , compensatory measures were absolutely necessary. Elmore never argued with a show director. He didn't want to get a reputation for being difficult to work with.

Then there was the large fake penis he needed to wear strapped to his inner thigh. Sweet Jane was always so gracious when she secured it, and when he was fully dressed and made up, ready to go on stage, she always said, "You are soooo like him, El! You're his living image!" She would top off the fake adoration with a vote-of-confidence kiss on the cheek, then push him in the direction of the stage door where she'd stand beside him in the wings, patting his nose with a powder puff. "You're gonna rock their socks tonight, Mr Elvis Presley!" she'd gush, beaming at him until they heard the MC introducing him and the audience beginning to scream and applaud — his cue to walk onstage into the limelight of the golden era of The Elvis Impersonator. In the mid-80s, Elmore was the best — in fact, the only one — in all of New Zealand.

Up until that moment, El always doubted himself, wondering whether he could pull it off again, wishing he could give it all up, wave a magic wand and become anonymous, retire up the coast to a small nondescript town where he could live an openly gay life and gradually fade away into old age. But when he heard the band playing the inimitable opening bars of *Love Me Tender*, a resurgence of dedication to the task overcame him, coupled by a renewed sense of pride in what he did so well.

Borne forth on the fringed glory of white bellbottoms and the faux glitter of royal-coloured rhinestones, embodying the aura of raunchy sex appeal and genuine ingenuousness of the performer he admired and revered above all others, he'd launch himself onto the stage in a strikingly accurate imitation of Elvis the Pelvis — tummy pulled in, shoulders squared, a big cheesy grin plastered across his face, with his crowning glory — a glossy Brylcreemed wig of thick blue-black hair — shining under the spots. He'd gyrate up to the microphone, run his hand through the lock of sharply angled fringe that had fallen across his forehead, and start lip-synching the song, bellbottoms flapping, hips swaying, arms reaching out, in supplication, to the audience.

Everyone, even the critics, said the way he moved was so *authentic*.

Throughout his performance, the thought of his dear mother sustained him. She was the person who had originally initiated Elmore in the art of artifice, when he'd been a young boy. From her, he had learned how to fabricate his appearance using costume and make-up and props, how to truly inhabit the character he was portraying, how to *embody* the role. She had been a master of the art; she, whose almond-shaped electric-green eyes had provided a consummate canvas for the curvy black Mary Quant eyeliner she wore along her lash line; she, whose curvaceous feminine form had been the faultless model for a tight-fitting faux-leopard-skin mini-skirt topped with a wet-look burnt-orange blouse that clung to and swung from the perfect cones of her pointy breasts; she, whose strawberry-blonde big hair, teased bouffant-style into an upswept chignon, reminded Elmore of candyfloss; she, whose immaculately smooth, super-long, Coppertone-tanned legs stretched up to heaven inside her plastic white thigh-high boots.

Elmore often reminisced about his early childhood in the seedy one-bedroom flat he and Mum had lived in on K Road. At night, after his mother had bathed, dressed, styled her hair and made herself up, she'd settle Elmore under a crocheted rug on the couch in front of their box-set TV, with a bottle of Coke and bowl of popcorn for company. Then she'd leave for work, returning very late. Her job must have been super important because when she got home — her hair tousled and her makeup smudged and her clothing askew — as soon as she'd donned her dressing-gown, she'd remove from her handbag a large wad of notes with the Queen's head on them and store them in neat stacks, secured by elastic bands, in a shoe box under the bed, together with her savings book.

When Mum and Elmore went down town to run errands, he watched, enthralled, as she counted the notes out, one by one, over the counter of the Southern Cross Savings Bank. The bank teller would re-count them, confirm the amount with a pinched look on her face, and record the figure in the correct column in the savings book which she would ceremoniously stamp and sign, then push rudely back across the counter. Elmore's mother didn't seem to mind, smiling graciously at the teller as she said, "Thank you, Ma'am." But as they walked away, she'd mutter under her breath, "Beware the Green-eyed Monster, Miss Prim and Proper," always making Elmore laugh.

Later, when they were sitting eating ice cream sundaes with all the other toffs at Smith and Caughey's Tea Rooms, she told Elmore that one day soon she'd have enough money saved to buy them tickets to travel on a jet plane — a jet plane! — across the Pacific Ocean to Memphis — *Memphis* in the U.S. of A! To be reunited with the incredibly famous man who was, she often reminded Elmore, his very own father. "Then that sour bank teller will have something worth writing home about, my boy," she'd say.

Some of Elmore's earliest memories were of sitting with Mum in front of her dressing table in the evenings, watching her in the mirror as she applied her make-up and helping her match the colours of her eyeshadow and lipstick to her outfit. Then, while she held a scarf up to her face, he was given the special task of applying hairspray to her back-combed Jackie Onassis flick-ups or her up-swept French roll, depending on her whim that day. Mum had also taught him how to paint her nails, praising his steady hand and neat strokes.

But his most important job was placing her 45s on the turntable of the battery-powered Philips record player she'd bought at Farmers Trading Company, and playing them for her again and again while she got ready to go out. She was batty for Elvis and listened to no one else. More than once, she told Elmore they'd had a bit of a fling back in the day and she knew Elvis was as crazy about her as she was about him. As far as Mum was concerned, Elvis was the King of Hearts. Let alone of music.

El wasn't surprised to discover years later that it was all fair dinkum. He'd been flicking through a Rolling Stone magazine in a dentist's waiting room somewhere in the States and had come across an Elvis interview. One of the questions Elvis was asked was whether he'd really slept with hundreds of different women. The journalist reported Elvis as saying, "Course I have. They're all different, you know! I even had a girlfriend from New Zealand once..."

One Christmas holiday, Elmore and his mum attended a summer picnic at Victoria Park. El's mum had taken some time off and they'd been on a few outings, to the zoo and on the ferry to the beach at Devonport. At the picnic in the park that day there were lots of people wearing strange get-ups — flares, tie-dyes, psychedelic shirts and colourful kaftans, leather sandals and platform shoes, with beads around their necks and flowers in their hair — and lots of different music was playing, songs which would later come to symbolise the era. Elmore's mum told him it was the Age of Aquarius and that Flower Power was the new politics. People were gyrating in the sunshine to the music with arms spread wide, smoking sweet-smelling cigarettes and swigging sherry from flagons.

The 'cigarette' smoke made Elmore feel dizzy and dreamy and he lay down on the picnic rug. While he dozed with his head in Mum's lap, he overheard her telling her friends how, before Elmore was born, she'd travelled to Hawaii as a hostess on a cruise ship, and later worked as an exotic dancer at the Flamingo Club in Las Vegas. After Elvis' shows at the International, he used to visit the Flamingo with an entourage of hangers-on, and he'd invited El's mum back to his hotel suite to party on. They had'd a really good thing going until Priscilla found out. A couple of Elvis' security heavies eventually dragged Mum to the airport and put her on a flight back to New Zealand. "I didn't realise it at the time," she said to her friends, "but I left the USA with a very special gift from Elvis," she said, pointing at El.

That afternoon a large crowd assembled along Fanshawe Street, and as the motorcade of visiting US Vice President Spiro Agnew drove past, they screamed abuse and threw flour bombs, paint, and eggs at his retinue, in protest over the Vietnam War. Elmore felt ripples of change eddying through his life, sensing it was beginning to extend beyond the confines of the small flat in K Road where he spent so much time alone. He was due to start school in the new year and that, in itself, would be a whole new experience.

Big changes did come, but not in the way he'd anticipated. One day, there was a knock on the door, and a man in a police uniform and a woman with a clipboard stood there, alongside the landlord. The landlord was telling them that Elmore's mother hadn't been home for a few days and the rent was overdue. He needed to get rid of the kid so he could rent the flat out to another tenant; he wasn't running a charity organisation, was he? Elmore stood there in shock while the policeman told the landlord they would be investigating his mother's disappearance as there'd been a spate of prostitute killings in the neighbourhood. The landlord replied it wasn't his fault if the woman was dead.

Dead. Elmore knew what the word meant. Once when his mum had been late getting back and his little budgie, Blue Peter, had been squawking nonstop because the bird seed had run out, El had grabbed the meat mallet he'd seen his mother using to tenderise steak and had hit the budgie with it over and over again, until it was finally quiet, so he could carry on watching TV undisturbed.

The social worker told Elmore to stop gabbling on and on about a dead budgie and to gather his personal effects, clothes, and whatnot. The policeman told him to get a move-on because he was a busy man with places to go and people to meet. Elmore did what he was told. He'd seen policemen doing some scary things to people on K Road from the flat's window. And he'd never seen such an ugly, cross-eyed woman before. She scared him silly.

While the policeman was smoking outside in the hallway and the social worker was visiting the bathroom, no doubt helping herself to some of his mum's expensive toiletries, Elmore emptied the contents of her dressing table into a toilet bag and packed it in his suitcase. He also grabbed an LP from her stack of records — *Elvis Presley* — and stored it carefully between his clothing. Most of Elvis' signature songs were on it: 'Blue Suede Shoes', 'Tutti Frutti', 'Blue Moon', 'Money Honey' — the tunes and lyrics that had been imprinted onto El's brain since babyhood, as had every inflection and nuance of Elvis' voice and singing style. Elmore discovered years later that the LP had been the first ever pop album to go gold on the US charts and was a treasured collector's item. He was glad he'd kept it; that he still had it in fact. He would never let it go.

Elmore also raided the shoe box and stuffed the savings book and stack of bank notes inside a jumper in his suitcase. Later, he discovered the savings book was in his name, which was a blessing. Lastly, he grabbed his mother's PYE Pockette transistor radio which he kept tuned to her favourite station for years afterwards. Radio 1 played all the pop tunes, meaning that El's knowledge of Elvis' discography continued to grow as each of his successive releases hit the charts.

Throughout Elmore's years in foster care, these precious memorabilia comforted him. Whenever he was able to manage a few private moments, when the other boys were at rugby practice (he was deemed too sickly to play) and his foster mother was next door drinking afternoon 'tea' (she always returned with watery eyes and would become overly affectionate, pressing him to her bosom and sometimes almost smothering him), he'd unpack his secret hoard and lay the treasured items across his bed. His mum's presence still lingered on in these precious keepsakes — the indents of her dainty fingerprints on the slab of cake foundation, the taste of her lips on the bright orange and dusky pink lipsticks, the almond curve of her eyes on the false eyelashes fanned out alongside each other in their little case, the moody colours and shimmering silvers and golds of her eye-shadow palette. Most precious, though, were the scent of her skin on her powder puff and the smell of her clothes in the little vial of Worth Eau-de-Cologne he often dabbed on his neck, wrists and ankles, like she had done. Until one day he discovered the bottle was empty.

His heart broke as he realised that he'd soon lose the scent of his mother for ever.

At around this time, Elmore started removing his foster mother's underwear from the laundry basket and trying it on when she was out of the house. Her bras and knickers were huge and discoloured from years of use; cheap discount store underwear as opposed to his mother's quality imported smalls. The pieces hung shapelessly from his underdeveloped body, yet he vaguely associated the experience with his mum, imagining her slender arms were wrapped around him, instead of his foster mother's huge hams accompanied by her foul gin breath.

One afternoon he got carried away and lost track of time. When his foster brothers returned home and burst into their shared bedroom, they caught him red-handed. It was the first time he'd ever heard the words, "poofter", "gaybo" and "sicko". His foster mother gave him a hiding and tipped all his mother's make-up into the bin, telling him he needed to stop playing with girly things. After this humiliating incident, he resolved to make his way to Memphis as soon as he could. And if Mum didn't turn up, he decided he'd just go on his own.

When, as a young adult, he finally made it to the States, Mum's savings having made the journey possible, he discovered in the wake of his death, Elvis impersonators were in high demand. His incredible singing voice and knowledge of Elvis' repertoire, combined with his strong family resemblance and innate talent for imitating the King earned him lots of attention. He travelled across the country taking part in Elvis Impersonation competitions, often winning large amounts of cash. Soon, he acquired all the gear he needed to polish his act: Stetsons and pointed snakeskin boots; sparkling white stretch-Lurex suits with hipster bells, sequin-adorned boleros and form-fitting tasselled jackets, red silk shirts, stud-encrusted belts that could handle a couple of heavy-duty holsters. And lots of bling.

Elmore returned to New Zealand when Elvis nostalgia was taking hold here. He brought the allure of the States back with him and was quickly able to establish his reputation, with shows that were huge sell-outs, promoted by billboards which read:

FORGET JOHN ROWLES - ELMORE IS THE REAL DEAL.

One night, when Elmore was gyrating his way through his repertoire at the Classic, lip-synching all those *uber*-famous songs (his voice had given out after years and years of performing), swinging those tassels, taming that signature quiff with his bejewelled hand, dropping his knee into Elvis' signature Catherine-wheel leg-circling movement (OUCH!) — the one which showed off the penis appendage to maximum advantage — a strange thing happened as the show was drawing to a close.

The audience was shouting, "Encore! Encore!" and Elmore decided to do *Love Me Tender* once more. It had always been his mother's favourite; he would never forget the way her face shone and her eyes glistened when he played it for her. The audience were on their feet and pressing forward towards the footlights when Elmore noticed an attractive older woman in the front row, blowing kisses and swirling a multi-coloured feather boa through the air. A long string of faux pearls hung around her neck, similar to one El's mother used to wear. Something about the tilt of her head, the set of her mouth, and the style of her hair and clothing were instantly recognisable. And there was that signature flick of the wrist, with those long, painted nails.

Suddenly, the woman collapsed to the floor, hidden from view by the bodies swaying around her. Elmore dropped the mic and leapt from the stage, pressing through the crush of people. When he reached the spot where the woman lay in a heap, he knelt down and lifted her head into his lap. Her false eyelashes parted in slow motion and she gazed up into his face and lifted a frail, cool hand to his cheek. Her lips moved and he leaned in closer, straining to hear what she was saying over the piped musical accompaniment.

"You were magnificent, my boy," she whispered. "Elvis would have been so proud."

Then Charlie was by his side, telling El an ambulance had been called and encouraging him to return to the stage. Sweet Jane also appeared and patted Elmore's nose with a powder puff while offering motivational talk. "Show's almost over, El!" she said. "And I've left you a little pick-me-up in your dressing-room!"

As Charlie pushed through the throng, guiding Elmore up the side stairs and back on to the stage, Elmore asked him if he'd heard what the woman had said.

"Silly old bat," Charlie said. "Don't take any notice."

"But what did she say, Charlie?"

"Something like, 'If life was fair, my boy, Elvis would still be alive.' Don't take it to heart, El. She's just a bloody cougar!"

Charlie pushed Elmore up the stairs but El kept looking back, trying to catch another glimpse of the old bird. When he tripped over the top step and fell to his hands and knees in the footlights, a hush travelled across the theatre. As the acoustic introduction of *Love me Tender* started up again, a solitary mirror ball turned slowly above him, reflecting a spray of rainbow-coloured lights. Elmore clambered to his feet, picked up the mic, and reinserted it into its stand. As the song's opening bars were coming to an end, he prepared to start lip-syncing and tipped the mic stand sideways, striking a classic Elvis pose as he did so — legs spread, arms wide, head cocked, his signature quiff flicked forward and shining blue-black under the spots. It was at this precise moment he felt the penis appendage abruptly parting company with his inner thigh and slipping down his trouser leg until it plopped out onto the stage floor.

The audience had thankfully turned away, distracted by the arrival of a group of paramedics bearing a stretcher, and some of the punters were already making their way towards the exits, to avoid the crush after the encore. El managed a choreographed bow while simultaneously swiping the lost prop into the wings with his foot, as if he was dispatching an unwelcome inner-city rodent that had dared cross the stage during the show. Then he started walking slowly backwards, into the shadows upstage centre.

"I do what I do for you, Mum," he whispered, as he slipped between the curtains and into the backstage area. "I wouldn't have it any other way."

Gone to Ground

Carolyn felt elated as she left the movie theatre and walked out into the bright afternoon. When the film she'd been to see had reached its totally unpredictable climax, relief had flooded through her and tears had flowed. On the fiftieth anniversary of their murders, Quentin Tarantino had given Sharon Tate and her unborn baby boy their lives back.

Now, the solace of retribution shone on her cheeks and twinkled in her eyes as she made her way to a café nearby for coffee and cake. She felt as if the cynicism and wretchedness she'd carried within herself for the longest time had drained from her like dirty dishwater down the plughole, leaving behind a pile of glistening squeaky-clean dishes drying on a spotless kitchen bench, sunshine streaming through an open window.

It had been fifty years of collective horror. Fifty years of inquiry down every bifurcation where meaning diverged. If the shocking events of the Manson murders could have been logically understood and a feasible rationalisation mooted, people would have been able to unravel the riddles surrounding the case and could have placed the heinous events in context. They would have been able to fit them into the accepted body of knowledge and could have boxed up the inexplicable horror and filed it away in the archives, putting it to rest.

Yet conjecture about the Manson gang and their monstrous actions had devolved into further questions, answers to which had proved elusive and fleeting, hidden perhaps just around the next corner — like the nameless creature of myth and legend who, with beckoning finger, entices the uninitiated deeper into the forbidden forest, only to disappear like a will-o'-the-wisp into the ether between the trees or down a dark tunnel, leaving the seeker irretrievably lost and hopelessly confused, about to be confronted by their deepest fears.

Until now. Until Tarantino's revisioning of the event in his new movie, *Once Upon a Time in Hollywood.*

The film's closing aerial shot stayed with Carolyn for a long time, pervading her thoughts and growing within her like blood spreads through water, diluting the intensity of the bleed. Filmed from the azure sky above Cielo Drive in Beverley Hills, a heavily pregnant Sharon Tate strides out of the front door of her house and into the lemon sunlight of a brilliant summer's day, then makes her way down the drive, arms swinging at her sides, her blonde tresses lifting in the breeze, walking without a care into her future and that of her unborn child.

In the weeks that followed, Carolyn began to wear a permanent smile and her once habitually hunched shoulders softened as wrinkles disappeared from her face. She felt as if she, personally, held the key to the vast underground vault where the details of the Manson murders had been kept hidden all these years; that she was party to their rediscovery and reinterpretation. Tarantino's revisioning of the outcome had made the truth malleable and elastic and open-ended; the awful facts of the historic event were no longer set in stone. As a result, it seemd as if the possibilities of Carolyn's life, of every life, had opened up.

"You seem so changed, dear!" friends teased. "Have you met someone? Or won the Lotto?" Wink. Wink. What her friends didn't say was that Caro's beaming face and positive demeanour suited her better than the angry scowl, rigid posture, and impatient bark for which she had formerly been well known.

Carolyn answered their queries by gushing about the film, as if a torrent of emotion had been unleashed in her and the dam of her heart had burst. "Oh, it's so clever, so moving. Tarantino has accomplished possibly the greatest feat of postmodern filmmaking! He's created a perfect fictive moment which radically alters the awful reality of those senseless murders, superseding the actual historic event by returning…"

"Oooh, spoiler alert," her friends interrupted, "Don't give anything away! We haven't seen it yet."

Carolyn's gush turned to a trickle. To others, the movie was simply a commodity, a vicarious entertainment experience they could purchase when they felt like a bit of 21st century escapism. They didn't appreciate the magnitude of what Carolyn wanted to share with them. But how could they? They had not lived Caro's life.

In 1969, when news of the Manson murders originally hit the airwaves, Carolyn had been a gangly thirteen year old, pimply-faced and knock-kneed, stranded in that awful ugly-duckling interstice between childhood and adulthood. She'd gleaned the gruesome facts of the case through the filter of adults speaking in low voices with expressions of shock and horror etched across their faces. While the media picked over the gory details of the case like a clan of hyena over a kill, speculating on cults, drug use, sexual licentiousness, hippie communes, Flower Power and other aberrations, the Ventura County Police's investigation ran into months of dead ends and red herrings. First, they aimed a spotlight on Sharon Tate and her husband Roman Polanski's bohemian lifestyle, conjecturing endlessly about motives and motivations, and who they had crossed, or who had double-crossed them. When those enquiries led to nothing, they cast the net wider.

Six months after the murders, when sensational scenes of Manson's arrest appeared on TV screens, the public were further outraged. Aside from widespread incredulity at his gnomic, soft-spoken appearance, people were shocked by the revelation that his gang of accomplices consisted mostly of females. Young women. Mostly teenagers.

Caro hovered like a shade, spellbound and riveted, in the corridors of her family home, her neck craned and an ear angled towards the lounge doorway, as her mother and friends sipped vodka tonics and munched through a tray of cubed cheese, pickled onion and pineapple skewers, discussing how young women cheapened themselves by wearing revealing clothing and sleeping around. In the den next door, her father and his cronies played darts and dunked cocktail sausages into tomato sauce while they knocked back Bacardi and Coke, slipping mysterious phrases into their conversations as slickly as they dropped ice cubes into their glasses: *dirty hippies, kinky sickos, hallucinogenics, sex orgies.*

"Go and play, Carolyn," her mother had said, waving her daughter away with a manicured hand. "What about making some clothes for your Barbie dolls? The basket is full of remnants now we've finished sewing your summer wardrobe."

"I'm too old to play with dolls, Mum," Carolyn mumbled indignantly, blushing to the tips of her fingers and toes because all the adults were now staring at her.

"Oh, nonsense," her mother retorted. "Playing with dolls teaches a young lady how to dress and behave. I played with mine till I got married! Just get out of my hair and make yourself scarce, for God's sakes. Find something *constructive* to do and stop hanging around like a gormless waif."

When Caro returned to her bedroom, bored stiff with waiting to grow up, she tried inserting balled-up socks into her training bra to see what she'd look like with real breasts. They looked lumpy and lopsided — false — so she gave up and flopped onto her bed, pulling a forbidden *Seventeen* magazine from its hiding place beneath her pillow. After much nagging on Carolyn's part, her older cousin, Molly, had swopped it for a 45 of *In the Year 2525* that Caro had nicked from her parents' record collection.

She flicked through the magazine, slowing down when she came to the Mary Quant makeup advertisements. If only her mother would buy her a tube of black eyeliner. But until she managed to persuade the witch she *was* old enough to wear it (which probably wasn't going to be anytime soon) she could at least learn how to apply it by memorising the step-by-step diagrams. She also studied the latest Vidal Sassoon hairstyles from Carnaby Street. Carolyn would have given anything to have her straight dark hair cut into a sleek angular bob with a back-combed crown like Cilla Black's, but her mother insisted she wear it in a ponytail which her nasty little brother pulled at every opportunity.

Carolyn turned to the latest band news, thrilled to discover the magazine's centrefold that month was a black-and-white poster-sized portrait of her idol, Paul McCartney. Imagining him leaning in for a kiss, she zoomed the magazine towards her face, but the experience soured when she got a whiff of the chemical-rich printer's ink. Then she remembered that Paul had married that year and was now off the market, so what was the use? She turned the page. Here the more hip, less clean-cut Rolling Stones posed, in garish super-saturated colours, against a seedy urban backdrop. Poring over the photo spread, Caro analysed their cocky poses and way-out gear until her eyes landed on the huge bulge in the crotch of Mick Jagger's tight-fitting jeans. Flushing red hot, she quickly closed the magazine and shoved it back under the pillow.

Her collection of Barbie dolls was lined up on a shelf above her bed and she looked at them now thinking she really ought to get rid of them — throw them out, or pack them away. She liked to do things to rile her mother; it was *so* gratifying. It suddenly occurred to her that Disco Barbie was almost the splitting image of Sharon Tate. She grabbed the doll from the shelf and examined her closely, noting the resemblances. Carolyn's mother had left her Queen magazine lying around and Caro had sneak peeked a look through it. Sharon Tate had been featured in a series of glamour shots, and she'd appeared in a Coppertone advert, reclining in a bikini on a surfboard held aloft by a bevy of muscly bronzed men, who'd been lined up on either side of the board like pallbearers.

Disco Barbie had the same curvy figure as Sharon did: cone-shaped, pointy breasts, a tiny, indented waist, and long legs that seemed to go on forever, ending in perfectly arched feet, moulded to fit high-heeled shoes. The last time Carolyn had played with the dolls she'd dressed Disco Barbie in a Lurex bikini and teased her mane-like blonde tresses into a tousled bedroom-hair look held in place by a rainbow-coloured headband, and she'd dressed Ken in surf shorts and sunglasses and slung a towel over his shoulder, pretending the couple were attending a pool party in Beverley Hills.

Carolyn remembered now how Sharon Tate had been wearing a bikini nightgown — whatever that was — when she'd been murdered. The adults had tittered about this, but Caro found out there'd been a heat wave in Los Angeles at the time of the murders. She remembered, too, how her mother had complained about the heat the summer she'd been pregnant with Carolyn's little brother, saying, "I'd give anything to be able to walk around in my swimming costume all day long!" Her mother hadn't, of course. Perhaps this was what made all the difference.

The Year of the Manson Murders was forever etched on Carolyn's mind. She obsessed endlessly about what had happened, wondering whether you had to be a sexy blonde movie star to get stabbed and murdered in L.A. Or anywhere else for that matter. Whether drugs, sex and rock music were the common denominator. Whether it was perhaps safer to be a plain, buck-toothed, flat-chested nobody, like herself, in order to escape such a notorious and brutal fate.

She decided she *would* sew Disco Barbie a new wardrobe. She'd make miniature versions of the same outfits her mother had made for her that summer: a denim pinafore, a floral knee-length high-waisted frock with a frilly collar, mid-calf-length bike pants and a boat necked top. No miniskirts, no boob tubes, no bikinis. And she'd ensure Disco Barbie's luscious long blonde hair was always scraped back into a demure ponytail. No more untamed long tresses. No more 'blonde bombshell'. No more 'bed hair'.

Disco Barbie's name had formerly been 'Jeanette'. When the doll's new wardrobe was complete, Carolyn renamed her 'Sharon'. 'Sharon Tate'.

Fast forward a few years. Carolyn was seventeen and engaged and getting married in the spring. She'd packed up her Barbie dolls, their clothes and furniture, and passed them on to the little girls next door. Murray was an insurance salesman, a junior at her father's firm. He was, her father assured her, a decent bloke with good prospects. If it weren't for the pastel-coloured safari suits he wore with plaid socks and white loafers, and the thick, black-rimmed Buddy Holly glasses he spent his life peering through, he might almost have resembled Ken Barbie. He was the exact opposite, however, of the handsome film director and widower Roman Polanski, who wore Renaissance lace shirts and velvet suits and blow-dried his hair into bangs to frame his androgynous visage. Murray also couldn't have been less like the dirty hippie, Charles Manson, with his diminutive build, psycho face, and unruly hair and beard. Murray was tall, clean cut, and fuller in stature. And the bulge in Carolyn's husband's trousers was totally unremarkable; he wore his trousers loose. Caro felt safe with that, inviolable. She was a *good* girl, after all.

A decade and more passed interminably by. She scrubbed the mint-green Formica bench tops in her kitchen several times a day until they lost their spearmint shine. She cooked TV dinners of meat and two veg until the meals began to taste like space food. And every night at 9.30pm on the dot, she'd climb into bed in her ankle-length winceyette nightie and lie very still, legs spread, while Murray did his darndest to impregnate her.

When he eventually figured out what to do, she had three children in quick succession. She sewed their wardrobes and knitted their pullovers and wetted their cowlicks into place. She sent them to Sunday school and made sure they learned the Creation Story and the Ten Commandments. She helped them with their homework and signed them up to Scouts and Guides and allocated them lists of household chores to help build their characters. She monitored what they watched on TV and listened to on the radio, and screened their friends and acquaintances, noting in her diary where they went, what they did, and with whom. If she sensed anything untoward, she stepped in immediately and put a stop to it. There would be no sex and drugs and rock and roll in her home.

But her husband had a cruel streak. And when he slapped Carolyn or pushed her or punched her, when he threw her on the bed and raped her, she knew it wasn't because she was beautiful and sexy and clever and rich like Sharon Tate, but because she was stupid, lazy and frumpish, had never learned how to properly apply black eyeliner, and had never had the kind of figure that justified wearing an itsy-bitsy, shiny-shiny, purple-wet-look, Lurex bikini. She knew this because her husband had told her so.

He told her so, so very often, that after a while, she began to believe him.

When, in her early thirties, Carolyn and Murray divorced, Caro reinvented herself. She attended university as an adult student, got a master's degree, and forged a career as a psychotherapist at a large teaching hospital. There, she met Allan, a junior colleague twenty years younger than her. The two became inseparable, and the part of Caro's psyche that had lain dormant since the summer of '69 was aroused, like a sleeping giant, from decades of slumber. Soon, she realised she *was* sexy, she *was* alluring, she had 'it', after all. She felt vibrant and alive for the first time in her life, every cell in her body on high alert, tingling with anticipation and exhilaration.

Her former existential loneliness evaporated into thin air as she and Allan embarked on a torrid love affair. Allan, who had been raised in a family of rough and ready country people, worshipped the ground Caro walked on. She was the calm and assured, sophisticated woman of his teenage fantasies, who wore silk stockings and pearl tear-drop earrings; the mature *femme fatale* with smoky eyes and manicured fingernails who made him feel like a man. To her, he was the trendy youngblood that she'd denied herself when she was growing up, who played grunge guitar and smoked weed on the weekends. Much tut-tutting took place behind their backs. But the couple were resolute. All is fair in love and war, after all.

Allan soon moved in with Carolyn and her children. The teenage boys tolerated him, mostly by avoiding him. But Caro's youngest and only daughter, Carla, became deeply attached to Allan, and he to her. He quickly fulfilled the role of surrogate father to the eight-year-old girl, taking the place of the moody, volatile Murray who had formerly made their home a living hell.

Five years on, though, the age difference between the couple had grown into a chasm, too wide to breach. One summer, Allan developed chronic hay fever, spending his days sneezing uncontrollably and producing vast amounts of catarrh, and his nights snoring so loudly he kept jerking himself awake. Over that summer, he transformed into a gaunt shadow of his former self, hollow-eyed and burnt out, questioning the relationship's future. His aunt, a self-proclaimed psychic and healer who practised all sorts of juju, told him his symptoms indicated a person close to him was very likely 'getting up his nose'. By autumn, he was gone.

The timing was bad: Carla's first year in college. She had been a quiet, gentle child, the kind about whom people say with a knowing look, "what an angel". Now she began to be bullied by her peers at school. Her older brothers had not long left home to pursue their own futures so weren't around to look after her any more. Pubescent and troubled, Carla fell in with a rough crowd for protection. Carolyn, grieving for Allan, was barely able to function, let alone be there for her daughter. Carla's problems escalated.

Years of trouble followed: truancy, bad boys, unrego'd cars, unlicensed drivers, drugs and alcohol, counsellors, social workers, rehab, relapse. Caro often felt as if she was running to keep up with herself. She'd been both mother and father, nurturer and disciplinarian, breadwinner and homemaker for that long, her resources were growing thin. As the years passed, she tried everything to keep a sense of family unity going, organising get-togethers at Christmas and Easter, never letting a birthday go by without arranging a celebration.

But Carla seldom turned up. News of her reached Carolyn and the boys occasionally, about trouble with men and trouble with the law. They started talking about Carla in hushed voices, in a coded language only they understood. "She's gone to ground. Carla's gone to ground again," they'd say to each other with a knowing look, when Carla remained incognito and incommunicado for long periods of time. As if Carla was a seasonal creature who had disappeared into a dark, subterranean burrow to hibernate for the winter. As if this behaviour was normal, to be expected. As if, when spring came, Carla would wake up, crawl from her burrow, return to the world of the living, and come home. But she never did.

They all knew, deep down, they'd lost her a long, long time ago. Or had she lost them? Maybe, she had willingly gone to the dark side. Maybe, *she* had discarded *them*.

As Carolyn's career advanced, research became her focus. She wanted to make sense of human behaviour, to get to the bottom of why people do the things they do, to come to understand what had caused her husband to abuse her and why her daughter had gone off the rails and why it had taken an affair with a man twenty years her junior for her to rediscover the dormant and stunted part of her own being. And like so many others — forensic experts, investigators, journalists, writers, psychologists and psychiatrists, cultural commentators, poets, and ordinary citizens — she wanted to understand what had motivated the Manson gang and why they had committed the atrocities they had — nine senseless murders!

Now, recently semi-retired, and with lots of time on her hands, Carolyn walked daily in the woods near her home, choosing the untrammelled paths, those that were dark and dank and overgrown, choked with fallen trees and dense undergrowth. She savoured these hours of pure solitude. They allowed her to silently process all she had experienced. She mulled over everything she had lived through and witnessed, fast forwarding or rewinding certain events, speeding them up and slowing them down, analysing them, deconstructing them, digging into their context and subtext and hidden meaning, erasing parts of them and reconstructing or revisioning others. As she willed. Or felt appropiate.

One evening, she noticed something incongruous lying on the ground in the middle of the path in front of her. She prodded it with her walking stick, recoiling in horror when she recognised what it was: the severed head of a Barbie doll with only a remnant of matted hair still attached to the back of its head. It repulsed her, but she felt compelled to pick it up, to cradle it in her hand. And once she held it in her palm, an awful shiver passed through her. She slipped the battered artefact into her pocket, *rescuing it*, she thought. She knew, even though she didn't quite understand how or why, that it was connected with her daughter, the one who, as a child, had been compliant and easy, quiet and good, naturally close. The one with the flat chest, knock-knees and thick ankles, like herself. The one who had given up on an ordinary life, as she herself had eventually done.

After Carolyn found the doll's head, her anxiety about Carla mushroomed within her chest like poisonous fungi multiplying in the dark. She couldn't eat, couldn't sleep, couldn't work, couldn't think. She felt she had to do more, make a final attempt to help her daughter, win her back, loosen her from the clutches of the underworld. Save her. Even though she'd tried many, many times before, and failed. She took the battered Barbie head out of her jacket pocket and placed it on top of the piano in her living room, from where it observed her, day and night. Even when she wasn't in the room, its face and demeanour remained etched in her mind; its fixed, immobile expression full of blank-eyed accusation, its disembodied presence an indictment of human nature, a reminder of the unmentionable: a place where no one would ever willingly choose to go. Or would they?

Caro felt confused and conflicted. She knew to remain sane, one had to believe that what one did, what one said, what one thought, made a difference. That it mattered. But this battered Barbie doll head defied that logic. It defied all logic. It was a reminder things could go wrong — horribly wrong — and that when they went wrong, they could always get *worse*. It was prescient of something far more sinister and more shocking, far less intelligible and less bearable than she had ever imagined possible. Something irretrievable. Something irrevocable.

Something like the Manson murders.

Carolyn sat on the piano stool night after night staring at the severed Barbie head, seeking answers. She decided to put into practice the Jungian theory that she counselled others to use; that the only way 'round' is 'through'. The monster grows smaller when you shine a light on it. When you take it out of your pocket and place it on the table in front of you and stare it down. When you examine it and prod it and poke it and turn it over and really become familiar with it, demystifying it.

She started by thinking back to Carla's childhood, combing through the accumulated evidence in search of markers that might explain what had happened to the girl, and why. Halfway through Year 6, Carla's school principal had called Carolyn in for an interview and recommended Carla be moved up a year, into intermediate. "Carla is too mature, too intelligent, too precocious to stay where she is," the principal had said. "She needs to be challenged, so I'm recommending advancing her."

Perhaps this was the beginning of what Caro had now come to term, the Turning Point. It started with Carla swimming out way beyond the breakers, needing to be rescued by life guards. Refusing a saddle at pony club and choosing to ride bareback like the more advanced riders until she fell from the horse. Putting her hand up when a volunteer was called for, causing others to turn and stare, because surely the task was beyond this child's ability? By the age of eleven or twelve, shortly after Allan left, she was leaving her bedroom window swinging on its hinge late at night, climbing walls and skulking in shrubbery, hooking up with boys and smoking dope. Carla had followed that will-o'-the-wisp to the dark side.

A counsellor had advised Carolyn: "Girls like your daughter are risk-takers, red-flag bearers; caution is anathema to them, they grab life by the horns and shake the guts out of it, this is the only way they know how to live. You will have to let her be, let her go. It's her life, not yours. The best you can hope for is that she grows out of it." When Carolyn tried to counsel her daughter and voice her concerns, Carla herself had said, "Mum, I'm fine. I can take care of myself. Stop faffing and fussing! You're smothering me!! I'm not a little girl anymore."

No, she was no longer a little girl. But she wasn't a mature adult yet either.

Carolyn deeply resented how Manson's accomplices were called *girls*; "the Manson Girls this, the Manson Girls that". It belittled them, infantilised them, victimised them, exonerated them. Had they really been as submissive and compliant as they'd been made out to be? The accepted narrative, that Manson had beguiled and bewitched them into carrying out his wishes, was entrenched. Their behaviour was proof of his charisma, the key to his allure. The standard story was that *he* had perverted *them*. That these young women were *victims*. That their agency as autonomous individuals, invested with free will, had no place in the accepted Manson mythology. They were mere accessories to the infamous cult leader. Accessories to the crime. Accessories after the fact.

But they were never granted bail. Aside from Linda Kasabian who was let off because she got immunity from prosecution for providing evidence, Krenwinkel was the longest serving prisoner in the state of California when she died, and the others were still incarcerated. Examples of what happens when women go feral and behave with evil intent... or inherent evil? Perhaps Carolyn's mother had been right. That dolls and make believe and 'love and marriage go together like a horse and carriage' were the safest way to heaven. Only girls like Sharon Tate and the Manson girls got into sex and drugs and rock and roll. Girls who ended up murderers. Or murdered.

Sharon Tate had been returned to the earth, buried in the Holy Cross Cemetery in Culver City, California, with her unborn baby swaddled in her arms. But she and her son had lived on in the public consciousness because of the horror of what had befallen them. And now, fifty years after their deaths, Tarantino had fully restored them to life by revisioning the ending of the Manson story in his movie. Once upon a time in Hollywood, anything was possible.

Caro decided she would do the same for her daughter. She'd change the ending of *her* story. Because she could. Because it was the only thing she had any control over. She would never again use the words "gone to ground" when she spoke of Carla. And she'd ask the rest of the family to refrain from using them too.

She wrapped the battered Barbie head in tissue paper and stored it carefully away in the large box of treasures where she kept the children's christening gowns, their threadbare teddies, their kindergarten handicrafts and miscellaneous school projects, their poems and pictures and stories and cards. She placed a large, framed photograph of Carla's beautiful 21st birthday portrait on the piano where she could admire it every day. From that day on, Caro would live her life with the belief — the conviction — that her daughter was safe and happy, thriving, even. And when she stood at her sink washing her dishes, she would imagine Carla standing at her own tidy kitchen bench with a satisfied smile on her face, watching as her children played happily outside, having scrubbed her pots and dishes and cutlery sparkling clean, and stacked them to dry on a rack in the sunshine that poured through the open window.

Corona is a Neighbourhood in Queens, NY

The events depicted took place during the Covid pandemic,

between December 2019 and December 2021.

At the request of survivors, names have been changed to

protect their identities.

WUHAN, CHINA

Roberto Romano arrived late at Tianhe Airport and was now pushing his way through hordes of passengers in the International Departures Terminal, trying to get close enough to read the overhead information boards. Red flashing lights confirmed what the milling crowds of people had already led him to suspect: all flights that night had been indefinitely delayed. A snowstorm had blown in from the Mulan Mountains, shutting down all transport systems in and out of the city.

Relief flooded through him that he hadn't missed his plane, followed swiftly by irritation. He would now have to kill time, waiting for a break in the weather. He wondered whether to return to his hotel and rebook for the morning — multiple flights flew direct, daily, between Wuhan and Milan and vice versa, so there was no shortage of options. But there'd be other passengers in the same predicament and seats would be at a premium. He decided to wait out the delay. It rarely snowed in Wuhan and the storm might soon abate. Besides, he'd promised his wife he'd be home in time for Christmas. Her mother's health was failing, and his wife feared this might be their last *periodo natalizio* together as a family.

Roberto made his way to the duty-free arcade where all the shops were doing brisk trade. After browsing for a while, he settled on Pokémon Go Consoles and White Rabbit toffees for his children, Chanel No 5 for his wife (so much cheaper in China!) and a Burberry cashmere scarf for her mother. He imagined his wife's shining, happy face across the candlelit table in their warm upmarket apartment in Basiglio, as they lifted their glasses in a toast on Christmas Eve. He could almost hear his children's squeals of delight as they opened the gifts he'd brought them, together with those from *Babbo Natale* and their devoted *nonna*. And his mother-in-law's sweet tears of mingled joy and regret as she basked in the bosom of her beloved family, would always be fondly remembered as they lived on without her.

Once he'd completed his purchases and stored them in his hand luggage, he returned to the main hall where long rows of seats were bolted to the floor, all occupied. When someone needed the bathroom or went to seek out refreshments, he would make his move. Roberto was an optimistic opportunist. Growing up on the streets of Genoa, the son of a dock worker and the runt of a rowdy litter of rough boys, he'd soon absorbed his father's favourite maxim: "There are only two kinds in this world. The quick, and those who go without." As a youngster, he had often gone without, and he'd soon learned that Papa was right: survival was dependent upon cultivating a keen eye on proceedings. And timing was essential.

It was these qualities that had contributed to his success in the fashion industry. He'd started on the cutting floor as a sixteen-year-old apprentice and had systematically worked his way up to the designer suite. A favourable marriage provided him with access to investment capital, and soon after, the dream of launching his own fashion house, Romano Couture, had become a reality. Building on his early successes, he'd stretched his bottom line as most other European fashion houses did, through subcontracting the manufacture and distribution of his range of designer apparel to price-competitive Chinese production houses in Wuhan.

Roberto leaned now against a wall near the entrance to the public toilets, scanning the hall. It was time he started flying first class, he mused. He could easily afford it. Right now, he could have been relaxing in the VIP Lounge sipping on an ice-cold glass of Tsingtao Beer with a steaming bowl of Kung Pao shrimps in front of him, instead of hawking for a seat in this crowded, noisy, international departure hall.

Soon, a man in a seat nearby stood up and Roberto moved swiftly to take his place. The woman seated beside him mumbled a feeble greeting. For a moment, he thought he recognised her. Maybe she worked at one of the many factories he visited on a weekly basis where he met with Chinese fashion industry executives to discuss textile choices, design alternatives, lines of supply, bottom lines, deadlines. The woman was deathly pale, her eyes ringed with dark circles. Beads of sweat dotted her forehead.

Roberto reached into his pocket to retrieve his phone, anxious to call his wife with an update on his travel plans. But the woman began to cough and Roberto turned away. He hadn't wanted to return home with the flu that was raging through China, but that was now probably going to be inevitable. *Grazie Dio*, his annual inoculation was up to date. He put his phone back into his pocket and clicked open his briefcase, scratching around among its contents until he found what he was looking for — a card of Vitamin C lozenges — and popped a couple into his mouth. He was as fastidious about his health as he was about Romano Designer Couture.

MANILA, PHILIPPINES

Jen-Lin's doll-like body lay on a makeshift cot in the corner of the sparsely furnished shack her mother rented in the slums of Payatas. The child had taken ill a few days before, becoming gradually more listless as an angry red rash colonised her torso. Ningning attempted to cool her daughter's fever by wiping a damp cloth over her forehead and chest, and, to keep her hydrated, she pushed a spoon of watery fish head soup down her throat. She didn't have enough pesos to take Jen-Lin by bus or taxi to the hospital across town; since the child had taken sick Ningning hadn't been able to get to her casual job at the fish processing factory on the docks where she worked when a catch came in.

That morning when Ningning woke, she found that Jen-Lin had deteriorated overnight. The child was breathing with difficulty and her eyes had rolled back into their sockets. Her skin was a mottled, dirty grey-blue, like the oily water that ran past outside their shack in the open drains. Ningning ran outside screaming for help and a neighbour responded, telling Ningning she'd try and get her cousin to come — her cousin was a community clinic nurse in a suburb nearby and might be able to help.

After a long and anxious wait, the neighbour returned with the nurse who rushed to the child's bedside to assess her condition. She immediately began to berate Ningning: "This child has advanced measles! You should have had her inoculated! Shame on you!"

Ningning shrank back, flinching. "Our pastor at church told us not to vaccinate; that it's a sin to put things into our bodies and our children's that are made from aborted babies..."

"You *dukha* people are so ignorant!" said the nurse. "If you had brought this child to the clinic regularly, as you were supposed to..." — she prodded Ningning on the chest — "... you would have had everything explained to you! Vaccines prevent serious illnesses like this. Vaccines save lives!"

"But my sister's boy died after receiving the Dengue Fever inoculation! There are many now, like us, who fear vaccinations," Ningning replied.

The nurse shook her head. "Your little girl has severe pneumonia, probably encephalitis. Because mothers like you listen to religious nutters, we now have an epidemic of measles in the Philippines! And as if we didn't already have enough problems, now Covid has hit us too..."

Ningning fell to the floor. "But... but... I work hard so I can feed her and clothe her! I look after her as well as I can. I have done everything I could!"

The clinic nurse shook her head, pursing her lips. Then she patted Ningning on her shoulder. "It's too late for science to save her now. Take her to your pastor and ask him to pray for her, to perform a miracle on her. That is all that is left for you to do."

NEW YORK, USA

Due to major staff shortages as doctors and nurses dropped like flies, Freda's shift overran by almost four hours that day. When she eventually signed out of the Critical Care Unit at Elmhurst Hospital in Queens, it was way past dark and sleet was falling, turning quickly to slush on the wet city pavements. She pulled her coat tighter and wrapped a scarf around her head, but she didn't have any boots. Her sneakers would soon be wet through. Too bad, she thought; she'd be home soon enough, and would dry them on the radiator overnight.

Blinking with tiredness and faint from lack of food, Freda made her way past a row of refrigerated trailers parked up beside the hospital and fitted out as makeshift morgues. Along the block, a motley queue of people inched forward towards the hospital's entrance where they would be triaged in field tents. As Freda and a few of her colleagues walked past, they clapped, and Freda smiled and nodded. But she knew the hospital was operating at 125% capacity; some of these Covid-infected patients would die before they ever made it to a ward bed.

When Freda reached her bus stop on Broadway, she noticed that other passengers were dispersing and walking away. An elderly woman was summoning an Uber on her mobile. "So many drivers are sick," she said, "they've had to cancel all the buses."

Freda's face collapsed, as if she'd just been told her dear Mama, two and a half thousand miles away, in México, had passed. After crossing the border as human cargo in the back of a truck and surviving the perilous journey north, followed by months of punishing overtime and the mental, physical and emotional strain of working with terminal patients, Freda was beyond exhausted and permanently weepy, not to mention constantly irritated by the itchy, sweaty rashes beneath her breasts and between her upper legs from wearing layers of PPE, and the rosacea which burned across her cheeks under the multiple face masks she wore for hours at a stretch.

"Are you alright, dear?" the woman asked her.

"Oh, yes, thank you for asking, *muchas gracias, señora*," Freda replied, bowing her head slightly as Mexican women do. "I'll be okay — when I get home." She trudged off in an easterly direction, heading towards the neighbourhood of Corona where she boarded with family above their Mexican food joint on the corner of 108th Street and 52nd Avenue. It was a two and a half mile walk and would take her the better part of an hour in this weather.

When Freda finally reached Café Empanadas, it had shut for the night. She wasn't surprised; her aunt and uncle could no longer operate the *cantina* as a sit-down eating establishment, and after 8pm, non-contact takeaway sales tapered right off. A short while later she was in her dressing gown, slumped on a chair at the kitchen table in their apartment, sipping a mug of chilli hot chocolate. Her young cousins clustered around her, hanging on her every word.

"How was your day, *chica*," her aunt asked, serving up a plate of black beans and corn for Freda's dinner.

"Don't ask, Aunty," Freda replied, her bottom lip trembling, her eyes black holes in her face.

"Oh, my poor girl," Freda's aunt said. "My poor sister's daughter." She put her arms around Freda's shoulders and gave her a big hug.

"They are saying that it's us Mexicans who are spreading the virus, because we live in overcrowded, multigenerational homes. But what about the blacks? They live like us also."

"*Neta*! They are just being racist. Because we're immigrants."

"*Sale, querida, Tía.* That explains it."

"When you came from México we had no idea this would happen," Freda's aunt continued. "But your mother will be pleased of the extra money. She needs every *peso* you can spare, *chica*, to look after herself and your little brothers, now that your father has run off with those *banditos...*"

"*Sí*, Aunty. I don't mind the hard work, really. I do it willingly, to honour *La Santa Muerte*. And to help Mama, of course."

"Of course, Freda. But there's something you're not telling me, *no?*"

Freda sighed. "The ward supervisor pushed me into the cleaning cupboard, and before I knew what was happening, he was pressing himself against me and threatening to report me, saying the government are deporting *mojados* — illegal immigrants. But maybe he was teasing? He was smiling and laughing. It's so difficult to tell with these Americanos... what they mean, *no?*"

"*No mames!*" Freda's aunt exclaimed. "But, Freda, you are *bien parecido* — a good-looking girl. Maybe he can't help himself?"

"It's sexual harassment, Aunty! Your generation might have had to put up with that kind of thing but this is the 21st century..."

"*Basta ya!*" Freda's aunt instructed her children to leave their cousin to eat in peace and go to bed. After everyone had kissed everyone else goodnight and the children had retired to their bedroom, she continued, "*Asi*, did anything happen, Freda?"

"*No!* But he is very handsome, Aunty. And a good kisser. Also, *lo más importante*, he's a *gringo!*"

"*Por tanto*, what will you do?"

"We give the most anxious Covid patients a sedative. It calms them and helps them breathe better. I always have a syringe ready, in my pocket. Next time he tries something — *pinchazo!*" Freda raised her arm and feigned a stabbing motion.

"But how will that solve the problem?"

"Five milligrams of Lorazepam will put him out of action for up to eight hours. He won't even be able to get up, let alone get *it* up!"

"But when they find out, they will fire you, *chica*, and send you back to México!"

Freda's uncle put his head through the door on his way to the bathroom. A cigarillo hung from his bottom lip and he was clutching a folded copy of the *Queens Daily Eagle* which he waved around in the air as he spoke.

"What is all the fuss about? Eh? New York is a sanctuary city, *Hola*? Besides, they need every single nurse they can get right now, even those without the proper papers, like our niece! *Por el amor de Dios*, let the girl eat and rest now! *Oye muy*, you *mujeres* are such drama queens!"

Freda and her aunt burst out laughing, and Freda wiped away her tears.

Tomorrow, when she was donning her isolation gown and masks and equipping her trolley with gloves, bleach, sani wipes and other medical supplies; when she was setting up ventilators for patients and administering Hi-Flo oxygen; when she was assisting them to communicate with their families over iPad screens; when she was comforting them as their heart monitors bleeped and their vents hissed and whooshed, and they stared at her with wide, frightened eyes as if she was the Angel of Deliverance, she would be batting her thick, dark lashes at the ward supervisor.

When he'd kissed her in the broom cupboard and fondled her breasts and told her he'd never wanted anyone as much, it had felt really good. She would do whatever was necessary to survive here in *Gringolandia. Lo que sea necesario.* She didn't want to go back to México. She did not want to live her mother's life.

JOHANNESBURG, SOUTH AFRICA

"Follow close! If we get separated..." Koketso led Lucky Boi down a labyrinth of narrow passages deep into the heart of a ramshackle shantytown. *Tsotsis* loitered on every corner, protecting their territory. Boi stuck to Koketso like glue as Koketso wove confidently between the shacks and hovels, calling out greetings to people they passed along the way: "*Dumela, sisi!*" "Whassup, bro?" He turned back to Boi, wagging his finger in the air. "And when we get there, Boi, remember... I do all the talking!"

Lucky Boi's fortune had recently changed for the worse. He'd fended for himself since the age of fourteen and done fairly well at it, hawking fruit and vegetables on the streets near Joubert Park in the CBD, where he slept in a doorway under a tarpaulin, his bagged produce tucked close around his body for fear it might be stolen. When his father had died from a lung disease contracted in the gold mines, Boi had been forced to leave school. His mother was a live-in domestic for a white Afrikaans family in an affluent gated community in the northern suburbs, and she, now a widow, could no longer afford Boi's boarding school fees, but her employers would not allow her son to live with her there in her backyard servant's quarters.

His grandparents grew the produce he sold on the streets of Egoli at their rural smallholding about an hour's drive south of the city. Sometimes they would bring corn, sometimes mangoes, sometimes carrots and sweet potatoes, sometimes squash and pumpkin; whatever the season brought forth. Once he'd paid off the self-employed street guards who allowed him to hawk on their strip of pavement, he'd give Ntate and Nkhono some *madi* towards their petrol, for seed and fertiliser, and some extra for themselves.

One day, the *bokgata* — the police — had turned up with paddy wagons and batons and told all the *spaza* pavement-stall operators to clear out. A bad disease was spreading through the community and everyone would die if they didn't get out of the city and return to their ancestral homelands.

"But there is nothing for us there!" he heard the woman at the stall next to him exclaiming. "We will die of hunger if we can't earn!"

"You will die here on the streets if you stay," the policeman had replied. "So, make sharp! Pack up and *voetsak*!"

Lucky Boi had abandoned his fruit and vegetables — there was too much produce to carry — and had jumped into a taxivan heading south to his grandparents when he heard someone calling his name. Soon he was sitting next to his childhood friend, Koketso, and sharing his predicament.

"Fok it, Boi, don't believe everything you hear," Koketso said. "The authorities are making up stories to clear the poor off the streets and out of the city. Tourists don't want to visit South Africa anymore, saying it's too dirty and too dangerous. So they're doing a huge clean up. Listen, I've got a job lined up, easy *madi*. And lots of it! You come with me, my china!"

Half an hour later, Koketso led Boi into a clearing between the township shanties where an illegal *shebeen* was operating. A few patrons sat at tables shaded by tatty beach umbrellas drinking *maroch* — traditionally brewed beer — and *kwela* music blared from large speakers. Three women with dazed, bloodshot eyes swayed on the dance floor, their garish clothing, bright eyeshadow and lipstick and western style wigs giving away their profession.

Koketso approached the bar. "We're here to see Skottel," he said. The barman motioned behind him. Boi followed Koketso through a doorway covered with plastic strips into a dimly lit container. The smell of *dagga* permeated the air.

A man came forward out of the shadows and Koketso greeted him the African way, palm to palm, grip to grip, palm to palm. The man looked Boi up and down. "Who's this?"

"My china from the homeland, Lucky Boi. He's *skraal* at the moment, Skottel; no work, no money."

"*Bakgat*! Able. Willing. And available. The best kind of recruit, *nê*?"

Boi felt nervous, wondering what would happen next, but the man seemed friendly and accommodating. He sat the boys down and handed them a couple of cold beers which he'd pulled out of a cool box. While they chatted about the soccer scores and the state of the nation, he passed around a reefer. Boi relaxed as the marijuana began to blunt his senses, beginning to drop his guard.

Soon, Skottel adopted a more business-like demeanour. "I want you *kêrels* to do the job tonight," he said. "You're gonna break into that animal rescue centre in Jeppestown. You know, the one run by that *Engelse teef* who's always on TV, telling us to stop trading wildlife. Man, the hypocrisy! The whites ripped off our natural resources for hundreds of years, and now think *they* can tell *us* not to! Bit rich, *nê*?"

Skottel began to laugh and Koketso joined in. Boi hadn't caught up on South African history having been forced to leave school early, so didn't quite follow Skottel's meaning. When Skottel noticed, he slung his arm around Boi's neck and pulled him closer.

"*Yekela*. Never mind. It's not every day you get to play with one of *these*, Lucky Boi," he said, as he pushed a paper bag with a solid, hard object inside it into Boi's hands. "Use this if you have to, *kêrels*. But make sure you clean up your mess. You fuck up, *o zo fantja*!"

Koketso slapped Boi on the back. "South Africa is one of the only places in the world where you get to commit a crime with a police issue handgun, my china! Now, that's bloody *befok*, isn't it?"

Boi screwed his face up. "Ow?"

Skottel smiled. "This one's still pretty green, *nê*?" he said to Koketso.

Koketso squeezed Boi's shoulder. "Listen, Boi," he said. "The *bokgata* get paid peanuts and sometimes they don't even get paid. They rent their *gats* out overnight to earn some coin and as long as we wipe our fingerprints off the pistols before returning them, no one is any the wiser. Seventy-five percent of crime in SA is unsolved anyway, so nothing to worry about!"

"Okay, listen up, *kêrels*," continued Skottel. "I've got a Chinese buyer and he's paying dollars. US greenbacks. He wants pangolin, as many as you can get."

Later, as the youngsters made their way back through the shacks towards the main road to catch a taxi to Jeppestown to break into the animal shelter, Boi asked Koketso, "Hey, how did he get that nickname? Skottel?"

"He killed a man with a frying pan. *Gif*, isn't it?"

AUCKLAND, NEW ZEALAND

"Hallooooo? Anybody home?"

"What a stupid question! Pandemic or not, you know I don't go out anymore, Joan! I haven't left home since my last hospital stay…"

"Of course! Anyway, how are you, Cecily?"

"Oh, bearing up, bearing up. Hurry up and get me my pills, will you? I'm feeling rather shaky today…"

"No worries. I'll put them on the brown saucer so you can easily see them, and I'll get you a fresh glass of water."

The home care nurse made her way through Cecily's living room into the open plan kitchen. A dinner plate with a meal laid out on it sat untouched on the bench. "I see you didn't eat the meal I prepared for you last night, dear." She raised her voice slightly; she knew Cecily was not only near blind; she was also hard of hearing.

Cecily remained where she was, reclining on a sofa in front of the TV, still in her stained dressing gown at four o'clock in the afternoon. "You don't have to shout, Joan! I'm not deaf!" she replied. "I couldn't manage it, not without my teeth."

"But I cut up everything and mashed it all together, like you asked."

"To be honest, I just couldn't be bothered."

"But if you don't eat, you'll fade away. You've lost a lot of weight since your last illness..."

"Oh, for Heaven's sake, Joan, it's not exactly my fault, is it? You know what happened — those stupid cleaners at the hospital swept my teeth off the beside caddy and into the rubbish! They probably ended up in the incinerator..."

"And you haven't been able to get new ones made because of the lockdown?"

"Exactly! Now hurry up with that water, will you? Otherwise, I'm likely to die of natural causes let alone this blasted Covis before I ever get to see my children and grandchildren again!"

Tears pricked Joan's eyes. The old bat was always so rude and ungrateful, no matter what she did to help her. And Joan had had an awful day, covering for another caregiver who'd developed Covid-like symptoms and was now isolating while awaiting her test results. Then there was the way in which Cecily persisted in calling the virus 'Covis' as if it was a variety of flower, like clivia, or crocus, or cosmos. If only. It might be shaped like an exotic bloom, but that was where the similarity ended. Didn't the old bat realise that in New York, a third of the population was sick, and thousands had died? The New Zealand government was doing the right thing by trying to eradicate the virus, despite how hard it was on everybody.

Joan took a deep breath. "I'm sorry you're upset, Cecily. It's hard on all of us. I haven't been able to see my children and grandchildren either..."

"Well, you can blame the government for that, Joan! Now, what are you going to cook for my dinner tonight?"

WUHAN, CHINA

Li-na stood at the kitchen bench portioning out her and her husband's evening meal. She put aside a small amount of rice and stew for their son's dog, who would eat his dinner later.

When ten-year-old Chia-Hao had first brought the pup home, her husband, Rong, had been annoyed. "Another mouth to feed! Someone else to take up space in this tiny apartment! More work for your mother, as if the songbirds don't already make enough mess. And what about your goldfish? You won't have time to clean their tank now!"

But the boy's obvious love and affection for the animal had, over time, softened his father. Chia-Hao spent every waking moment playing with the pup and they shared a bed at night. Sometimes his parents overheard the boy talking to the pup as if it were a human being, a friend or sibling — perhaps the brother or sister the boy's parents were prohibited by law from providing for him. Soon the dog had become a member of the family and had been given a name: Xin-ai, Beloved. But Rong had insisted on disciplining the animal. "No food until we have eaten, and then, only if there's some left over! No treats until he learns how to sit and stay and walk on his hind paws! And no more sleeping on the bed! It's not only unhygienic but the dog will grow too big and will suffocate you, Chia-Hao. We will install a doghouse on the balcony."

Now, Chia-Hao was nineteen and went by the name of Charles and was living and studying in New Zealand. He had been unable to return home for Chinese New Year because of the Covid-19 lockdown in Wuhan. Besides, he had a part-time job at a service station in Auckland and needed the money. His parents had been forced to close their dry-cleaning business because of the lockdown, and were struggling to keep up with Charles' overseas study and living expenses.

When he'd left home, Charles had charged his parents with taking care of the aging Xin-ai. In Charles' absence, the dog was some consolation to his parents. His presence comforted them, almost as if they still had one child at home. And Xin-ai reminded them, always, of their beloved son who now lived far away. Every time Charles phoned home he asked, "How is Xin-ai? How is my old friend? How is my brother?"

Li-na placed her and her husband's bowls of food on the table and sat down next to Rong. He extinguished his cigarette and they began to eat.

"We're running low on rice, Husband," Li-na said. "One of us will have to go out soon."

"But the army is patrolling. No one is allowed outside, Wifey."

"Tut-tut. There isn't enough left to feed us all," Li-na replied.

"Some are saying the virus is spread by dogs and cats," said Rong. "It's all over Weibo."

"What? Is there proof?"

"They claim Covid has jumped the species barrier, from animal to human. Western governments are pointing fingers at the Huanun wet market, saying the virus spread from there."

"Tut-tut! All this anti-Chinese propaganda! We're not the only people in the world who eat animals, Husband!"

Rong pushed his chair back from the table and relit his cigarette. "Wifey, I wonder ... are you aware? Others are... disposing of their pets? There are photographs on Weibo."

Li-na threw her chopsticks down on the table and spat her mouthful of food at her husband. "Are you asking me to throw our son's dog out of the window to his death as others are doing?"

"I'm sorry, Li-na, but we may have no choice," he replied.

Li-na's face went dark and her eyes burned with anger. She stood up and tipped her leftovers into the dog's bowl, then opened the door to the balcony. Freezing cold air sucked into the room and Rong blanched.

"Xin-ai will eat my food from now on, Husband," she said. "And I will sleep in the doghouse with him until our son comes home."

Transit of Mercury

"Ata Mārie. Good morning, everybody. Come in, please. Haere mai."

"Morning, Miss."

"Kia ora, Whaea."

"Hi, Mrs B."

"Mōrena."

Mrs B stood at the door nodding and smiling as her Level 2 English students filed into the classroom. The students had always called her Mrs B — her surname, Boroughgoode, was a jawbreaker, easily mangled. Besides, she encouraged a less formal relationship, knowing it fostered a more positive teaching and learning environment.

She noted that many of the students were chewing gum — someone must have shared a bulk pack around at interval. There were also the usual uniform violations. R'Nia had folded her skirt over so many times at the waistband it barely covered her backside and a couple of the boys were sporting Alien Weaponry hoodies instead of the college's regulation jumpers. Mrs B had an eagle eye for noticing student misconduct; she could even intuit it when her back was turned and she was otherwise engaged — writing on the board or marking student work at her desk. The students often joked about her having eyes in the back of her head.

A group of lads known as the Rugger Buggers jostled each other as they passed her, curses slipping from their mouths in a slick hierarchy of one-upmanship. These boys made up the forward pack of the first fifteen which had recently ascended to the top of the Northland Interschools' rugby table. Staff had been instructed by the principal, who in turn had been petitioned by the sports coaches, to ensure these lads re-enrolled next year. The school didn't want to lose them to other educational pathways or the lure of employment if they were to maintain their status as the top team in Te Tai Tokerau.

"Totally inappropriate, boys," Mrs B admonished them now. "Remember what we learned about 'register'— how language should always fit its context? This is not the locker room!"

"Sorry, Miss!" they chanted in unison as they made their way to their seats.

Some of the girls were wearing ridiculously long eyelash extensions. Mrs B was horrified at how tarty and simply *ludicrous* female fashions had become. The school's ban on make-up and jewellery did not even exist as far as these girls were concerned. If only they understood, youth and beauty were shallow and fleeting; the life of the mind was the sole thing one could count on. Mrs B's favourite mantra was a line from a D.H Lawrence poem: *Thought is a man in his wholeness, wholly attending*. Its message went above the heads of some of her students and she had to explain what it meant, but they'd heard her quote it that often, she hoped it would be seared into their memories for posterity.

Jaxon, the Year 12 heartbreaker, and the new girl — what was her name again? — entered the classroom last. Jax pinched the girl's backside as they parted company to take their seats. Mrs B instantly put two and two together. He'd already worked his way through all the available talent, both male and female, in the Sixth Form.

"Okay, everyone, settle, please!" she said, clapping her hands.

While the students scrabbled in their bags for their study materials, Mrs B considered giving them a dressing down. It did not do to let them get away with the blatant flouting of rules. But if she brought up their list of transgressions, she'd have to issue behaviour notes. And if she'd missed something, it wouldn't be fair on those she *did* punish. It'd also take up valuable lesson time; time she'd planned to spend on revision for the upcoming exams. It was well into the fourth term and the students were soon going on study leave. Careful revision was essential; it made all the difference between a fail and a pass, between a merit and an excellence. She also had to ensure the Rugger Buggers got enough credits to encourage them to return in the new year.

She decided to ignore every infraction this morning and focus on what mattered, teaching and learning. In this particular case, text analysis. It often paid to let the students think they'd got one over you — strangely, it made them more cooperative and compliant. At these times, when her students *were* receptive and responsive, Mrs B remembered they were human after all, not merely clusters of preprogrammed pheromones controlled by the reptilian brain. It heartened her to know they were capable of at least one sophisticated emotion, even if it was only pity. For her.

"Right, quiet, everybody! Time is marching on! I've got some helpful exam tips for you today — remember, your success will depend on how well you understand what it is you need to do in order to achieve…"

Just then, Jaida burst through the door, late for class. The girl's eyes were hazy and bloodshot. She mumbled an apology and shuffled to her desk. Mrs B had been on duty at interval and had seen Jaida skulking in the treeline on the far side of the sports fields, a halo of smoke around her head. It wasn't the first time the girl had come to class stoned; nor would it be the last. Jaida had probably been addicted to cannabis since babyhood, probably from the womb in fact. But Mrs B had never reported her; expulsion would have only exacerbated the girl's problems. She was far better off *in* school. Mrs B was convinced Jaida was intelligent and resourceful enough to find a way to break the cycle of destitution and hopelessness she had had the misfortune to have been born into, being a member of a gang family.

She welcomed the girl now with a warm smile. "Right, we're all here at last! Before we get started on our exam revision, I wanted to enquire, are any of you planning on going to the Tuia 250 celebrations this weekend at the Town Basin? I have the programme here if anyone is interested."

"Huh? What?"

"It's the 250th anniversary of Captain Cook's arrival in New Zealand." Mrs B continued.

"Nah," said Shanae, "why would we want to celebrate the arrival of Pākehā in Aotearoa? Kāpene Kuki was an imperialist and an A-hole. He stole our land, Whaea!"

An uncomfortable silence filled the room. The Ihumāteo protest was still fresh in everyone's minds, and lengthy discussions about it had already lost Mrs B valuable lesson time; as pertinent as those discussions had been. But the syllabus didn't teach itself, after all. There were so many distractions and interruptions: field trips, sports events, special assemblies, fire drills, and, worst of all, social media. Social media was like cocaine to young minds. While Mrs B delivered her carefully planned lessons on text types and language features, she'd scan the room to gauge student engagement only to see heads bent over screens and fingers scrolling and tapping away. At times, she felt the literary luminaries who populated the posters lining the walls of her classroom were the sole entities paying any attention, albeit with the blank stares and deaf ears of dead poets and writers.

She forged on. "That's not exactly how it happened, Shanae, it's a lot more complicated. And Captain Cook didn't have anything to do with it, really. The land confiscations took place much later, after the Treaty had been signed. In fact, some Māori willingly sold their land to the Crown, and to colonists. If History was a compulsory curriculum subject, you would have had the opportunity to study this."

Orion interrupted her: "Some Māori. Our iwi didn't even sign Te Tiriti and they still took our land. No way are we gonna celebrate the arrival of the invaders who helped themselves to our motu and destroyed our people and our way of life!"

Mrs B started seeing black spots in front of her eyes. When she got stressed, they swam across her vision and she'd become disoriented, wondering whether she was seeing things, or whether there was something wrong with her sight. Menopause had been difficult for her, constantly surprising her and undermining her self-worth with its uncomfortable symptoms and debilitating quirks. Perhaps this was another. Or perhaps not. She'd read somewhere that seeing spots was symptomatic of a psychoneurotic tic, a turning away from conflict, perhaps. She wasn't good at conflict. She took a deep breath and blinked a few times, trying to make the black spots disappear. Thank God she was retiring at the end of the year and only had to get through a few more weeks before the exams started.

"Okay, okay, everybody, we're getting side-tracked. Please understand, I'm in no way minimising Māori land issues or the negative effects of colonisation. I am the first to admit that many wrongs were done to tangata whenua and am an ardent advocate for redress. The Tuia 250 event is to celebrate Māori and Pacific seafaring traditions, as well as European exploration. A flotilla of oceangoing vessels, with waka hourua and a va'a tipaerua from Tahiti, as well as a replica of Captain Cook's Endeavour and a few other tall ships, are sailing around New Zealand as part of the event. It's all about recognising what an incredible achievement it was for our forebears — *all* our forebears, whether from the Pacific or from Europe — to cross the ocean without modern technology, following birds' migration patterns and using only the stars to guide them."

"But Cook's men killed some Māori at East Cape and Ngāti Porou are still pissed off about it, Miss," said Tae, a short, stocky lad who had been elected as a school leader for the new year, as had his twin sister, Kaitirea.

Mrs B knew she ought to interject here once again to remind the students not to swear or use slang in the classroom. To develop context-appropriate communication skills in the learner was an essential part of the English syllabus. She had already overlooked Shanae's use of the 'A' word because she hadn't explicitly *said* the swear word. Now Tae had used the 'P' word in full which was a step too far. But it was already twenty minutes into the lesson and she needed to wrap up this discussion so they could focus on the programme.

"They didn't intend to kill anyone, Tae. They came ashore to make contact with Māori, thinking they might be able to trade with them. Something went wrong, a misunderstanding. Later, Māori down in the Sounds killed and ate a few of Cook's men. So, lives were lost on both sides."

"Gross," said Sylvie. "That's totally S.I.C.K! And not in a good way."

"They shouldn't have come ashore in the first place," Arena chimed in. "Their bad!"

Mrs B cleared her throat. "Look, history is complex. There are always at least two sides to every story. History is like a tapestry; made up of many threads travelling in different directions. It's important to consider *all* the evidence and to draw balanced conclusions instead of defaulting to a point of view that suits your own personal take on things…"

"Whatever! You're just racist, Miss!" R'Nia was pointing an accusing finger at her.

Mrs B felt a hot flush coming on. The last time she'd had to deal with a crisis in the classroom had been when Greta Thunberg had been all over the media and some students had accused Mrs B and her generation — boomers — of being responsible for the climate crisis. One of the girls had started sobbing, blurting out how sick with worry she was because the world was going to end in ten years' time. Mrs B had had to think quickly to avert a disaster. "Don't worry, dear, that's not going to happen," she'd said in her most reassuring voice.

But when she'd seen twenty-two pairs of eyes staring back at her, incredulous and dissatisfied with her answer, cell phones totally forgotten in that frightening moment, she'd realised these implacable young people deserved more than mere platitudes. She needed to come up with something more convincing; a reason why, in her view, the world wasn't going to end any time soon. "Because good people are going to do good things and find workable solutions to climate change, pollution, and overpopulation — all the big problems you're worried about," she'd said.

There! At least she'd backed up her statement with a justification. Something she was always encouraging her students to do in their essays and speeches. She considered reassuring them, also, by reminding them about all the other disasters mankind had survived: meteorite strikes, ice ages, major world wars, plagues, genocides, famine. But these young people had no History. Many of these historical events were beyond their frame of reference.

The sound of Trent's voice pulled Mrs B back into the present. "She's not racist, R'Nia! And her reo's improving."

"But her pronunciation is way wrong," interjected Orion. "She sounds like a poncey pommie immigrant!"

Mrs B's bottom lip started trembling. She was usually so good at keeping it together, but she'd had a few lapses lately, losing her temper in front of the students and once even muttering the F-word over and over like a person with Tourettes while she clutched at her hair like Mad Bertha in *Jane Eyre*.

The incident had probably shocked her more than the students. But still. If only they knew how deeply she cared about them and how much she would miss them next year as she rattled around her home alone, waiting for old age to overcome her. She gazed around the classroom now, taking it all in and storing a freeze-frame in her mind: the earnest faces focused on what she'd say and do next; the battered desks and chairs graffitied with lewd symbols and corny jokes and studded with globs of discarded, germ-infested gum; the huge fans spinning overhead like choppers in a Vietnam war movie; the dim haze still hanging in the air even though chalk had been outlawed donkey's years ago; the shelves at the back of the room groaning with defaced books filled to bursting with words of wisdom that had barely been read.

She remembered the first time she had asked the students to be more respectful of school property, explaining it was their parents' taxes which paid for all the school facilities; the reason why they should treat the school's resources as their own. They had stared back at her disbelievingly, faces filled with shock and horror like rows of wide-eyed, wide-mouthed emoticons. Many had never even made the connection before. She often despaired that the general knowledge and life skills the education system *didn't* teach would take these young people a lifetime of struggles to learn. They needed to know this stuff now — yesterday! — for it to make a difference to their lives.

How could she get them to understand that even without pollution and climate change, life was fragile? That every day women still died in childbirth, drunk drivers crossed the middle line, aeroplanes disappeared off the radar, terrorists discharged suicide bombs, people starved to death in squatter camps, and children were sold into slavery or prostitution. That a strange invisible illness could strike you down even if you *had* been vaccinated?

The words of the literary legends who had informed her entire life ran through her mind in jumbled fragments: *Now therefore, while the youthful hue/Sits on thy skin like morning dew / / The world is too much with us; late and soon,/Getting and spending, we lay waste our powers / / This goodly frame the earth, seems to me a sterile promontory; this most excellent canopy the air, look you, this brave o'er hanging firmament, this majestical roof, fretted with golden fire / / The intellect of man is forced to choose/Perfection of the life or of the work / / Know then thyself, presume not God to scan;/The proper study of mankind is man / / Thus, though we cannot make our sun/Stand still, yet we will make him run...*

Trent came to her rescue again: "Tell us more about this Tuia 250 event, Miss!"

Mrs B composed herself. She had always found a smile worked wonders, and she smiled broadly now, softening her features and her posture, allowing her eyes to float around the room and make soothing eye contact. When she saw the rows of youthful shining faces staring back at her expectantly, she continued:

"It's a commemoration of all the voyagers and explorers who first navigated their way to our shores. Tuia means to weave or bind together, so it's an acknowledgement of our shared ancestry and destiny. They're going to be celebrating the life of Sir Hec Busby too, one of Northland's best-known kaumātua. A master carver and builder of waka, he led a revival in celestial navigation which has restored its mana as a strand of knowledge. You might remember, he visited us here at school a few years ago. Tuia 250 is a celebration of the contribution of mātauranga Māori alongside that of modern astrophysics..."

Mrs B glanced up at the clock at the back of the room. The lesson would soon be over. How had she lost almost an hour? Her bullshit detector kicked in. Were the students playing her, derailing the lesson into any juicy topic they could dredge up as a pretext to avoid doing any actual syllabus work? It wouldn't be the first time. Language was her subject, not current affairs, not race relations, not New Zealand history, not world history. Language: that dynamic, contestable, constantly-evolving mode of signification that is mankind's only tool for describing the universe and trying to make sense of it. Language: that semantic system of denotation and connotation which exists on a continuum between hot and cold, loaded and unloaded, opinion and fact, cogency and improbity, yours and mine, theirs and ours.

Oh, to hell with the syllabus, Mrs B thought. This was language in action: Text. Context. Subtext. Her students needed to understand how the development of human knowledge was the result of a constant process of interrogation, negotiation, refutation, reformulation and accretion. They needed to learn how to factor in historical, political, geographical, philosophical and cultural contexts to be able to appreciate that different interpretations could stand alongside each other in a non-hierarchical manner.

"Interestingly, history is about to repeat itself in a cosmic way too," Mrs B continued. "On the 12th of November the planet Mercury will orbit between the earth and the sun. Its silhouette will actually be visible — it'll look like a black dot moving across the solar disk. It's a rare event that only happens a few times each century.

"An astronomer who travelled with Cook on his first voyage in the late 1700s was the first person to observe and record the transit of Mercury. In fact, when the group had been in Tahiti a few months earlier, they'd also observed the transit of Venus, enabling scientists, for the very first time, to accurately calculate the distance between the earth and the sun. Some maintain the purpose of Cook's journey was political, but in actuality, it was scientific more than anything else. He had been charged with finding the great southern continent, as yet undiscovered back then..."

The bell rang and Mrs B's voice was drowned out by the scraping of chairs and the eruption of loud chatter as the students packed up and began to exit the classroom.

Jaida came up to Mrs B and gave her a hug. "You're the coolest teacher we've ever had, Miss."

"Thank you, Jaida. Glad you enjoyed the lesson."

After the students had left, Mrs B crossed the room intending to close the door. She had a non-contact period now, time to collect herself before her next class, time to brace herself for the next onslaught.

She paused in front of a large poster of the human brain that dominated the front of the classroom. She often pointed to it during class, saying, "Why are we here, people?" The students would chant their answer in unison, as she'd taught them: "To grow brain cells, Mrs B." Then, she'd recite the words in block letters that framed the poster: "Because *THE LAST REMAINING UNEXPLORED TERRITORY IS THE UNIVERSE OF THE MIND*, right, everybody?" "Yes, Miss," they'd chorus in answer, rolling their eyes.

Her eyes grew wide now as she noticed the text on the poster had been defaced with a black vivid. Someone had crossed out the words *THE UNIVERSE OF THE MIND* and scribbled, in their place, *THE SPACE BETWEEN A GIRLS' LEGS*.

Mrs B began to laugh, so loudly and hysterically, that students on the way to their next lesson paused in the corridor outside her classroom. She waved them on, but they continued to stare, looking at each other with raised eyebrows and questioning expressions. Had Mrs B totally lost it? Rumours had been circulating for some time that she was close to having a breakdown. But Mrs B looked really happy — she was doubled over and clutching her stomach, tears of mirth streaming from her eyes.

After all these years of teaching English, and despite her very best efforts, one of her students still didn't know how to use the apostrophe correctly.

Refining Him

Thinking that earth would never mind it,
He stole her oil, and then refined it.
Now it's her turn — and she's engaged, withal,
Refining him till nothing's left at all.

Bruno Becker lay flat on his back, arms and legs splayed, head resting on his neatly folded jacket, his body forming a human barrier between three or four idling twenty-tonne trucks and the chained and padlocked steel mesh gates of Marsden Point Oil Refinery. The ground was hard and cold, and gravel dug into his back through his shirt, but he lay perfectly still, watching small puffy clouds passing overhead, swirling, dispersing and reforming high above him in the bright blue sky. He could sense men darting back and forth nearby, vaguely heard them sharing information and shouting the odd instruction, but he felt strangely detached — silent and inanimate even though positioned centre stage — a passive witness to the scenario unfolding around him.

A picket line which consisted of two uniform rows stood directly in front of the locked gates; good, keen, working men — fitters, turners, welders, riggers, scaffolders, sheet metal workers — with expressions of resolve on their faces and arms slung round each other's shoulders in solidarity. A festive mood prevailed, as if they were attending a social gathering rather than assembling outside their place of employment, conducting a serious strike. As they talked among themselves, breath condensed around their heads in the thin, cold air. Occasionally, when the headman gave them the nod, they would quieten their chatter and yell out slogans and catchphrases in unison.

The idling trucks — loaded with valves, piping, prefabricated spooling and other plant and equipment for delivery to the refinery expansion project — were stalled now in an untidy row, engines rumbling, tailpipes belching exhaust fumes, their drivers leaning out of their windows and heckling the strikers whose industrial action would cause them to be late with their deliveries all day.

Refinery personnel who were not part of the union but who'd also been locked out congregated on either side of the road, leaning in small groups against their vehicles or sitting astride their push bikes, yarning and smoking, conjecturing on the possible outcome of the day's events, dipping into their lunch boxes, pouring hot drinks from their thermoses and discussing the Cavaliers' controversial rugby tour to South Africa.

Members of the refinery's management team huddled in a group nearby conducting a stand-up crisis meeting. They would need to nut out a proposal which they could present to the Engineers' & Boilermakers' Unions in an attempt to end the standoff. Union officials had parked up a large caravan nearby to serve as an on-site office for meetings, placard production, and moral support. If negotiations stalled and a resolution not be achieved by sundown, they would adjourn to the Kingsgate Hotel in Whangārei where the management was used to accommodating them at short notice and they had an open tab at the bar.

A large group of rubberneckers, representatives of the press, assorted family members and hangers-on had also congregated near the gate, this unexpected high drama more riveting than any of their other daily concerns, or anything they might watch on Television New Zealand that night.

Beyond the security fences the refinery's eighty-metre-high, red-and-white-striped flue loomed overhead, spewing out waste gases from the oil refining process. Nearby, the even taller flare stack — the refinery's 'foo-foo valve' — fired balls of yellow flame high into the sky. Across the harbour, multi-peaked Manaia, ancestral mountain of the Whangārei district and named after local Māori's earliest tipuna, towered over the scene like a row of sentinels, their mana and repute wrought from the story of this land: Aotearoa.

Bruno's mind drifted as time passed. He'd volunteered without hesitation at a recent meeting when union bosses had asked for someone to up the ante during the strike and act as a human shield in front of the gates, preventing entry to the refinery. But he was still wondering why he was always so quick to shoot his arm up. The current rolling strikes were, frankly, petty — the trumped-up ruses of union agitators, designed to disrupt the refinery expansion project as far as possible — and there wasn't much substance in their current allegations of employer misconduct. Yes, former action had been warranted, gaining workers huge improvements in working conditions. But they were pushing their luck with their current grievances; everyone knew that — union bosses, refinery management and workers alike. Bruno had no choice now, however, but to continue to lie in front of the gates as he'd said he would; a lot of argy-bargy would still have to go down before he would either be told by the union rep to abandon the strike, or be dragged away by the police. Or lauded as a hero if the striker's demands were met.

Mount Manaia, across the water, dominating the local landscape, always reminded Bruno of the massive multi-turreted castle fortress that dominated the town in eastern Germany where he'd spent a few years during the latter part of the Second World War. He'd immigrated to New Zealand in the seventies, when the country had been actively importing skilled labour from overseas to work on Muldoon's Think Big projects, including this $1.5 billion refinery expansion. But forty years before, he'd been a young lad living in Berlin with his parents, attending school, and spending his afternoons and weekends participating in Hitler Youth programmes.

Within these structured curricula, he'd been thoroughly indoctrinated in Nazi ideology. By nature, he was an earnest fellow, always eager to please, responding with enthusiasm when volunteers were called for, and accomplished in his delivery of any tasks allocated to him. His contributions had been handsomely rewarded, testified to by the row of badges and insignia he wore across the breast of his Hitler-Jugend uniform. He'd became well known among the youth corps' leaders as the obedient and talented boy from Siemensstadt who goose-stepped like a professional soldier and saluted and shouted "Sieg Heil!" faster than any other *junge* in the brigade.

Thus, he was held up to other youths as an example of dedication to the cause and an exemplar of its aim, which was, according to the Hitler Youth motto, to produce young men who were 'swift as greyhounds, tough as leather, and hard as Krupp steel'. Bruno was also a near-perfect specimen of Aryan racial purity — well built, with fair hair thick as a sheaf of wheat, petrol-blue eyes (like Hitler's), and a ruddy complexion — except for an irritating cowlick which always caused him grief, no matter how much spit was used to try to tame it into submission.

When the Führer visited during an inspection tour, Bruno was chosen to lead his brigade, and after they'd performed their marches and exercises for the esteemed visitor, Bruno was selected for the coveted photo opportunity. For the duration of the war, a framed copy of the front page of the local newspaper, featuring Bruno with the Führer's arm around his shoulders, was prominently displayed on the Becker family's mantelpiece, to be fawned over by his proud parents and admired by all who visited their humble abode.

Fairly early in the war, Bruno's postal worker parents had been conscripted and put to work in a Siemens factory in their district, on a production line that engineered electrical and electronic components for the war industry. When Berlin was heavily bombed by the Allies in early 1942, many factories, together with their employees, were moved to secret locations in German military-occupied rural areas.

However, they remained targets, and Bruno's parents decided, at this juncture, to send their twelve-year-old son to live with his widowed grandmother in the village of Königstein near the Czech border, where his safety would be assured.

Here, his grandmother worked as a dairy maid on a large farming estate on the outskirts of the village where she lived in a timber-framed cotter. She was grateful when her grandson came to stay: she not only adored the boy, but he was fit and willing, and she was able to make good use of him, teaching him how to milk cows, separate cream, and churn butter. For the first time in her long life of manual labour her chores were completed much earlier in the day, and she was now able to spend the afternoons soaking her bunioned feet in a bowl of warm water in front of her fire, occasionally rousing herself to stir a pot of *erbsbrei* for their evening meal. Bruno was also seconded by the farm manager to run important errands, one of which was to deliver the day's supply of dairy produce to the grocer's shop in the village, after it had been accounted for by the farm manager and much of it removed, to be delivered, also by Bruno, to the local Nazi garrison up at the castle, on military orders.

One day as Bruno pulled his cart along the castle ramparts where its small, barred, dungeon windows flanked the road, he heard shouts and screams. He bent his head to look within and the sight that greeted him chilled him to the bone. Gestapo officers were torturing a man who was tied to a chair; a man he recognised as the mayor of Königstein. The mayor was bruised and bleeding and crying and pleading with the officers, saying, "But they are innocent! They have done no wrong! They are good citizens!"

Bruno was deeply disturbed and wondered why the Nazis would torture a German national. He had been taught that only Jews, blacks, mixed-race individuals, homosexuals, leftists and trade unionists were enemies of the state.

At *Herschel's Lebensmittelmarkt*, where Bruno made his delivery every afternoon after he'd been to the castle, he soon befriended the young daughter of the couple who ran the shop. Little Ruthie, aged about four or five, was a regular presence in the store where her parents weighed and dispensed weekly rations of sugar and flour, coffee, soap and paraffin, and sold bacon and other supplies to the local inhabitants. Her older brothers, however, were always upstairs in the family's living quarters, hunched over the dining table with piles of books, being tutored by a man who apparently had very long curly sideburns and wore a wide-brimmed black felt hat and long coat. Or so Ruthie had told Bruno; he'd never laid eyes on any of them. The tutor arrived each day well before sunrise and left after dark, and the boys weren't allowed outside, or even downstairs, to play or exercise. Bruno knew that education was important and was concerned that his own had come to an abrupt halt because of the war, but he didn't envy the Hershel boys whose lives seemed very dull in comparison to his own.

Ruthie's pinched little face soon endeared itself to Bruno — those dark, gypsy eyes squashed too close together on either side of her pointy aquiline nose, the downy black curls that framed her animated face. He was entranced by her tiny hands which fluttered about in the air like butterflies when she spoke, and her dainty doll-like feet fascinated him, encased in little handmade leather shoes with mother-of-pearl buttons, propelling her through space as if she was a dust-mote fairy. The little *mädchen* was sharp as a tack and often made curious observations or passed sardonic comments to which Bruno reacted with entranced surprise. She reminded him of the baby blackbird he'd come across in the hedgerow behind his Oma's cottage, chirping away in high spirits and preening itself with gusto. Whenever he saw Ruthie, he was overcome with the same sensation he experienced when he watched the fluffy little fledgling: a feeling of deep tenderness and solicitude which he now shared equally between both delightful, animated creatures.

Ruthie would wait for Bruno in the afternoons and after he'd made his deliveries they'd talk and play. Unless the Little Spinning Top — Bruno's nickname for her — had run out of energy, which was when he knew to look for her under the wooden counter at the back of the store, where she would be curled up on a shelf, fast asleep; a little bundle of rags, the black curls framing her face whited out by the drifts of flour which seemed to hang in the air at all times, the result of her parents sifting, weighing, and bagging copious amounts of it for their customers all day long.

The sound of a vehicle approaching at speed distracted Bruno from these memories and he turned his head to the side to see the Refining Company's general manager's burnt-orange Jeep Wagoneer belting down the road towards the refinery gates. The 'Generalissimo' (as the GM was referred to behind his back) had acquired the ostentatious vehicle on a trip to the US and had had it shipped over to New Zealand, courtesy of last year's Christmas bonus. The workers resented the fact that the GM had even received a bonus; the expansion build was two years behind schedule and the workers' bonus that year had consisted of a single scrawny turkey, instead of the usual slap-up party and Father Christmas' bulging brown envelope full of an extra hundy in small notes — easy enough to divvy up between the wife and kids for their Christmas shopping with enough ready cash left over for a 40 ounce, and to splash out on a keg if a couple of mates pooled their leftover dosh.

Roy Blaikie's jeep snaked past the line of stalled trucks and skidded to a halt a few metres away from Bruno, spraying metal into the air. A few stones hit Bruno on the face and body and he winced. He wondered again how much longer the strike was going to carry on for; he'd almost had enough. But he couldn't let his mates down by abandoning the protest; besides he'd volunteered, hadn't he? And he always did what was expected of him.

He watched with interest as Blaikie alighted from his vehicle, wondering what would happen next. The circle of suits standing in a huddle nearby broke rank and turned to greet the GM, nodding obsequiously as he strode towards them.

"What are you all standing around for?" Blaikie barked. "Somebody drag that bloody prick off the road!"

The Refinery's 2IC, Jim McClean, stepped forward. "We can't touch him, Roy. He's not on refinery property."

"Come again? I've got twenty thousand bucks going up in smoke every hour this shitshow drags on! The whole bloody country is following this fiasco with bated breath, and every paid-up union member and his dog on every other Think Big project throughout the land is gearing up to follow suit. Muldoon and the whole bloody guv'ment is breathing down my neck, telling me to deal to this situation quick smart, and you're telling me we can't move the idiot who's deliberately blocking the entrance to my refinery?"

"That's what I said, Roy."

Blaikie stamped his feet and all five foot one and a half inches of his barrel-shaped body shuddered as if he was about to erupt. He raised his arms in a gesture of despair. His team of managers, lawyers, and number crunchers huddled around him now in a deferential semi-circle, shifting uncomfortably from foot to foot, searching each other's faces for a solution as Blaikie eyeballed each of them in turn.

"How in God's name are we going to resolve this? Any ideas?" he asked them.

"Um, we thought that's why you'd decided to come down here, Roy — to sort it," McClean said sheepishly.

Roy's face collapsed as if he'd just sucked a lemon. "Well, I'm not frikking happy!" he shouted.

The ensuing silence was punctured by a lone voice from the picket line: "Which fucking dwarf are you, then, Mr Blaikie?"

A rumble of laughter broke out and Roy's face darkened to an even riper shade of tomato than it had been a moment before. He turned to his heavily-pregnant secretary who had tottered across the road two steps behind him, clutching a clipboard and pen.

"Write that joker's name down, Samantha!" he said. "And while you're about it, find out who this prostrate martyr is, blocking the road. I also want all those men on the picket line identified. No one is getting away with this! I'm going to convene a disciplinary inquiry into these shenanigans..."

Jim McClean put up his hand for permission to speak again.

"What? What is it?"

"We can't penalise the staff for striking, Roy."

"So, you're telling me, I've got a $2 billion world-class refinery idling in semi-shutdown mode, with a brand spanking new state-of-the-art hydrocracker ready to rock and roll — not to mention, a hundred and seventy kilometres of squeaky-clean new pipeline ready to pump fuel to Auckland at a rate of four thousand litres per minute, and twenty of the best operators in the southern hemisphere standing by in a bombproof control room, their fingers poised on the fire-it-up switches — but I'm being held over the barrel by a few dozen engineers and boiler makers? All because their tea isn't hot enough and the tea ladies aren't wearing short enough skirts?"

"That about sums it up, Roy."

Blaikie clutched his head in his hands. A few tense moments passed. Then Samantha tripped over to him and whispered something in his ear.

"What did you say? Jesus, girl, let me get this straight — the man blocking the gates is a bloody Kraut?"

"Yes, sir."

"And Muldoon expects *me* to sort out this shitshow when *he's* the one responsible for importing all this frikking foreign labour? Including the ten-pound commie poms who now run all the fucking unions in this country?"

The semi-circle of suits started mumbling; suddenly everyone had something to say. As they entered the fray with pertinent comments, Blaikie seemed to visibly relax, unhunching his shoulders and lowering his flailing arms. He'd had a lightbulb moment.

"Right, men," he said, "time to bring in the big guns. I've never seen the poncey new Beehive — I could actually get quite excited about a tiki tour to Wellington. I hear Courtenay Place is where all the action is on a Friday night. And mark my words, by the time I'm finished with Muldoon, I'm picking this guv'ment will be passing urgent legislation to prevent this sort of carry on ever happening again! After all, we've got the crude, we've got the hydrocracker, we've got the pipeline. But if we ain't got the labour to complete this last critical hook-up, we can't transfer any frikking fuel, can we? I'll have Muldoon on his knees before you can say, 'Cheryl bloody Moana Marie'."

The semi-circle of suits conferred, heads nodding in agreement.

"Darn good idea, boss."

"Our hands are tied. What choice do we have?"

"The government could do with a rev up. 'Bout time they stepped up and put a stop to these shenanigans!"

"Yeah, too bloody right."

Blaikie picked up the chorus line: "Read my lips, team: 1984 will go down in New Zealand history as the year the unions stopped squeezing the balls of free enterprise!"

He pulled himself up to his full height. If he stretched his neck and lifted his chin it made him look an inch taller. He knew it did because he often practised in front of the mirror. He needed to shut this circus down. Otherwise, things could escalate, turn nasty. Hell, the press was already having a field day, and some jokers would do anything to get themselves onto a TV screen or the front page of a newspaper. He knew from experience how quickly a strike could turn violent.

He indicated for one of his aides to hand him a megaphone. It was time to rise to the occasion. Holding the large metal cone made him feel braver; more confident. He spun around in a tight circle, scanning the crowd, projecting his voice as well as he could:

"Right people, the carnival is over. I'm closing the refinery until further notice. You might as well pack up your picnics and head home. Peacefully, please. I don't want to have to call the cops down here. Members of the press — see me for a statement after everyone has dispersed."

At this precise moment, a giant of a man unfolded himself from the doorway of the union caravan and stepped down onto the roadway. Minutes before he'd been twitching the curtains inside, watching Blaikie make a fool of himself. He began to walk across the gravel to where Blaikie and his subordinates stood, near the poor bugger who was blocking the gates.

Bully Durham was a bovver boy and an ex-heavyweight boxer from the back streets of Glasgow; a bear-sized man and a rigger who'd worked Clydeside in his former life and been active in the Shipbuilders' Union back in the old country. Now he was hitched to a handsome Māori wahine half his age who wore hibiscus flowers in her hair as if she'd just stepped out of a Gauguin painting, and he had a bevy of golden-brown children who rode on his shoulders and clung to his trouser legs as he measured out in giant strides the fertile land he owned near his wife's marae at Takahiwai, where he was farming beef for his retirement.

Bull, as he was more formally known, had spent years building up the Engineers & Boilermakers Unions in New Zealand into the powerful organisations they were today. He knew for certain he had far more clout in this situation than Blaikie did. He crossed the gravel slowly, walked right up to Blaikie, then stared down at him, dwarfing him in shadow. Blaikie tilted his head back and looked up at Durham, narrowing his eyes, trying to look fierce. He noticed that Bull's forehead was furrowed with deep craters and the man's ample moustache twitched when he pursed his lips, as if a small rodent was clambering across his face.

"Sounds like you're working harder than a fiddler's elbow to make some noise on that instrument, yet only a weak warped sound is coming out of it," Durham said to Blaikie, pointing at the megaphone. "Might be, the person in charge here should be telling these men when they can disperse. Or not. And that person would be... *me*," he said, stabbing Blaikie in the chest with a finger the size of a salami sausage.

Blaikie knew that Durham knew his onions, and he was always horribly mismatched in any contest of words with the big fella. Any contest, actually. Besides, he was beginning to get a crick in his neck.

"Fair enough," he said. "I'm not going to argue with the likes of *you*, you commie sympathiser!"

Bull snorted, stabbing his forefinger further into Roy's sternum. "Don't push my buttons, Cunt," he said.

Blaikie stepped back, tensing up again. "Don't call me cunt, Cunt!" he said, in a shaky voice that had travelled a few semitones up the scale since he'd last spoken.

"Or what?" The huge Scotsman started laughing like a stuck bear, and the captive audience began to titter as the sound of 'ooh' and 'aah' and 'ouch' travelled up and down the picket line and through the crowd.

When Bull finally stopped guffawing, he smiled ingratiatingly at Roy, gave a slight bow, and extended his hand: "Mr Blaikie, Sir! I'd like to cordially invite you to meet with me in my office for a coffee and a chinwag. There's some important guff I'd like to share with you about why my boys pulled the pin on this here operation and downed tools, what our demands are, and how long we're intending to continue this strike action. We do actually have some serious concerns about health and safety, Blaikie. Stuff that needs to be addressed. Stuff you're really going to need to know about when you're standing in front of Muldoon shaking in your boots and on the verge of crapping your duds, while he's holding you accountable for this situation..."

Roy gulped. It didn't sound pretty. And it didn't take much to persuade him. He needed to at least be *seen* to be trying to broker a solution. The boilermakers and welders were desperately needed back on site to complete some critical tie-ins to the new plant before it could be fired up, and he would be the fall guy if the dispute wasn't resolved soon — existing stocks of petrol and jet fuel would soon run out if the standoff continued for much longer. He quickly decided it would be in his best interests to oblige. Not to mention, the country's. He would be conciliatory, negotiate in good faith. He knew from experience that a bit of palm greasing went a long way with these union stalwarts.

"Thanks for agreeing to be civil, Mr Durham" he said, as if the chinwag was his idea. He knew Bully was purported to add a liberal dose of Johnny Walker to a hot drink, and Roy felt in dire need of a snifter right now. That, in itself, would be worth swallowing a few mouthfuls of humble pie.

Bruno watched as the two men retreated to the caravan and the crowd and picket line settled down again, poised for the duration. He groaned inwardly as he realised he'd now be expected to lie where he was for a while longer.

As more time passed, Bruno started thinking about Little Ruthie again. One afternoon, he'd arrived in the village with the day's parcel of butter for *Herschel's Lebensmittelmarkt* to find a couple of Gestapo jeeps pulled up outside the store. Shouts and screams could be heard from inside and when he entered, he saw Herr and Frau Herschel backed up against a wall where an officer was holding them at gun point. Frau Herschel was sobbing and begging the officer not to shoot, while her husband entreated her to be quiet. Bruno heard noises on the stairwell and looked up to see two other officers herding a small, frightened group down the stairs from the family's living quarters above — obviously the three Hershel boys and their tutor — hitting them with their rifle butts and shouting at them to get a move on:

"*Schnel! Schnel! Juden raus*! Out with the Jews!"

Bruno couldn't help staring. He noticed how dark Ruthie's brothers' hair was, how black their eyes, how sallow their skin. Their tutor was as strangely attired as Ruthie had described him to be. How had he not realised before that the Hershels were a Jewish family?

"We heard there was a girl too," the officer holding the Hershels at gunpoint barked. "Where is she?"

Dread filled Bruno as his eyes searched the interior of the shop for little Ruthie. She was nowhere to be seen and he knew immediately where she could probably be found — under the counter, fast asleep.

In the pregnant pause that followed, a muffled cough was heard, and shortly Ruthie emerged from beneath the counter rubbing her eyes. Her cheeks and clothing were covered in a fine dusting of flour, as if she was a doll-sized gingerbread girl. She took the situation in with one glance and blinked a few times, but her pasty, drawn little face didn't betray a single flicker of fear.

"There she is!" one of the officers said.

But before he began to move towards her, Ruthie said, very firmly, "*Nein*. No." She pointed at Bruno. "*Ich bin bei ihm*. I'm with him."

The Nazi officers looked confused and scanned each other's faces, each one hoping that one of the others would make the decision about whether to take the girl with them, or not. Ruthie took advantage of their hesitation and ran over to Bruno. He hugged her to him, then stepped forward smartly, clicking his heels, and saluting the soldiers.

"Heil Hitler!" he said. "Long live the Führer!" He addressed the officer who seemed to be in charge, the one who'd mentioned they were also looking for a little girl.

"If you please, Commandant, this girl is with me," he continued. "She's my little sister, Gretchen. The Hershels look after her while I'm out working in the fields, milking cows, and churning the butter which I deliver to your mess at the castle every day. My parents are away, working at the Siemens factory, manufacturing munitions for the war effort."

"Is this correct?" One of the soldiers had jammed his pistol against Mr Herschel's temple, cocking it.

"Oh yes, quite so," Herschel replied. "She's very naughty, a real handful, always playing in the flour, messing up the shop. She doesn't listen to me, or to my wife. Her brother fetches her at this time every afternoon. We always sigh in relief when he arrives, so happy to see the back of her."

The Commandant looked unconvinced. "But she is dark and he is fair?"

"Their mother was a postal worker before the war," Mr Herschel continued. "You know what they say about postmen, eh? Well, the women are just as bad!"

The Commandant started laughing and the other Gestapo officers joined in. Ruthie took Bruno's hand in hers and made eye contact. She tilted her head sideways ever so slightly, then gently tugged his arm, and they walked out of the shop.

Bruno eventually dozed off where he lay in front of the refinery gates. Time passed. He slept on until he heard footsteps approaching across the gravel and a woman's voice, with Germanic inflections, speaking nearby:

"I'm with him," she said to the groups assembled nearby. "I mean," she corrected herself, "he's with me."

Then she was by his side and he heard her voice again: "Wake up, Bruno. You can come home with me now, *Schatz*. Get up."

Bruno looked up to see his wife peering down at him with those deep-set narrow eyes, her face framed with soft greying curls. He noticed her apron was dusted with swathes of flour, as were her hair, cheeks, and arms.

"They called me on the telephone, told me to come down here and fetch you home. It's all over."

"*Gott sei Dank*," Bruno replied.

He raised himself with some difficulty; it had been a long vigil and he was stiff and sore. His wife dusted him down while he stretched and shook the pins and needles out of his arms and legs.

"The Generalissimo has already left for the airport," she continued. "Apparently when he came out of the caravan, he was bowing and scraping and clicking his heels together like the most ingratiating of Nazis! Then the big union boss came out and gave a speech of thanks to all the strikers for their forbearance." She smiled. "He said everyone can take the rest of the day off and return to work tomorrow."

Bruno looked up to see waste gases from the refinery's flue curling into the sky and tracking across the water towards Manaia. He threw his arm around the woman's shoulders.

"Well, Ruthie," he said, "Our castle in Königstein has stood strong against her enemies for a thousand years so I guess Mount Manaia is not going to fall down any time soon. There'll be time enough to refine oil into petrol tomorrow, don't you think?"

"Oh yes, quite so," she said. "I've got *erbsbrei* bubbling on the stove. You must be starving, *Schatz*..."

Bruno smiled at his wife. "*Liebling*, what do you think? Maybe it's time for me to stop putting my hand up for stuff," he said. "Other men can do the dirty work from now on."

"Maybe. But sometimes it's for a worthy cause, *ja*? Sometimes it's a matter of life and death."

"*Jawohl*," Bruno replied. " But sometimes it's also a matter of *herzenangelegenheit*, isn't it? A matter of the heart."

Terror and Self-Loathing in Te Atatū

That particular morning, you should have known your number had come up, Jerome. You really ought to have, man, because when that day dawned — so bright, so awful — every cell in your illness-racked body went on high alert as the news of the closeness of your death travelled between them like Chinese whispers.

Yet, you continued to resist the inevitability of it all. You were gung-ho, hacking it, still riding the wave even though you barely had the strength to drag yourself through another twenty-four hours. The Great Pretender, the Invincible Man. But even comic book heroes have use-by dates, mate. You knew that, surely? This was the day on which the enormity of what you'd have to face sooner or later was to come suddenly upon you. Notwithstanding your unpreparedness. Despite your denial.

The fact is, dawn always comes too soon when you're loath to face another day. As you surfaced uneasily to consciousness that morning from the depths of Hieronymus Bosch's Hell, where you'd spent the last few hours in the company of creatures more animal than human, engaged in acts more surreal and bizarre than your waking mind could ever conceive, it seemed as if a cosmic switch had been activated. The dense pre-dawn blackness you'd been staring into for the longest time was instantaneously replaced by the bright unforgiving glare of the sun, as its vengeful beams penetrated a chink in the curtains, piercing you where you lay.

You waited, still as death, face to the wall, as a woman crept from your bed. You wanted to say something to her. Honest you did. You wanted to reach out to her in some way and share some kind of tenderness. But it was so much easier not to.

You heard her shuffling around your room, pictured her dressing in last night's hastily discarded clothing, then sensed her closeness and felt her hot breath on your face as she leaned across the bed. A long, quiet moment followed. *What was she doing?* Next thing her lips brushed across your cheek and she was gone, her footsteps echoing down the hall. The front door clicked as it closed behind her. You heard her car starting up and accelerating through successive gear changes until it merged with the distant grumble of commuter traffic on Te Atatū Road. All those suckers — the working poor — crawling towards their dead-end jobs in the city. Not you, though. You'd never worked a regular job, ever; had no conception of an ordinary life.

You sighed and rolled over onto your back. *Just another cruisy weekday morning in the life of me, myself, I,* you thought. Your body felt like someone else's. Your limbs ached and the hollow in the pit of your stomach felt like a bleeding ulcer. Your head whirled and throbbed and you felt like you were floating above yourself, somewhere between life and death. The glowering sun continued to bore holes in your retinas, even when you closed your eyes. Unbearable.

You felt for your shades on the bedside table, the compulsory accessory of the habitual dope smoker. They were the cheap ones, like alien eyes, which wrap around the sides of your face, cutting maximum light. The relief when you shoved them on was indescribable.

Curry jumped onto the bed and delivered his usual foul-mouthed early-morning greeting: a long, plaintive "Meoooooow." He tiptoed across the rumpled sheets and started pawing at your shoulder. You slapped him away. He stood his ground nearby, glaring at you as if to say, "You pathetic lazy excuse for a human being. Get up you sod, and feed me." He was so like Garfield, you often questioned your sanity in choosing to cohabit with him. A chick — the one before the one before the one who had just left your bed — had left him behind when she moved out, so you'd been kinda stuck with him. He was a poor excuse for a flatmate, but at least, in his cupboard love kind of way, he cared whether you lived or died.

You forced yourself up and made your way shakily to the bathroom where you slumped over the basin. Pulling off your shades to wash your face, you caught your reflection in the mirror. A parody of your former self stared back at you. Your once striking blue eyes, now faded and sunken in their sockets, looked scarily vacant. Your skin was sallow, and the sharp protruding cheekbones your illness had left behind were exacerbated by a five-day growth. *Maybe it was time you shaved. Maybe not. What difference would it make?*

An overwhelming sense of vitriol overcame you. You cast about for something strong and hard to break the mirror but all you found in the vanity were a few threadbare towels. You grabbed one and wrapped it around your fist. After a last look at the spectre in the mirror, you lunged for it. You were in the ring with the Tua Man. It was fight night, and you — you were the contender. When you finished, the basin was unusable, filled with fractured fragments of broken mirror. *Better purge myself,* you thought. *Better scrub away all the shame and pain that threatens to overwhelm me.*

You flicked the shower on and limped into it. Hot water gushed over you, and you slid down the wall and slumped in the corner, where you sat, curled in a stupor of sudsy vapour, until the water ran cold. It was only when you heard the shrill ring of the phone that you came to your senses. While trying to dry yourself, you tripped over the cat a couple of times and kicked him out of the way. Catching a glimpse of your naked self in the full-length mirror on your cupboard door, you blanched. Your body resembled the carcass of a strange beast hung out to cure. *Bugger,* you thought, *I'll have to get rid of this mirror too.*

Spurred on by his growling stomach, Curry tried his luck again. This time you kicked him and sent him flying across the room. He hit the wall, spun off it into the air, landed on his four feet, and bolted from the room. "Stay out of my way, Peabrain!" you shouted after him. "Or else!"

You sat down on the edge of the bed and tried to collect yourself. A wave of self-revulsion swept over you. *Why were you always so mean to him? Why had you been so offhand with her? Why were you so angry with everyone and everything?* You pulled on your trackies, a T-shirt and jumper, and what last night's lay had referred to as your 'old-man' slippers. The smell of her lingered in the room. You remembered how good it felt when you got your dick into her at last and let rip, got your rocks off good and proper after all the inane small talk and seduction repartee. *What a hard-up grot she was.* She said you were the only man she'd even known who could undo a bra with one hand. "Must be due to all the practice I've had," you'd said. She hadn't even batted an eyelid. "Aren't I the lucky one, then," she'd said.

After you'd got dressed, you shuffled through to the kitchen, chucked on the jug, and threw a few Friskies on the floor. "Here, Puss, Puss," you called, but Curry was making himself scarce. No surprises there. You took your coffee into the lounge where you fell onto the couch and switched on the TV. The picture shimmered into view. That gay cunt was on; the metrosexual who hosts the Good Morning Show. You shuddered. A red-nailed sophisticate with her hair teased up into a French roll was showing him how to cut and sew an apron. "And after that," she said, with a wicked gleam in her eyes, "he'll be wearing this cute little apron while we bake yummy blueberry muffins for morning tea." *Oh fuck, spare me!* you thought.

The phone blinking on the coffee table distracted you from the banality. You remembered someone had tried to call and dialled message retrieval.

"Jimmy... Jerome! This is your mother (as if you needed an introduction). Why can't you record an ordinary voice message instead of that God-awful cacophony? Lead Zebras? Anyway, what I want to know is, when is your hospital appointment?

"It's bad enough *you're* sick (voice shrieks up to a crescendo) but Nana's not too good either. She wants you to come down and see her; says this time she's certain she's... (blubber, blubber). You were always her favourite, Jimmy. Remember how she used to call you Jiminy Cricket?" A bleep sounded and the message cut out.

Fuck, she could go on and on, just like the Energiser bunny! Didn't she ever run out of puff?

You retrieved the second message. It was Mum again.

"As I was saying, Jerome, Nana needs you. Remember when she'd pretend to be the Blue Fairy and told you your role in life was to be Pinocchio's conscience, to save him from all ill deeds. She'd pat your bottom and say, 'Now run along and play, Jiminy; time enough for you to be serious another day (sniff, sniff).'

"Dad will pay for your air ticket. I suppose you haven't any money as usual (sigh). It's about time you came home, Jimmy. Your brothers want to catch up too. And your birthday's coming up. You could spend it with us, just this once, in Dunedin."

The message timed out again.

You rolled a cigarette and lit up, relishing that first drag of the day. *Oh tobacco, the perfect complement to sweet, metallic, instant coffee.* Your mother's voice continued over the lame TV programme, a pre-recorded tape in your head: "You've got to pull up your socks, Jerome, clean yourself up and make an effort, take better care of yourself. Cut out the alcohol, coffee, cigarettes, and anything *else* you're on, dear. You know what I mean. Eat lots of fruit and vegetables. Remember what the doctor said! Come home and we'll help you through this, take care of you..."

Yeah, more likely, drive me to my own demise and hammer the nails into my coffin as fast and firmly as you can. Man, Mum is such a control freak! How had Dad put up with her all these years...?

They lived on another planet, as if the latter part of the twentieth century had passed them by. Dad was an accountant who cooked a lot of books. And a serial philanderer. No surprises there. Said he spent his life at the office and the RSA and the golf club servicing his clients, but we knew otherwise. He'd shifted out to New Zealand as a young man from the 'Old Country' as he liked to call it, on a sponsored immigration programme. He was your typical Ten Pound Pom. Had the aura of a gentleman about him, and that la-di-da way of speaking, *the Queen's English*, he'd say. But most people knew he was a charlatan and a cheating son of a bitch.

Okay, you had to admit, Dad had his uses and you ought to cut him some slack. The old fart was quite wealthy now and since your life had gone pear-shaped he always sent you cash if you needed it, no questions asked. It was probably a guilt trip thing, but it was a help.

As for Mum, she wasn't as easy to manipulate, but she meant well. At least she kept in touch. She liked to call herself a 'home executive' — her positive slant on the drudgery of housewifery, underpinned by longstanding memberships of Probus and the Women's Institute. A craft fetish and Tupperware containers full of home baking were her definition of happiness. These domestic pursuits took the edge off the perpetual premenstrual tension she inflicted on all and sundry. She always kept a large card of Valium in her knitting bag, which was handy for both you and her. Mother's Little Helper.

She actually looked really pretty in her wedding photos, the ones hanging in the hallway of the family home; dewy-eyed and innocent, wearing a sixties getup. Back in the day, couples married pretty young — the only way they could have legal sex, basically. It must have been hard on her having three babies in a row before she was even a proper adult, especially with Dad always away from home. Why hadn't she stood up for herself and demanded his loyalty?

As for your brothers and their successful professional careers, brand new houses in new subdivisions with late-model beamers and SUVs in their garages, the national average of children between them, and wives with horsey teeth who were book club and wine club freaks. They didn't give a stuff about you and why would they? You were a failure in their eyes.

Oh, that fucked-up town at the arse end of the world. Dunners. Populated by people you were stuck with by an accident of birth. If only they'd just fade away. But no, they endured, like cockroaches. Armageddon could come, and they'd still be out there on a Saturday morning mowing the lawns and pruning the roses, baking date scones for afternoon tea, reading the weekend papers in the sunroom, while

Nana wandered around the neighbourhood in her urine-stained nightie chanting nursery rhymes. Nana was the archetypal 'Blue Fairy' all right, and she had the blue rinse to go with it!

Nothing in their paltry lives could ever equal the way you'd felt when you'd been at the top of your game, driving home from your 'office' in Newtown with a couple of K in tidy bundles in your briefcase, trance pumping from the JVCs in the boot of your Commodore Club Sport. The matchless high you'd felt when you parked up outside your Grey Lynn villa and walked through the stained-glass front door, your long black leather coat swishing across the kauri floorboards, your hand in your pocket stroking the loaded Smith & Wesson .45 nestling there like a hard-on. The slow wink of the Siamese cat as she stretched out in front of the wood burner on a white Flokati rug. The hum of the refrigerator in the stainless-steel kitchen, where bottles of bubbly sweated at four degrees. The cracking good blow you snorted from the marble vanity in your bathroom as you sat with your bum on the side of a claw-foot bath filled with rose petals. The smugness that lit up your face when you snapped open that loaded briefcase and tipped all that fucking success and happiness onto your king-size waterbed where a blonde in a push-up bra and G-string lay waiting for you, smiling like a Cheshire cat.

Everything was relative. Relative as, you thought. *Like, hadn't your family ever heard of Einstein, for fuck's sakes???*

Okay, you had to concede, things were different *now*. You were down and out. A no-hoper. A loser. And you weren't even *in* Dunners. Haha. You were the dark secret your folks had pushed under their garish seventies lounge carpet, the unholy terror they burned in their annual Guy Fawkes bonfire, the spoilt baby of the family gone bad. *So what? A short life on the edge was infinitely preferable to banality.* Soon enough, the hospital would up your morphine and you'd die on your own terms. Just like you'd lived. It was way better to burn out than to fade away. Wasn't it?

Something pricked you in the buttocks. A hoop earring. You must have nibbled it off last night's lay's ear at some point during the proceedings. 'Crystal'. Not her real name — you'd picked her up on NZ Dating. For fuck's sakes, it was so lame — she hadn't even been able to come up with an original handle! Yours was Seven_Nation_Army, after the White Stripes song.

You swung the earring around your bony finger hula-hoop-like, thinking about 'Crystal'. You'd never found out her real name. Never asked. No matter. You weren't exactly champing at the bit to see her again. But you had to admit, there was something about her that was... *vaguely* intriguing. For one thing, she was ...dark. Dark skinned, dark haired. You'd only ever gone out with blondes, and man, you'd been through so many they'd all merged into one. Haha, you had a stock joke you always used on them. You'd ask them to describe their hair colour and they'd say *ash* blonde or *strawberry* blonde or *platinum* blonde, and you'd reply, 'Nah, bottle blonde, surely?' Most of them were so thick they didn't even get you were taking the piss.

Actually, you did hang with a chick, once, who was a *natural* blonde. A *real* blonde. Mercedes. She had squinty eyes like Karen Black, that actress in *Easy Rider*, your fave cult movie. You were hightailing it back to Auckland once, coming down after smoking a lot of bad shit up north with the bros, and she'd gotten up your nose about something. That's right — she'd broken your designer Versace aviators! You'd been mad as a snake and dumped her in Maungaturoto; hadn't seen her since. And thank fuck for that! She'd been super ditzy, with her new age mumbo jumbo and her 'carpet bag' full of incense and Buddha effigies and tarot cards and whatnot. She was always trying to read your fortune; told you the cards said you were cruising for a bruising.

Whatever. How can your future be predetermined? What about freedom of choice? What about being the master of your own destiny/ Helloooooo?

'Crystal' is bit 'different', alright. Quirky. She's short and curvy and her feet seem to stick way out in front of her, like that's all you see coming towards you. When she talks it's about weird stuff like how she likes to push her face into a full-blown rose and inhale the perfume. She says roses make her so happy she can't stop herself from tearing the blossoms to pieces and eating the petals! *Weird,* you thought, *way weird.* She had a cute smile, though, and her mouth was all velvety. Like a rosebud's. Yeah.

Mmm, it's not like you to wax lyrical, Jimmy Masters. You never get sweet on a woman, ever. That's when they start expecting stuff. Like deep conversations and joint bank accounts.

Last night's lay didn't though; she just up and left, didn't even try to organise a repeat date. Maybe you were losing your touch. You'd been a real looker once; you'd pulled chicks with a Woody Harrelson stare and a flick of your fringe. Not anymore. You had to lure them in now by posting old photos on dating sites.

You threw Crystal's earring into the empty fruit bowl on the table. The gay dude on TV was stuffing a muffin into his cakehole, looking like a total dick in the frilly apron he'd made, while the bitch beside him jumped up and down with glee. *Rather him than me,* you thought. Thank fuck it was Wednesday, your regular meet up with your connections down at the local gang headquarters. You'd drop a couple of pills, smoke a few pipes, down a couple of Woodys, play a game or two of pool, ya-de-ya about the old days. *Bring it on, man.*

You needed to ring Dune to remind him to pick you up. Your wheels were off road right now, parked up in your front yard, unrego'd and unwarranted, with ferns growing through the engine bay and knee-high grass covering those to-die-for mags. You closed your eyes when you walked past the wreck; it was absolutely gutting to see.

Oh well, you thought, *the wreck made a far better garden ornament than a sad collection of chipped garden gnomes with fading paintwork, like Mum had, back in Dunners.*

Your cell was busted and the landline bill was overdue, so Telecom had put a call bar on it. *Different name, different address, same shit,* you thought. The old bat next door always let you use hers though; she was petrified of you and did anything you asked of her, even if it was mostly just a cup of sugar you needed. You got up and made your way down the hallway towards the front door, clutching the walls to guide yourself. *Were you imagining it, or was the pain worse?* Sweat beaded your forehead and you felt faint.

You opened the door and were standing at the top of the steps with your foot poised in the air ready to step down when a marmalade-coloured flash sprinted across your vision. It was Curry; he'd shot out of the kitchen and crossed your path. *That fucking stupid moggie!* You folded at the knees and hit your head on the banister on the way down. *Boing. Boing. Boing.*

There were only three steps but the concrete path at their bottom was the exact opposite of a soft landing. You lay there incapable of moving — not one iota — as something wet gushed from an abrasion on your temple. The sun burned in your eyes until it became the bright white light of the tunnel of death. That's when you realised your number *had* come up, Jiminy Cricket; that you were in the departure lounge and they'd just called your flight. That you were simply another nameless, faceless passenger travelling through this world of trouble and sickness and woe on a one-way ticket to salvation. Or was it oblivion?

Hang on a minute, you thought. *All that stuff about the tunnel of death is just a physiological reaction induced by the body's chemical response to a lack of oxygen. Just a lie, like all the other crap and nonsense and bullshit and psychobabble people make up to help them face reality.* You'd decided as a child to reject all that shit. And that was OK. You could hack it. You'd have to. You had no choice.

But you couldn't hack the light, man; it was just too fucking bright. The sun burned down on your retinas, and you cursed yourself for overlooking the one and only rule you lived by. *Never... repeat... never... ever... go anywhere without your bloody shades!*

If last night's lay hadn't decided to come back for her missing earring, it would have been tickets for you, Jerome, that bright, sunny day in Te Atatū.

Golden Girl

Jake Lazarus was an early riser, the comfort of deep and extended sleep no longer something older people take for granted. After rising well before dawn and shuffling through his morning routine which consisted of relieving himself (a lengthy and difficult procedure what with his prostate problems); letting the cat out (dangerous, because one might trip over her in her enthusiasm); making a cup of strong tea which he delivered to his wife's bedside at 7am (tricky because he possessed few natural domestic skills); and slowly dressing himself (which might have been the easiest task of his morning routine if he wasn't so arthritic, as he merely pulled on the clothes he'd thrown over a bedroom chair the night before); he ventured outdoors at daybreak to spend the long mornings of his life lazily tending his beloved flower garden at the front of the house.

The only interruption to his morning routine was when Madge called him in for his cooked breakfast of fried blood sausage, eggs and toast, accompanied by a pot of strong tea; a necessary refuelling of the body through which he suffered the interminable garrulousness of the female specimen to whom he was attached — she who spoiled the pleasure he'd otherwise have taken in this repast by preaching forth on a variety of subjects including the weather, the rising crime rate, and the effects of inflation upon the household budget.

Jake's afternoons followed a different pattern, however, tending to dissipate into uncertainty as far as gardening weather was concerned, due to the vagaries of the South Island climate. Thus, after devouring a couple of luncheon sandwiches and more tea, he spent his afternoons dozing in his living room in a fat armchair which had shaped itself through long use to the contours of his body, in front of a large picture window that provided him with a wide-angle view of his garden and the quiet street beyond; a street which suffocated itself in its clean and regimental ordinariness and lack of interest, come rain or shine.

In this way, Jake could still enjoy his garden while also observing the comings and goings on Orchard Street, Tākaka. Having been an investigative journalist and war correspondent in a former incarnation, he was an innately inquisitive fellow and liked to keep vigil, lest anything untoward take place in the neighbourhood. Yet his ability and desire to participate in the life of the community had long been reduced to that of a mere observer. It never occurred to him he might, in any proactive way, become embroiled in any other life, other than his and Madge's.

So, mornings saw Jake moving slowly around his front garden and communing with his beloved plants, petting them with his hands and talking to them with such gentleness and unhurried affection one might think they were endowed with human attributes. From time to time, though, he would pause to look up and down the street, checking all was in order. When satisfied that it was, he'd return his attention to his gardening chores, dipping into his grubby gardener's apron for a pair of secateurs to deadhead his roses, or pulling the trigger on a bottle of pest spray to dispatch without remorse any unwelcome creepy-crawlies that had dared colonise one of his prized shrubs. If any strangers appeared in the street, he'd eyeball them, letting them know in no uncertain terms that he was on guard; similarly, if any weeds dared show their heads above ground level, he was merciless, immediately culling them with a weed puller and throwing them on a bonfire in the back yard.

In the afternoons, settled comfortably in his stuffed out old La-Z-Boy, he could be seen from the street reclining resplendent in an egg-stained button-up jersey and wearing a pair of worn tartan carpet slippers, the Dominion spread across his lap keeping the burn of the sun at bay in summer and warming his knees in winter, the coarse grey stubble on his slack jaw and his bowed head nodding in the Land of Naps completing the picture of a contented retirement.

This was how he filled his time when Madge was out of the house, working the afternoon shift at the local fish and chip shop to earn the extra income they needed over and above the pension to make ends meet. But in the evenings, when he heard Madge's footsteps outside, or if he'd been dozing when he heard her key in the lock, he'd jerk upright, push his bifocals back up the bridge of his nose, brush away any spittle that might have dribbled down his chin, grab a blunt pencil from the folds of his lap, and pretend he'd been working on the crossword all afternoon. Then, when Madge started rattling around the kitchen preparing tea, he'd switch to his evening routine, which he always referred to as 'going to see a man about a dog'.

So it was, now Madge was gone, he'd find himself coming to with a startled feeling at precisely the same time every evening, and as was his long time custom, he'd rise from his chair, stretch, scratch his crotch, then shuffle through the kitchen (where he had always pecked Madge on the cheek in passing), out of the back door (which he had invariably slammed shut behind him, causing Madge to wince), and make his way along the cracked concrete path to his shed at the bottom of the garden. En route, he'd pause at the same place to relieve himself — the same spot the cat always used — noticing with smug satisfaction how the grass never grew there.

When he reached the shed, he'd fumble for a while with the padlock on the door; a nuisance it was — his arthritic fingers could no longer manage intricate tasks. But since Madge had reported she'd heard there were bad elements about, they'd both decided to be more cautious. Besides, all his treasures were in his shed and he didn't want any old stranger poking about amongst them and helping himself to stuff now, did he?

He relished the feeling that overcame him when the door eventually sprang open, allowing him to enter. He'd pause on the threshold and inhale the smell of pipe tobacco and two-stroke oil that lingered inside, then totter in and sit down on an upturned beer crate in the back corner. He stored his pipe within easy reach on a shelf beside him, and soon, he'd pick it up, and pack it with Port Royal from a worn leather pouch. After a few puffs, when his throat started feeling scratchy, he'd reach for the half-jack of whisky he kept tucked away behind the crate and take a long swig. "So good for lubricating the old joints," he'd say to Marge when he asked her to restock, despite her pinched mouth's disapproval.

The alcohol always fired him up somewhat. He'd notice his hard thumping heart still doing its job, sending his thick blood coursing through his sluggish old veins. As his worn synapses fired in the depths of his brain, the few remaining hairs on his head would prickle with anticipation. And in his mind's eye he'd randomly relive scenes of derring-do from his past, when he'd been a strong, capable man of the world, who after an early career in construction and a few dead ends, had ended up as a journalist, travelling widely for his job. Expressions of pride and the satisfaction of a life well lived and a job well done would flicker across his face as the shadows of his former selves gleamed there again for a short while.

One evening, as he searched his memory for past exploits, he became distracted by the sound of something vague and near — obscure snifflings and scratchings in the wood box abutting the shed. Shifting from side to side on his bony buttocks and listening more attentively, a feeling of foreboding overcame him as he remembered Madge's warnings of bad elements in the neighbourhood, combined with an acute sense of loneliness now that she was gone.

Perhaps a possum was scratching for pickings, but the compost heap was on the other side of the yard. He switched up his hearing aid to full volume and leaned in closer to the wall. He still couldn't identify the sounds he was hearing, yet knowing instinctively they were made by some living creature, he waited, patience being a quality one learns well in old age. And in the silence of his mind and the quiet of the autumn evening, he heard what he thought sounded like human sobs, interspersed with gasps of breath.

He did not know what he'd do if he had to deal with a *situation*. Now that Madge — the more practical one of the two — was no longer there to refer to, inadequacy overcame him. He took another deep swig from his half-jack, then looked for a gap in the sarking to peep through. When he found one, all he could make out was the back of a head of yellow curls that rose and fell in concordance with the sobs emitting from the sorry little creature huddling there.

Madge had always insisted Jake keep a tin of biscuits in the shed for his low blood sugar. "If you come over queer before I call you in for tea, you'll have something to nibble on," she'd say, "to counteract the side effects of that God-awful whisky, not to mention that devil's weed you smoke. And don't you ever think I don't know what you're up to down there in that darn shed, you old curmudgeon," she'd scolded, far too often than he cared to remember. She had also warned him shortly before she died that he was becoming increasingly doolally, and even though she had always been prone to exaggeration, he wondered whether she hadn't perhaps got to the heart of the matter. Right now, he felt so shaky and confused, he reached for the tin and slipped a wine biscuit into his mouth, chasing it down with another swig of whisky. Madge's high-pitched admonitions continued to ring in his ears. *I must get this hearing aid seen to*, he thought, certain it was playing up on him.

When he heard another wretched sob or two he knew for certain the child hiding in the wood box was in deep distress. The voice of his long dead mother took over from Madge's and he heard her say, "Better do the right thing, my boy, and share." He slipped a couple of wine biscuits through the gap in the wall and let them fall. The muffled sobbing stopped immediately and he heard a deep intake of breath. When he peered through the gap again, he saw a tiny hand moving one of the biscuits towards a cherubic little mouth which opened like a trap, then clamped shut again, and began chewing.

Jake felt perplexed. He'd never noticed a curly-headed child playing in the street before, vigilant as he was regarding the coming and goings of the neighbourhood. Who could it be? He pushed a few more biscuits through the gap and watched, intrigued, as the child munched ravenously through them.

After a few minutes, he ventured a gentle, "Hello?"

All activity on the other side of the wall came to an abrupt halt. A dirty, little, tear-stained face turned to see where the voice was coming from, and their eyes met. Jake did a double take; he had never seen eyes that colour before and was momentarily distracted trying to think of a descriptive for them. There was a violent scrabbling in the wood box, and he heard the lid squeak open, then slam shut. When he looked through the gap again, the child was gone.

The child was Mercedes. 'The Golden Girl from Golden Bay', as Jake later came to call her. Jake had loved only two members of the female sex before this tiny blonde-haired, violet-eyed child had turned up totally unexpectedly in his wood box; his mother who'd been tender and true and done an exemplary job of raising him on her own, and Madge who had gifted him her youth, her beauty, and her loyalty. He'd had a narrow escape in his early twenties when a girl named Samantha had gotten herself pregnant by him to try and get her hooks into him, but after a life-threatening run in with her irate father, he'd met Madge and her family, and they had nursed him back to health. Even though Jack and Madge had been unable to have children, Jake had never felt their lack nor longed for them. The softness of Madge in his arms and the way she cleaved to him in the night when he returned home from an extended overseas journalistic posting made him feel he could let go of the horror he had witnessed in hotspots across the world through her; that her receptive feminine goodness negated it all, restoring him to himself.

Yet, as time passed, he came to love this golden-haired little girl more deeply than even Madge and his dear mother. He loved her with a selflessness formerly unknown to him, a devotion purer than anything he'd ever experienced. Mercedes, Mercy for short, visited often, spending long hours hiding in the wood box, fleeing from what horrors Jake knew not. During her visits they'd whisper a truncated form of communication through the gap in the wall. She was always hungry, and Jake broke a larger hole in the slats so he could pass her bunches of sweet black grapes from the old vines at the back of the section, leftover lamb chops, cold from the fridge, ripe cherry tomatoes warmed by the sun, a cup of milk, a slab of buttered bread, and anything else he had to spare. The child devoured everything he offered her, as if she was half starved.

As time passed the little girl grew braver, coming to trust old Jake. He was different from the constant string of rough blokes who passed through her mother's abode, who caused upsets and meted out discipline, who took but never gave. She'd call in to Jake's place on her way home from school, grubby and unkempt in her over-tight, green- and white-checked smock and scuffed sandals. Jake waited for her like he'd waited for Madge, parked in his Lay-Z-Boy, watching the quiet street from his picture window through the tall heads of his flowering hollyhocks. And when he heard Mercy letting herself in through the front door, he'd always call out, "Here comes my Golden Girl."

As they became better acquainted he allowed Mercedes to sit at Madge's dressing table and use her things. First of all, he taught Mercy how to remove the knots and tangles in her hair with Madge's boar-bristle brush. Then he showed her how to trim and file her fingernails with Madge's manicure set and let her use Madge's cold cream to soothe her scuffed knees and elbows. When she'd cleaned up, he'd give her a glass of milk and make her a sandwich, then sit beside her in front of the old upright in the hallway, teaching her how to play scales and read music. Soon she was picking out the melodies of songs she knew, her fingers skittering across the keys like dragonflies across a pond. And as Jake sat beside her marvelling at her musical aptitude, he could smell his garden in her glorious hair.

When the weather was dry, Jake often went outside again in the late afternoons to check everything was shipshape, in the garden and in the street, with Mercy at his side. He taught her the names of the birds and the flowers, how to drown snails and slugs in a tin of sugar water, and how to rescue hedgehogs. She pulled the weeds he pointed out, and when he was puffed, she turned the soil with a spade as he'd taught her to, counting the number of earthworms she came across so Jake could determine whether the soil was in good health or not.

Sometimes, when things had gone wrong for the child at home or school, Jake would dry her tears, wiping them away with one of Madge's scented tissues, marvelling once again at the unusual colour of her eyes — moody blue, they were, like the cornflowers growing in his garden, and ever so slightly crossed, the way a cornflower's petals fold imperfectly over one another.

One afternoon as Jake dozed in his armchair, a loud rapping on the front door roused him. He jerked awake to see a patrol car pulled up outside. A small crowd of neighbours had gathered and were tittering and pointing. When Jack opened the door, two police officers stood side by side, formal and aloof in their starched uniform blues and highly-polished, police-issue brogues.

"May we come in, Mr Lazarus?" one of them said. "We need to discuss a matter of some importance with you."

"Why, yes, of course..." Jake stood aside, but as they passed him to access the living room, he felt alarmed, certain they were the bearers of bad news. He leaned against the entrance-hall wall to steady himself. "Has something happened? Has something happened to Mercy?" he asked.

The police officers exchanged cryptic looks. "Not exactly, Mr Lazarus. We've received a complaint from the child's mother involving yourself."

"Pardon? I'll just switch this hearing aid up."

"Perhaps you'd better come in and sit down," the senior cop said.

Jake toddled towards his Lay-Z-boy, glancing through the large picture window to look out for Mercy who'd be along from school any minute. He noticed the hollyhocks were drooping; he'd need to get her help to water them later.

The police officers shuffled awkwardly from foot to foot waiting for Jake to seat himself. Then the senior officer launched into a short formal speech: "Mercedes' mother has lodged a complaint against you, Mr Lazarus, regarding your relationship with her daughter. As you're probably aware, the girl is only eleven years old. Her mother feels it's... er... very inappropriate she should spend so much time with you here at your house."

Jake didn't know what to say. He stared out of the window.

"We're going to need you to answer some questions, Mr Lazarus," the junior officer chipped in, flipping open a notebook. "We expect you to cooperate in this matter."

The senior officer continued. "Firstly, how long has Mercedes... er... Mercy been visiting you here, at your home?"

Jake racked his memory to fix on a time frame yet his days had merged into one another for so long now, the passing of time had become irrelevant. When he didn't reply, the officers glanced meaningfully at one another again.

"We're going to have to press you for an answer," said the junior officer.

Jake leaned forward in his chair, trying to focus. "Um, it's been a few years now," he said. "She was only a little thing when I first came across her in the wood box."

"The wood box?" The junior officer recorded this information on his notepad, then looked up again. "So, she's been visiting you here at your home for a number of *years*?"

"Yes. If she's eleven now, that would make it about six or seven years, I guess."

"How old was she when she first started visiting?" continued the junior officer.

"I'm not exactly sure," replied Jake. "She was very small, maybe four or five. I've never had any children of my own, so nothing to compare with really."

"Did you initially invite her to visit?" asked the junior officer.

"Well, no, she just turned up here, occasionally at first, and then more and more regularly."

"And what would you say is the nature of your relationship?" the senior officer continued.

"Well, I'm not really sure," said Jake. "I mean, we do things together. She helps me in the garden, and she likes to play the piano... I've been teaching her. She has a marvellous voice, sings like a bird."

"Right. Have any of her siblings ever visited your house? She has a brother, Rover, and two sisters, Jaguar, and... er.... Porsche?" The officers exchanged another meaningful look.

A sudden commotion outside diverted their attention. Mercy had dropped her school satchel on the sidewalk and was running up the garden path towards the house. She burst through the front door. "What's happened? Is Jake okay?" she called out.

When she entered the living room, she stood still for a moment, assessing the situation. Her school shift barely fitted her and her arms and legs splayed out in all directions, totally out of proportion with the rest of her. Her hair, as always, was a tumble of golden curls, unbrushed, unkempt. When she saw Jake across the room, she ran over to him.

"I got a fright when I saw the police," she said. "I thought something had happened to you." She pulled his tattered rug back up over his knees, patting it into place. "He hasn't been well lately," she continued, addressing this comment to the police officers.

They didn't answer.

She peered at them, her expression changing from concern to suspicion. "Right, I get it," she said. "My mother sent you, didn't she?"

The cops nodded. "Yes, she did, Mercedes. She has some serious concerns about your friendship with Mr Lazarus," the senior constable said.

"I knew it! Bloody witch! Just because she can't be around a man without something happening doesn't mean everyone is like that."

"Well, perhaps *you* can tell us why you visit Mr Lazarus?"

"Jake's my friend! I've never had a father, don't even know who he is. Let alone grandparents. Jake looks after me. Lets me play his piano. And I help him in the garden — he's not able to manage on his own anymore. What the hell is wrong with that?" Mercy's cheeks flushed red and her eyes flashed with emotion.

"Don't upset yourself, dear," said Jake, patting her on the head. "I'm sure we'll be able to sort this out."

The girl jumped up and smoothed down her school tunic. "I'll sort it out, alright," she said to Jake.

Turning to the policemen, she continued: "Listen here, you lot!

Think I like living in a cramped trailer at the campground with all those unruly kids who aren't even my proper brothers and sisters? Then there's Mum's endless stream of good-for-nothing 'men friends'." (She made quotation marks with her forefingers.) "There's never enough food, let alone any peace and quiet! Jake often helps me with my homework. I'd never get it done otherwise and would probably still be in primary school. Because Mum is a useless parent; because she is a child in an adult's body and never learned how to take any responsibility for anything. The day I stop coming to see Jake is the day I shoot through, five minutes after I turn sixteen and I've packed my bags and I'm on my way out of here. Get it? Now, how about you drop these stupid charges and go and do something useful, like solve an actual crime, or something?"

The policy enquiry soon blew over, but the incident made Jake realise how little he knew about Mercy: where she lived, who the other members of her family were, why she visited. She'd always avoided speaking about her life at home. All he knew was, she wasn't very well cared for or very happy there; that much had always been obvious.

As the seasons passed, marked by the growth and decline of Jake's garden, Mercedes grew lithe and graceful, her yellow curls a crowning golden halo, her dusky-mauve eyes with their alluring squint a distinguishing feature for which she was known throughout the district. She excelled at college and won the 5th Form Music Prize.

When old age overcame Jake, his mind growing duller and his body weakening, his sight and hearing failing, Mercy did more and more for him, concocting meals out of the meagre supplies he had in his larder, running errands for him, and relaying information about the goings-on in the neighbourhood. She read him the paper and filled in the crossword for him, and she played the piano and sang each afternoon while he dozed in his La-Z-Boy. Each evening, as he'd taught her to, she tended to his beloved garden, reassuring him that his hollyhocks were growing tall and beautiful, and that all was well on Orchard Street, Tākaka; the place where nothing out of the ordinary ever happened.

But one day, Mercy came no more, and the long extra years she'd added to Jake's life began to run out. His garden soon fell into disrepair, the ground covered with rotting fallen blossoms and decaying leaves, lying in drifts across the concrete path. Jake took to his bed and district nurses and caregivers visited him, fighting their way to his front door through thickets of weeds and long grass. Blight overcame the grape vines and their stems grew gnarled and barren. Morning glory and black-eyed Susan grew in abandon at the back of the section, overwhelming the veggie patch where only a few leaves of silver beet struggled on, soon covering Jake's shed, hiding it beneath a tangle of unchecked vines.

As Jake lay dying and the world outside his room ceased to exist, he drifted in the sea of his bed thinking only of Mercedes, the Golden Girl from Golden Bay. Who would listen to her bell-like, pitch-perfect soprano, her sweet chatter, her perfect laughter? Who would teach her the names of the butterflies, the birds, and the flowers? Who would lose themselves in her beautiful liquid eyes and wipe her tears away?

And who would reach out to her through a hole in the wall and pass her morsels of sustenance?

Dead Ball Zone

The game of rugby is played on a pitch; a two-dimensional space, one hundred metres long, seventy metres wide. Life is played in a field called the universe; an infinite, multi-dimensional space consisting mostly of emptiness. In rugby, the pitch is divided into zones demarcated by white lines, the goal posts are exactly five point six metres apart with a crossbar at a height of three metres, and a typical game is limited to fifteen players a side, with predetermined rules. Play lasts for strictly eighty minutes, extending into overtime only in rare circumstances. In the vast mysterious domain comprising the universe no such demarcations or restrictions exist. An uncountable number of contenders play their games in an undelineated field; there are no sides, no rules, no parameters, no time constraints. As the universe expands, the goal posts are continuously floating ever further apart...

Darren Wood turns fitfully in his sleep, these convoluted thoughts drifting through his consciousness like a bad dream. When his baby's insistent cries intrude, he jerks awake. An early riser, he usually gets up for Bub in the mornings so Layla can lie in. He has to be at Headquarters for a 7.30am start anyway and often doesn't get home till late — sometimes not at all if something major is going down at work — so he often misses the little one's bedtime. He appreciates it's tough on Layla being stuck at home with three kids under five, a never-ending merry-go-round of domestic chaos, so he tries to give her a break when he can.

But as he opens his eyes to the washed-out, wintery, mid-afternoon sun warping its feeble light through the bedroom window, he remembers it's not a weekday morning after all, and the day's events return in a rush to his addled brain. He rolls over onto his back, groaning with anger and disappointment.

The baby's cries become increasingly plaintive, and he wonders where Layla is and why she's not responding. He crawls from the bed and searches for something to chuck on over his boxers. His All Blacks supporter's jersey is lying on the floor where he tossed it a few hours ago. He can't bear the thought of wearing it now but it's the nearest thing to hand; the clean washing is still jumbled in the overflowing laundry basket at the end of the bed. He finds it immensely irritating that Layla is always behind with the housework.

He pulls the jersey on and makes his way into the room next door. When he sees the special smile his baby always saves for her daddy, he doesn't mind being disturbed quite as much. He scoops the child into his arms and wanders through to the living room. Darren and Layla's other children, Nancy and Josh, are parked in front of the TV, watching cartoons in their pyjamas. Their mother is outside on the deck hanging listlessly over the balustrade.

Darren yanks the ranch slider open. "God, woman, you know the weekends are the only time I get to rest!"

Layla turns towards him. Her face is puffy and her eyes are red and blotchy. He notices the half-empty bottle of wine on the patio table, the full ashtray, the disappointment in her eyes.

"For fuck's sake, Layla, it's only a game!" he says. "Get it together, Hon. Cindy's woken from her nap and needs her bottle!"

She glares at him. "Since when did I ever give a damn about the rugby, Darren?"

"Eh? Well, what's the fucken problem then?"

He steps out onto the deck to hand the baby to Layla. Next thing he's doubled over, and the baby is hanging from the crook of his arm like a rugby ball awaiting a calculated pass. He notices now that shards of broken glass are strewn across the decking. And he's just stepped on one.

"Fucken hell! What's going on here?"

"Give her to me," Layla says. "And how many times do I need to tell you not to swear in front of the kids?"

Layla takes the baby and Darren flops down into a patio chair and starts examining his foot.

"Jesus!" He pulls a chunk of glass from a deep gash in his heel. "This is all I need right now. For fuck's sakes!"

The baby is pulling at her mother's hair, burbling, "Mama, Mama..."

Layla sighs dramatically. "You know, Darren, you're not the only one around here who could do with a rest," she says, stepping carefully across the deck in her UGG boots, making her way inside.

Balancing Cindy on one hip, she starts heating the baby's bottle in the microwave. As she waits, she scans the disarray on the bench: the sink full of dirty dishes, the floor littered with toys and other domestic debris, including a basket of wet washing needing to be hung on the line. Her eyes prick with new tears.

Darren calls to her from the deck. "Layla?"

She ignores him.

"Layla!" he shouts.

Nancy and Josh are jumping up and down on the couch. "We're hungry, we're hungry," they sing in unison as if they've invented a new nursery rhyme.

Layla lies the baby down on a cushion in her playpen with her bottle, then fills a couple of bowls with coco pops and sloshes milk into them. "Okay, kids, come and get it!" she calls from the kitchen. "Eat your food nicely at the coffee table and watch TV. Call me if Cindy grizzles, okay? Daddy and I need to talk."

In the bedroom, Layla leans against the headboard snivelling into a tissue. Darren limps in, slams the door, and goes into the ensuite. Layla hears water running, then the sound of the vanity squeaking open and objects being pulled out and thrown across the floor as he rummages around for the first aid kit.

"Layla, I'm worried about you," he calls through the open door, "your drinking and smoking. What sort of example is *that* for the kids?"

She doesn't reply. She can see Darren through the slit in the half-closed door, sitting on the toilet. The lid is down only because she closes the toilet after he's used it. She's given up reminding him their inquisitive baby loves playing in the bowl. She hears Darren muttering under his breath as he cleans his wound and slathers antiseptic onto it.

He hops back into the room. "For crying out loud, woman, what the fuck is wrong with you? I really don't need this shit right now, not with that big court case coming up. I'm under a lot of pressure, for fuck's sakes! My promotion is hanging on this investigation. The whole country's in mourning. So what? It's not the end of the frikking world!"

"You're having an affair," she says.

Darren stops mid-hobble. He throws his hands up in the air and rolls his eyes. "I thought we sorted that out. You forgave me, remember? We got on with our lives, with our marriage. For the kids' sakes. Because we love each other. Right?"

Layla leaps off the bed and stomps over to Darren. Earlier, out on the deck, she'd looked pathetic. Now she looks crazy, crazier than he's ever seen her. "I'm not bloody stupid, Darren!" She spits the words into his face, then backhand slaps him. The large protruding diamond in her engagement ring grazes across his cheekbone, drawing a line of blood.

Darren is momentarily dazed and stumbles to the edge of the bed where he sits down. Layla keeps talking, but she sounds far away. "After you fell asleep, I went through your phone and guess what? I found multiple texts to and from a woman named Kelly, about how you'd give anything to see her again. Soon. Real soon. About how you're hanging out to fuck her again! And it appears the feeling is mutual..."

A rush of adrenalin hits Darren's empty stomach and bile rises up into his oesophagus; the acidic residue of the copious amounts of beer he'd downed that morning at the rugby final.

"What?" He swings out and grabs Layla's wrist, jerks her towards him and throws her onto the bed, then rolls across her, pinning her down with his forearms, a tree-trunk-sized thigh slung across her hips.

"If I've told you once, I've told you a thousand times, woman, don't ever go through my fucken phone!" he hisses inches from her face. "You could come across classified information which could endanger you and the kids!"

Layla struggles. She's not sure where the bravado to confront him like this has come from. All she knows is there's something awful bursting out of her she can't control and the tender soft heart of her has morphed into a raging beast. "So, what're you gonna do about it, you big bully?" she screams into his face.

Darren grabs both her wrists with one hand and pins her arms to the bed above her head. With the other, he pulls Layla's skirt up and shoves his hand roughly between her thighs.

"Stop it! You're hurting me!" She squirms and wriggles beneath the weight of him, trying to break free of his hold.

"Shut up," he says. "You know you want it. You know you need it. So I'm gonna give it to you, good and proper!"

"What about the children?" she sobs.

"Oh, that's rich, coming from you. They're still in their pyjamas and you're feeding them cereal at four o'clock in the afternoon. The TV is babysitting them while you're out on the deck in full view of the neighbours, smoking and drinking and breaking wine glasses. You're so self-absorbed, you didn't even hear Bub crying!"

He forces his way inside her and gradually she acquiesces, his guilt meting out an assuaging form of discipline upon her. In his arms, she finds a short-lived ecstasy. Besides, she is too weak to escape his bruising domination; he's a hulk of a man, built like a front row forward — the position he's played since he was thirteen years old.

"That'll teach you, Layla — for being a bad mother, for cutting my foot, and for breaching police security regulations," he says between gritted teeth as he withdraws.

Layla lies motionless on the bed in a state of subdued shock, like a dead butterfly pinned outstretched in a sterile museum case. Darren rolls off her and limps across the room towards the laundry basket. He rummages through it until he finds his trackies, pulls them on, then grabs his keys, mobile, and wallet off the bedside table.

"I'm taking the kids over to my sister's and leaving you to your pity party," he says. "When you get it together, let me know. Bear in mind, I've got a whole lot on my plate right now. I could do with some support, Goddamit! And clean this fucken place up before I get back!"

When he leaves the room, Layla turns on her side and draws her knees up to her chest. She's shivering now and pulls the duvet over herself. Her cheeks are burning and her skin feels tight as streaks of salty tears dry on them.

She hears Darren calling to the children down the hallway: "Get some clothes on, you monkeys! We're going over to your Aunty's."

"Yay! Yay!" comes their reply as they thunder down the corridor to their room to get ready. She hears Darren rummaging around in the baby's room next door for the nappy bag. A few minutes later the front door slams behind them, and the house descends into stillness. All she can hear is the muffled sound of the TV blaring in the lounge. The kids have obviously switched the volume up again. It's exhausting trying to control them and their fascination with knobs.

The weekend papers are strewn across the bed and Layla remembers how she and Darren had cuddled there together earlier, after lunch, when the baby had gone down for her nap, reading over each other's shoulders, squabbling light-heartedly over the best bits. Before he fell asleep. Before she went through his texts.

She finds herself staring absentmindedly at a full-page Warehouse advert on the sheet of newsprint lying inches from her face:

FINAL CLEARANCE OF ALL WINTER STOCK
CLOTHES, SHOES, UNDERWEAR, ACCESSORIES

Dead Ball Zone

FOR THE WHOLE FAMILY - MEN, WOMEN AND CHILDREN

Rows of photos line the page showcasing merchandise, including a range of patterned women's Wellington boots, *NOW ONLY $19.95*. Some have bright floral designs, others are covered in animal print or camouflage. How wonderful it'd be to own a pair, Layla thinks. How practical, but also how 'out there'. She imagines herself wearing them to the rugby club on a Saturday afternoon; sees herself crossing the sidelines and walking out across the rain-soaked grass, squelching through the sweat-filled trenches of mud and clay and blood and sweat and snot, out onto the centre of the pitch. All the roiling and running and ra-ra-ing would cease and the game would come to a sudden standstill, the players frozen in various attitudes of play.

She'd stop right there in the middle of it all, in front of Darren, right in his face, in the centre of his precious bloody game. He'd look up from the ruck, surprised, confused, questioning. And he'd *see* her, really see *her*, not just his wife, the mother of his children, the maid, the cook, the convenience, the obligatory sex partner. He'd make eye contact and give her that how-dare-you look, the kind only a cop-bully can make. But he'd be powerless, unable to react, unable to abuse her in front of all his macho teammates, in the public eye. And she'd gain possession of that slippery, mud-encrusted, elliptical rugby ball, long forgotten now and abandoned on the wet grass, and she'd tuck it securely under her arm.

Then she'd turn away, and start walking. She'd turn her back on Darren. And she'd just keep walking, through the muck, dross, confusion and chaos, across the halfway mark, past the 22-metre line, through the centre of the goal posts, into the dead ball zone.

Darren drops the kids at his sister's. Once the kids are settled with snacks in front of the TV, he drives over to the rugby club. When he enters, it's like he's joining a wake; the glum-faced crowd are staring at the TV3 news coverage of that morning's World Cup Quarterfinal:

'The magic moment for the French came in the 68th minute when they got away with a blatant forward pass enabling them to break through and score a try. Scrumhalf Jean-Baptiste Elissalde's conversion of Yannick Jauzion's try brought the score to 20-18 heading into the final minutes. In the last minute of the game, New Zealand fullback Leon MacDonald missed a drop goal that would have won the game for the All Blacks.'

Darren queues at the bar for a couple of handles, then walks over to join his mates. By the time he reaches their table the sports news is over and everyone is talking, all at once.

"Chokers, ay? The ref's bad calls shouldn't have made any difference. On paper the All Blacks were so far ahead, poor refereeing decisions should only have affected their winning margin, not the outcome of the game!"

"Sure, but three warm-up games against minnows left our boys feeling invincible. And let's face it. They've been treated like a bunch of namby-pambies over there, swanning around the French Riviera like movie stars."

"Our guys should have kept the ball in hand or kicked it out. It's common knowledge the French excel in open running play and they often come back strong in the second half."

The debate and drink swilling goes on around him but Darren is preoccupied, even though he's as gutted as anybody. He says 'yeah rights' and 'fuck no' when appropriate. But his personal situation is a bigger failure. He had it all going for him, like the All Blacks did. But he blew it, as they did, because when the crunch came, he didn't get his game together. Because he allowed unexpected changes, random mishaps, and the stress of it all to distract him from the ball in play.

"Player rotation and conditioning's the problem. Graham Henry's new strategies lost us the game. He should have stuck to traditional rugby."

"Let's face it, the French won the coin toss. They won the jerseys. They won the national anthem. They won the haka. They won the game, fair and square!"

"Yeah, I had a bad feeling from the start. The way the French stood up to the haka gave them the psychological advantage. And it didn't feel right seeing the All Blacks in silver-grey — the jerseys were indistinguishable. That has to have put our boys off!"

"McAlister's unjust sin binning was the nail in the coffin. It's what cost us the game in the critical moments, being one man short."

"The All Blacks had seventy-three percent possession and sixty-eight percent territory. There's absolutely no excuse for them losing the game."

Something inside of Darren snaps and he jumps up, slamming his handle down on the table. Beer flies everywhere and his mates wipe it from their faces with their sleeves. "For God's sakes, guys! We lost a game, not a war. Get over it!"

Silence follows his outburst. Everyone is staring at him.

"Aw, fuck it!" he says. Grabbing his other handle, he storms outside onto the deck where it's dark and cold and quiet.

He leans against the balustrade, taking the weight off his injured foot. It's painful, though nothing worse than any other injury he's suffered on a rugby field or in the course of his job as a cop. He's tough, probably way too tough, he thinks, over-conditioned to be the aggressor, both on the field and in life. He looks out over the new fields it took the club years and years of fundraising to finance, fully floodlit tonight, glistening with dew, smooth and sparkling and glorious; a monument of green grass and white lines, framed at each end by its towering parallel poles. Shrines to the national game.

He rubs his eyes, taking in deep gulps of frosty air. He's exhausted, he realises, from trying to keep it all together, trying to find a way through the muddle of his life: the lack of sleep, the miserable wife, the stress at work, the long hours, the increasing financial pressures of escalating mortgage interest rates and rises in the cost of living, the demands of his growing family, the need to be a paragon of virtue in the eyes of the community. And what's worse, deep down inside, he knows he's a hypocrite of the worst kind — the lying kind.

If the All Blacks had won this game; if he hadn't been so down after the loss of the match that he'd overdone the drinking and passed out; if rugby wasn't so bloody important to him and he'd stayed home instead of insisting on watching the match at the club with his mates; if he'd helped Layla around the house and made more of an effort to spend quality time with his family; if he'd had the *nous* to delete all those texts to and from Kelly in the bloody first place, everything'd be different now.

But deep down he knows there's no excuse for his infidelity or his brutish behaviour. No excuse at all.

He'd met Kelly when he'd been stationed up in Wellsford investigating the case he was now preparing to take to court. She worked the night shift at the truck stop where he had his evening meal before retiring to his motel. She was as hard as the truckies and bikies, late night revellers and mystery travellers who passed through, and as crass. But, she was a cute little thing, like a tiny fragile bird, petite and flighty. A real chicky babe. Her tittering and tatting and fluttering about the place, chatting to customers and serving them, smiling and laughing and flirting, reminded him of a fantail flitting from tree to tree.

He'd rooted her up against the trash cans in the back yard of the takeaway outlet next door to the cop shop. Wriggling and giggling, with her jeans around her ankles and her black apron pulled up above her waist, she'd said, "Well, well, this is a first for me; the first time I've ever been with a *detective*." Kelly was so carefree, so much fun, so different from Layla with her postmodern angst and high seriousness, her impossible expectations, her overwhelmedness. He'd already put Layla through hell once. Not that long ago, Layla'd ankle-tapped him into a confession about a previous indiscretion, and that first transgression had already nearly cost him his marriage. He remembers how relieved he'd been when Layla had forgiven him.

Now he realises that, in a weird kind of way, her letting him out of the sin bin then was like the 'resume play' whistle for him to keep two-timing. He needed something easy, uncomplicated, unburdened with significance, untainted by his guilt and the damage he'd already done. Kelly was easily satisfied with what little he had to offer. And she looked up to him; thought he was important. And he was, wasn't he? It wasn't easy being a senior detective. Fuck, it was the pits sometimes, what he'd had to witness and cope with.

How the hell could he sort this? There was no way he could sidestep this. And if Layla red-carded him, he'd be lost. Because she was a far better person than him. Because she was good and kind and decent; the reason why he'd married her in the first place. And he had so much to lose — his children, their future as a family.

Darren's mobile rings and when he sees who's calling, he has no option but to answer. It's his boss from Auckland Central.

"Have you read the psych report on the Rawhiti twins yet, Darren?"

He hasn't. "Um, I'm getting through it," he says.

"Riveting stuff, eh? Reads like a novel."

"Yeah, bloody interesting."

"We need to make a strong case, mate, but I can't help thinking, kids like these should be given a little slack. The defence is likely to argue their behaviour was a cry for help, anyway; the consequence of the trauma and abuse they'd been subjected to. You can't help admiring them, really, especially the girl."

"Yeah, Kitty is something else. I remember interviewing her when we tracked them down and brought them in. Hard, defiant and cunning, she was, no pushover. She told me they were on a mission to get their Dad back. She was also very protective and nurturing of her twin brother who's a bit of a sissy, as I recall."

"Seems she masterminded everything, did all the scheming, while the boy is apparently stuck in a permanent state of arrested development. Just the pawn she used to carry out the arson attacks. They might have been encouraged in the whole thing by their one time carer, Violet Nene, but it'll be impossible to prove so there's no reason to drag her into this. Anyway, just a heads up, we're meeting with the prosecutor on Monday. We need to appear to be sympathetic, you know, what with all the current negative media attention the cops are getting."

Darren's boss rings off and he heads back inside to the dunny where he washes his face with cold water, then pulls off his jandal to examine his foot again. It's throbbing painfully and the jagged cut is covered in gungy dried blood. He's taking a slash when the posters plastered all over the walls catch his attention, about the *Blow the Whistle Campaign*, launched to coincide with the World Cup. It's been funded by the 'Campaign for Action on Family Violence'. Darren remembers now how the club's bar counter and tables are covered in coasters promoting the campaign. Red buckets full of gimmicky pea-whistles have been placed in prominent positions around the club with a notice on them inviting punters to help themselves to a whistle and take it home, and to use it whenever a domestic situation is getting out of hand.

The bright poster shouts its message at him now from the white-tiled urinal wall; two screaming faces covered in rugby war paint, followed by the message: 'Blow the whistle on violence! Play fair on the field and at home!'

Standing between his past and his future, urine draining from his stressed out body, and psychological stress and physical pain the only buddies standing alongside him right now, Darren realises what a fool and a bastard he's been and wonders how he's going to get that elusive elliptical ball back into play.

First and foremost, he's going to have to get a handle on his drinking. It's totally out of control. As a fourteen or fifteen year old, he and his young team mates had been initiated into 'the inner circle' after matches, when, down in the dank smelly changing rooms under the club rooms, they'd been introduced to the drinking culture that's part and parcel of being a rugby player in this country.

The pub that sponsored the club would drop off a few crates of Lion Red each weekend for the players to help themselves to after the game. It was the promise of ice-cold beer that urged them on during games that took place in lashing rain and freezing cold, that made them brave when they were being pounded and pummelled by Islanders twice their size. It was the reward that made them sprint faster and push harder, with the sole focus of scoring tries in the dead ball zone. Despite the cost. In spite of the pain.

At the end of the season, a couple of kegs would be delivered, accompanied by a length of tubing and a funnel. They funnelled beer till they raged and raved and all but blacked out. "This is what makes you tough enough to become an All Black, boys," the coaches chanted. To think he'd been that wet behind the ears, he'd actually believed them!

He'd never made the grade though; the brown boys were always bigger, better, harder, tougher. He never even got through the provincial selections. Soon, he will enrol his son in Little Rippers and the cycle will start all over again. But does he really want his son following in his footsteps, well on the way to becoming an alcoholic by his mid-teens? And the club wants Darren to coach. Maybe he should. Maybe he can change things, change the culture.

But he'll have to park that dilemma for now. There's other shit to sort out.

He leaves the club and calls in at Pizza Hut where he orders Layla's favourite, an extra-large Seafood Deluxe. While he's waiting for it, he paces up and down, thinking that the best thing to do is to revert to the tried and true and fall back on his training. No more player rotation. No more conditioning. No more distractions. No more excuses.

When he lets himself back into the house, Layla is still lying where he left her, asleep in a sea of newsprint on the bed. She's been dreaming that she's wearing a pair of bright floral gumboots, walking in space — floating, flipping, flying, tripping — attached only by her lifeline to what actually matters. No floodlights illuminate outer space, but starlight is bright enough to see the rugby ball she has kicked through the centre of the ever-widening goalposts travelling into endless orbit.

Darren puts the pizza into the oven and hobbles around the house, tidying up as quietly as he can. When he returns to the bedroom, Layla is sitting up in bed. He is struck by her cool, dark beauty; how her level gaze is like a blackbird's, fixed, focused, penetrating.

"The laundry still needs folding and putting away," she says.

"Shush, Hon," he says, "you rest, I've got it covered."

He tips the washing basket out onto the bed, and the laundry falls in a heap on top of the weekend newspaper, covering the Warehouse advert and all the quick fixes consumerism offers in exchange for a man's hard-earned coin. He starts working through the pile, item by item, folding the clothing as best he knows how, placing it in neat piles on the dresser like he's seen Layla doing, night after night until she eventually falls into bed beside him,.

"Where are the kids?" she says.

"At Bonnie's. She's keeping them overnight, Hon, not to worry."

"Okay." Her voice is so quiet he can barely hear her.

"I'm gonna try and get time off work," he continues. "We need to sort ourselves out, get back on track somehow." She ignores him, but he presses on. "I'm gonna get help, request counselling. I promise you, things are going to change around here, big time."

"Whatever," she says, cutting him off. She looks away, and Darren follows her gaze as it travels to the window where the curtains are still open even though it's way past dark.

"The sky is super bright tonight," she says.

"Yeah, they've got the floodlights on down at the club; they've lit the whole place up like a bloody Christmas tree, as if an international game is about to kick off. God knows why, probably in commiseration for the All Blacks' doozy of a loss today, I guess. Those poncey pikers all deserve the bloody sack if you ask me."

"That won't change anything," she says. "What they should do, what they ought to do, is ban the game before our son grows old enough to play."

Darren doesn't reply. He knows Layla will never agree with him on the importance of rugby to the national psyche. He also doubts whether his hollow promises will cut it this time. She's heard them all before.

When the laundry is out of the way, he pulls his guitar from under the bed and sits down. It's a relief to get the pressure off his wounded foot. He hasn't held the instrument in a while and it feels good in his arms. He tunes it up and starts playing the opening bars of the song he courted Layla with.

"Layla, you've got me on my knees, Layla, I'm begging darling, please..." he sings, looking at her with entreating eyes. She's still staring out of the window at the night sky, unmoved, unmoving.

"I'm so sorry, Hon," he says.

Layla's voice when she replies is flat, resigned. "How many more times am I going to have to forgive you, Darren?" she says.

Queen of the Night

Those of you who know anything about the living arrangements of cats will be acutely aware — probably as a result of having been taken endless advantage of — that they attach themselves to human beings, often seeking out a form of communion (not unlike the religious kind) and communal living situation (not unlike the conjugal kind). This behaviour is not so much based on need (whatever!) but rather on the fact that, because they are so psychologically in tune with mankind, cats and humans make natural companions.

Lilith, the resident and Lady-of-the-Manor as it were of Apple Tree Cottage, was no different from the rest of human kind (on the surface, that was) in the sense that a cat always seemed to attach itself to her. But she had never consciously sought to be a 'cat owner' and was not by nature a 'cat lover' or even a 'cat person'. Yet, somehow, she was never without one. Companions of the feline variety always seemed to 'come to her' through bizarre or tortuous circumstances involving ex-lovers, ex-friends, or ex-acquaintances. Or, sometimes, they just turned up on her doorstep unannounced, promptly moving in on the basis of a tacit invitation.

Predictably (you will soon discover why), they were always black males and their names were usually interchangeable: Claw, Paw, Fang, Satan, Beelzebub, Mephisto, Grim (short for Grimalkin or Grim Reaper) etc. And so, it followed that Lilith always enjoyed the company of a resident *familiar*. In the case of her current feline accessory, Claw II, he was obliviously unaware of his role vis-a-vis his mistress and believed himself to be a) self-employed in an industry and profession entirely of his own choosing b) living the self-sufficient lifestyle he had personally engineered for himself.

Please indulge me, while I explain...

Conscientious to a fault, Claw maintained a careful vigil over the gardens at Apple Tree Cottage by day, yet by night he guarded them all the more fiercely, when the dangers of dark forces were that much more likely to be prevalent, under the cover of... *darkness*. This personal mission — with which he had endowed his life with existential relevance and by means of which he was able to experience a high level of job satisfaction and fulfilling self-actualisation — was one to which he was well suited by virtue of his species, his gender, his natural aptitudes, and the many years he had invested in the honing of his innate skills.

He was thus, at one and the same time, self-employed and self-appointed to perform the distinct yet overlapping duties of both daytime security guard and night watchman (depending of course on whether it was daytime or nighttime), as well as those of CEO of his own limited liability company: a profession or undertaking or even a *calling* (his word) that he imbued with the utmost sense of gravitas. The fact that his various roles and their implicit duties dominated his life around the clock was never for him a burden too great to fulfil; in fact, it would have been almost impossible to detect on any given day or night that he was actually on the job, were it not for certain telling details...

Ever vigilant, he patrolled the grounds at regular, predetermined intervals, leaving no path untrodden, no bush uninspected, no vista unscanned, no flower bed unexplored, no corner unturned. All observations, relevant data and other (possibly pertinent) associated information — in short, the sum total of his investigations — were relayed back to 'The Boss' for analysis and possible further inquiry. (Claw had an almost uncanny, mercurial ability to switch effortlessly between roles, as required). Eventually a decision-making process got under way that, depending on any extenuating circumstances, resulted in certain actions being taken, or not, by a member of Claw's security detail, as befitted the situation.

The manner in which he carried out these different yet equally essential components of his business operations always appeared leisurely and nonchalant; moreover, the magnitude of this huge responsibility and undertaking never seemed arduous or burdensome to him (as I've already pointed out).

It was obvious to Lilith from the start of Claw's tenure at Apple Tree Cottage that this enterprising tomcat's modus operandi were thoroughly... *thorough* and methodically... *methodical*. No field mouse, sparrow, daddy-long-legs, weta, cicada, huhu grub, cricket, grasshopper, or any other intruder was able to come and go at Apple Tree Cottage unobserved, unapprehended or uninterrogated. Bigger threats — "game" as Claw liked to call them — came under even more severe scrutiny. A wood pigeon, for instance, preening on the overhead telephone lines in the cool of the morning would be surreptitiously observed and investigated from every possible angle and perspective. Sometimes, these bigger threats were subjected to even more drastic action. If any vermin considered, or worse, dared attempt a run-and-grab-and-run assault on the freshly-filled rubbish bin or fragrant (to vermin) compost heap in the dark of the night — a lengthy pursuit on an empty stomach was all they would have to look forward to till dawn rendered both the pursued and the pursuer exhausted.

Claw was acutely aware that subject to 'The Law' (always voiced in an American accent), all employees must be afforded their due breaks (a minimum of fifteen minutes per three hours of work). And since he was both the boss as well as the only employee on duty at any given time, '24/7' (he actually hated the expression, but popular parlance demanded its use), this computed in his estimation to an absolute minimum of thirty minutes per three hour period plus an extra five minutes either side of the break to clock off and clock on, i.e. forty minutes per three hours (he was, after all, a generous employer).

During breaks, Claw would lie in the shade in pre-designated staff rest areas and appear to be taking a catnap. But on closer inspection, one couldn't help noticing that the stipulated spot not only had an excellent vantage point but also that a grossly unnerving, hairy eyelid was always stretched wide open with a disconcerting, rotating eyeball duly noting every shiver of leaf, flutter of wing, or articulation of miniature mandible — even the capture of a tiny dust mote in the fragile thread of a spider's web.

Claw didn't wear a uniform; an unnecessary expense he felt. He'd been through all the catalogues and come to the considered conclusion that his natural attire would do just as well, since it suited his purposes, so very... *suitably*. Incidentally, he also believed in the practice of flat management and therefore that both employers and employees were equally valuable members of the organisation. Consequently, they should not be distinguishable by virtue of their attire or designations.

As a result of this eminently wise executive decision, during the day he was highly visible, as any security guard ought to be (the deterrent factor!), his glorious, thick, shiny-black fur coat easily visible from rooftops and treetops, telephone poles and electricity supply lines, as well as at ground level, even when glimpsed through dense foliage or long grass. Yet, by night, he passed under the cover of darkness, black on black, blending with and bleeding into the amorphous shapes of witching time; unseen, unnoticed, moving from shadow to shadow, incognito.

For many of the creatures living at Apple Tree Cottage, as well as for those that dared venture an unexpected visit, the sight of Claw on patrol or even at rest was a disconcerting blur on what would otherwise have been a perfectly idyllic landscape, consisting as it did of a rambling, Devonshire-style cottage set in an English country garden with an ancient orchard and carefully tended vegetable and herb gardens, surrounded by a couple of paddocks where sheep and cattle grazed contentedly in knee-high grass. Situated such as it was at the foothills of the Tamahunga Ranges, near the innocuous service town of Warkworth (named after a town in Northumberland, England) in the verdant countryside of rural New Zealand, bordered on two sides by a river flowing through native bush and on the other by a curving road that separated it from extensive vineyards, it proffered the perfect lifestyle for those seeking to escape the modern world's overpopulated, over-frenetic, over-polluted urban world.

The only time Claw allowed himself any significant respite from his onerous (not to him though, as I've pointed out a number of times now) responsibilities and duties, was when he took his annual leave, in January — twenty working days now, according to 'The Law' (a very welcome, recent amendment to the Employment Act), which meant that with the addition of statutory holidays and weekends he usually had a full month off.

In the manual of company regulations (which he had compiled, naturally), annual leave always officially started when the Queen of the Night that grew alongside the west wall of the cottage came into bloom. This stipulation was non-negotiable for there was something about the scent of the flowers that induced in Claw a drug-like state of such inertia that, coupled as this event usually was with the languorous, intense heat and extended, long, lazy days of high summer, all his resolve, accountability, and self-discipline immediately dissipated.

Thus, when his annual leave commenced, his commitment to his usual multifarious activities was instantaneously foregone as he fell beneath the night-flowering jessamine and lay there comatose for days and nights on end, while the Dama De Noche gently dropped its prodigious tubular-like miniature flowers upon him where he lay prone and prostrate beneath it, suffusing the air around him with their insidious perfume, the sickly-sweet sensuous scent of them promptly penetrating his nostrils and ingratiating itself upon his highly susceptible sinuses. This divine scent had a direct link to his synapses with an effect not unlike serotonin uptake, the result of which served only to prolong indefinitely a hedonistic state of absolute apathy and lassitude as it pervaded the whole being, body and soul, of this otherwise highly responsible cat.

In my considered opinion (as the all-seeing, all-knowing Eye of God), the focus of Claw's choice of career was entirely misdirected, for in the world of man that existed cheek-and-jowl with his own, far more dangerous and subtle forces were at work to which his gravely serious attentions could have been redirected to better effect. And so it was that one year, when Claw was on leave, dreaming away the long lazy days and brief twinkling nights of January in a state of euphoria and inertia under the Ike He Po, a chain of events in the world of men was set in motion that would result in the sudden termination of his (completely taken for granted) annual summer holiday.

Now Lilith, Claw's current conjugal human companion, was a work of art as much as Claw was a work of nature. She'd been around since the dawn of time and had lived through many reincarnations since her original claim to fame as Adam's first wife. Thus, she had become a master (or rather, mistress) of her own destiny; a master (or rather, mistress) of the particular art of artifice that served her life's (or more aptly, her many lives') purpose. And since she'd been around the block a few times throughout the long and convoluted history of mankind, she'd had the opportunity to add a great deal of experience to her own, particular, innate abilities and sensibilities.

She was a busy woman and had her finger in many pies. She was a popular socialite in the local community, an accomplished cook and gardener, and a woman who excelled in a variety of other ordinary as well as nefarious pursuits, all of which either directly or indirectly supported her present life's purpose. Currently that purpose involved a man named Rove. She'd been introduced to Rove (short for Rover) at a Christmas function by a mutual acquaintance, and he had ingratiated himself upon her during the course of the evening in such an obsequious manner that she had immediately recognised him as being a man in dire need of 'retraining', in the sense that he had gotten away with so many misdemeanours regarding his relationships with women and their (sometimes, actually often *his*) children during his lifetime, that he desperately needed, in Lilith's opinion, what she termed *corrective* treatment.

Now the strange thing about Lilith was that, even though she stopped traffic and people gasped when they saw her for the first time, most men (ordinary men, decent men, that is) gave her a wide berth, because something subliminal inside them knew they could never match her, and, to phrase it in common parlance, they really didn't want to go there.

Tall, willowy (she towered above Rove who was, although perfectly formed, a rather small man), raven haired (it flowed down her back to well below her waist like a black bridal train and on closer inspection one might have noticed the odd spider resident there, in amongst its web-like tresses), moon skinned (even in daylight), rosy cheeked and red lipped (without the application of makeup), she inspired the kind of awe and respect in men that brought them instantly to their knees (metaphorically speaking), and had them dutifully rushing home to their wives or girlfriends the minute they could stand again without trembling (metaphorically speaking).

So, when Rove attached himself to Lilith at the Christmas party, she knew immediately what kind of a man he was (it was always the same 'type' that had the audacity to approach her), and her every inherent sensibility and long-practised skill rallied to her command. You see, Rove was of a type that Lilith instantly recognised — Archetypal Gnome, Leprechaun, Rumpelstiltskin — the kind of man who is by nature miserly, mercenary, and cruel; a taker and perverter of every good thing; the kind of man who is incapable of love other than that of the most narcissistic kind. Which, in Lilith's book, was the epitome of a certain kind of male personality disorder that demanded the employment of dire... No! drastic and ruthless measures. Uncompromising measures, to say the least.

On returning home after the Christmas 'do' Lilith promptly consulted her almanac on the forthcoming position of the planets, calculated the phases of the moon, and induced in herself a deep trance-like state by means of an herbal concoction, in which she could exactly divine what Rove's karmic acts of selfishness towards women and children had so far entailed, in order to devise how to deal with him appropriately. And so, she set about preparing herself to bait the trap she would lure him into; the trap that would not only be his undoing but also his nemesis.

She invited him to join her for an intimate dinner at Apple Tree Cottage on the 12th of January, a Saturday. When he turned up on that exceptionally sultry summer evening and banged the brass knocker on the front door (a cheeky little cross-legged elf) to announce his arrival (the door was wide open, suggesting, he thought, that Lilith would be wide open to his advances) she was fully ready to deal with him in the most merciless of ways.

Floating towards him, Lilith twinkled in a midnight-blue chiffon gown that appeared in the darkening evening light to have been studded with sequins, welcoming him in with a twinkly wave of her delicate bejewelled hand. She noticed that he had the self-satisfied look on his face she knew so very well: the expression of thousands of men just like him who had crossed her path through the ages, whose grasping ego-bound need for self-gratification cannot be disguised when they believe they are about to get lucky with a Queen of the Night without much effort on their part.

Lilith played Rove slowly so that she could savour every moment of his gradual undoing, leading him first into the cool conservatory on the east side of the house where she had prepared dinner for the two of them. She handed him a silver goblet into which she poured a generous amount of her well-chilled, homemade gooseberry wine from a cut-glass decanter, toasting him with such a promising sparkle in her well-practised eye it induced in him a look of crooked-smiled lecherousness that revealed a set of ugly rotting teeth.

Her chest expanded with a sigh in anticipation of the wine's effect on him as he swallowed his first sip of the syrupy golden liquid, and she watched bemusedly as his eyes dropped to her ample heaving décolletage, returning to her face via the gracious curve of her swanlike neck. She knew full well that it was highly unlikely he would ever have tasted such nectar of the gods before (he wouldn't have been in need of reforming on this particular occasion otherwise!) and she awaited its inevitable result with great glee — a few small sips and he'd become intoxicated with a lust so all-consuming that any vestige of self-protection he might have arrived at Apple Tree Cottage with would be instantly eroded.

Shortly he began to exhibit the behaviour she was expecting.

"Lilith, my dear, your beauty overwhelms me," he said as he lurched towards her, wrapping his arms around her tiny waist, and, finding that, because he was so much shorter than her, his face now nestled conveniently between her ample alabaster breasts. He couldn't resist the urge to slobber a few wet kisses on them but she tittered sensuously and drew away.

"Rove, Rove, what's the rush? We have all night, darling. And I've prepared a delicious dinner for us to share over an intimate *tête á tête.*"

Lilith bade him sit down and moved behind him to tie a large, starched napkin around his neck. As she leaned across him and the scent of her heavenly perfumed person wafted into his nostrils, he felt a violent stirring in his groin. Behind him, she grinned cheekily at the ludicrous sight of the pogo-stick-like protuberance in his trousers that was now pointing heavenwards. She moved away to light the candles and as they flickered and caught alight, he noticed how sheer her gown was and how her porcelain skin glowed like moonshine through its silken folds.

All too soon, however, the throbbing anticipation he felt mounting in his groin area gave way to a compellingly vague discomfort in the region of his throat. The napkin that Lilith had tied there seemed to have tightened, ever so slightly, and as he pondered this unpleasant development, it tightened again, and then again — almost imperceptibly, as if some invisible hand was tugging on it — until it became uncomfortably taut.

He reached up a nervous hand to loosen it off, as best he could. "Whew, it's so warm tonight," he said by way of explanation.

Lilith smiled benevolently at him. "Yes, that it is, darling," she said, winking at him, "and it's going to get much, much hotter as the night wears on, my love."

She seated herself graciously beside him and proceeded, with a flourish, to remove the high domed lid from the large, ornate silver serving platter that dominated the table. *Voilà,* the sickly-sweet smell of some sort of braised meat in a creamy shallot sauce permeated the air, causing Rove's nostrils to flare wide open with greedy anticipation. The meat was garnished with a ring of nasturtiums and poor man's capers in which quail's eggs nestled cosily. Rove noticed with a gasp of surprise that the nasturtiums were still growing; in fact, from the moment Lilith had removed the platter's lid, their tendrils had begun to creep over its side and spread their nubile fingers across the white tablecloth towards him.

He was a trifle unnerved at their tenuous creeping embrace, but Lilith's indulgent attentions distracted him as she served him an ample plateful of food, and he returned to thinking about what the rest of the evening held in store for him. He was very much aware of the fact that he'd downed a whole goblet of gooseberry wine in a couple of gulps and the thought occurred to him that he'd better slow down, or he might not be able to perform to his best ability later on.

Within a short while, Rove had licked the platter clean and had sucked every delicate bone dry. He did not think he had ever tasted anything quite as delectable, even though he'd always made a point of shacking up with and living off women with excellent culinary skills. Lilith hadn't even had a solitary mouthful, and he was overcome with a momentary feeling of incredulousness that he'd single-handedly devoured all the food. But she looked so happy and glowing that this uncharacteristic lapse of self-centredness passed over rather quickly.

Had he been any the less self-absorbed — perhaps even one iota less — he might have seen the fresh stick-mounted possum pelt stretched out to cure against the glass panels of the conservatory. He might even have noticed the occasional flicker of concern that crossed Lilith's face as she wondered whether she would be able to raise Claw to action from his comatose state under the flowering Jessamine to fulfil *his* role in the evening's developments, while she silently rehearsed the spell she had prepared to ensure that eventuality.

But Rove didn't notice anything amiss. Rove only had eyes for Lilith.

During the meal, he talked incessantly about himself and was gratified to see that Lilith hung on his every word, laughed when he laughed, and tut-tutted solicitously when he shared his sad stories about how badly women had always treated him and how it was always their doing when things didn't work out. He made a point of explaining that he had always been honest about his feelings, had always told them that he could not be blamed if they loved him more than he loved them. If they'd been foolish enough to keep chasing him, taking care of him, even having his children, children that he never wanted, and, God forbid, never wanted to take any responsibility for, was it *his* fault?

"And so, Lilith," he heard himself say, "I have left a trail of broken hearts and fatherless children because I knew all along that one day, I'd meet a woman like you; someone worthy of me, someone I could be truly myself with."

How right you are, she thought, smiling sweetly all the while.

As soon as he'd made this confession, he baulked at himself — he'd never, ever, admitted to anyone before, least of all a woman, that he was basically a selfish bastard and a user and a taker. Moreover, he'd never complimented a woman so freely before, usually keeping them guessing as to his true feelings. But Lilith didn't seem to mind or even notice, continuing to smile indulgently at him, saying, *"Mon tout petit choux-choux"* in the most solicitous tone, as she wiped the dribble on his chin with the napkin hanging from his neck.

"And now, dear one, some dessert?" she said.

"Oh yes. Lovely," he replied.

As if by magic a huge bowl of trifle replaced the bone-filled dish in front of him: sherry-soaked sponge, crystallised plums suspended in raspberry jelly, all topped with meringue nipples floating in a sea of frothy crème anglaise — amazingly trifle was the favourite treat his mother plied upon him with utmost devotion every time he returned home seeking succour and solace after some or other woman had finally seen through him and sent him packing. Once again, he couldn't help himself, and gobbled it all down so quickly, he started burping and farting uncontrollably.

"A little stroll in the garden, Rove, to aid your digestion?" Lilith said. He loved the way she uttered his name, the way she rolled the "R" over her tongue and her lips pursed into the shape of a kiss as she sounded out the "V". It looked and sounded like an invitation; an invitation to the zenith of personal gratification.

"What a good idea!" he said, gleefully anticipating that he could reduce the physical distance between himself and Lilith far more easily when he was on his feet.

He leapt up enthusiastically but was overcome by a sudden head rush, quite unlike the many drug-induced ones he had enjoyed over a lifetime of indulgence in every kind of chemical high. He grabbed the chair back for support and realising that he had single-handedly drunk the entire carafe of gooseberry wine, he berated himself silently for his lack of artificial good manners. But when Lilith took him by the arm and their skin made contact through the sensuous sparkling fabric that barely hid her voluptuous feminine form, every vague qualm he was feeling immediately dissipated. He fell in beside her, floating alongside her through the French doors that led out into the garden.

A profusion of roses of every possible colour, size and shape grew beside the path they followed (naturally! roses were Lilith's eternal flower), and that night, to Rove, they seemed like the soft velvet faces of all the good, trusting women he had defiled over the years with his lewd thoughts and selfish actions; yet tonight they inclined towards him with faces beaming with the purest gratitude and devotion. At their feet the sweet innocent visages of innumerable pansies and violas smiled up at him, reminding him of the children he had begotten and promptly forgotten, yet tonight they whispered "Daddy, Daddy, we love you," as he passed by. He had never felt so good, so justified. So self-satisfied.

When they rounded the corner of the house a wall of such intense perfume wafted towards them that Rove was almost overwhelmed by its cloying sultriness. He closed his eyes and sucked in deep breaths of sweetness such he had never known. It was almost as if Lilith's arm (around his waist now) held his body slightly suspended above the earth as they moved dreamlike past the flowering Queen of the Night growing alongside the house.

Of course, Rove was in no fit state to notice a certain black cat lying comatose at the base of the magnificent flowering shrub. If he had seen Claw there, beast that he was, with paws the size of a dog's, and a jaw like an animal trap, he might have come to his senses and taken flight, avoiding the inevitable that was yet to come. But he was so consumed with the delicious anticipation of having his lust assuaged at the earliest opportunity, that he remained quite oblivious to each and every warning.

Lilith spoke a few words in what sounded like a foreign tongue, and Rove, recalling that she had used a sprinkling of French earlier, thought it sweet that she would woo him in another of the sonorous romance languages she was obviously so fluent in. He couldn't quite place which one, but what did it matter? The language of love was universal, wasn't it?

He turned to smile indulgently at Lilith, failing to notice that upon her indecipherable utterance, Claw had instantly leapt to his feet. Realising that he had been summoned by a power far greater than any he had formerly known, to face a challenge and adversary far more sinister than any he had heretofore ever encountered — far more daunting and worthy therefore than any of his former, now petty concerns — Claw had immediately rallied to attention, responding with dutiful enthusiasm to the call to action. He fell in now behind Lilith and her visitor as she'd hoped he would, slipping from shadow to shadow, incognito.

A haunting siren song, juxtaposed with what sounded like the wailing of children, started up somewhere in the background, and the thought crossed Rove's mind that Lilith had perhaps put on a CD without him noticing — not his taste in music certainly (he only listened to heavy metal), but how romantic of her to set the mood for their romantic tryst, he thought.

Lilith led Rove through a rickety, squeaking gate into an orchard where ancient quinces shone like lanterns in the moonlight and the flowers of the Deadly Nightshade vines curling up the trunks of the trees twinkled like billions of stars. They left the path and Lilith guided him across lush ankle-high grass, telling him she was taking him to her cosy little love nest overlooking the river.

Rove's excitement was mounting by the second but he was momentarily distracted by a black shadow that leapt and pranced in his peripheral vision. When he noticed that a gentle breeze had sprung up, he deduced that the swaying branches of the plum trees under which they were now walking were casting moving shadows.

He thought it strange that a wind had picked up, though — it had been perhaps the stillest and hottest day of the entire summer, and that evening's report had not mentioned any unexpected change in the weather.

He started to feel a little cold and shivery — a sobering thought, because he wasn't that well-endowed. Moreover, he was acutely aware of the fact that the rapidly falling temperature would adversely affect the size of his manhood in inverse proportion to him rising in Lilith's estimation.

Suddenly however, she stood before him in all her glory, floodlit by a shaft of moonlight. She beckoned him closer, saying, "Come my love, come to me". As he lunged towards her, her gown began to slip from her shoulders, revealing the most magnificent bosoms, delicate waist, and curvaceous hips he had laid eyes on in a long time. She stood between the columns of the entrance to some sort of mausoleum, but since he was overcome with relief that they might have reached her little love nest at last and now needed to concentrate more than ever on not 'jumping the gun' as it were, he didn't give the setting a second thought.

He fell upon her like an eagle upon its prey and she took him welcomingly into her arms, drawing him inside. The temperature within her 'love nest' was decidedly colder but Rove was only vaguely aware of this fact; the warmth of Lilith's hands as she undressed him and her naked skin as she cleaved to him rendered him oblivious, mentally at least, to the freezing draft that swirled around them. She ran her hands over his buttocks and squeezed them encouragingly, but Rove became concerned that further progress would be hampered by the fact she was so much taller than him.

He considered asking her whether there was a bed in there, somewhere in the darkness, but she seemed to have read his mind, for she whispered sensuously in his ear, "Darling, you're covered in goose bumps! Lie down and let me cover you..."

He was overcome with how she anticipated his every need and desire, and when she pushed him gently down onto a cold concrete slab and an awful smell of death and decay rose around him, he couldn't help ignoring it as she lay down on top of him. There was nothing he liked better than the woman-on-top position and he couldn't believe his luck; it was as if Lilith knew everything about him, every secret of his lascivious soul.

"You're the perfect woman for me Lilith," he said. "I am in your thrall ..."

"How right you are, *mon amour des époques*," she whispered in his ear, as she began to make love to him.

Rove succumbed to her enthusiastic ministrations and was soon transported on waves of mounting pleasure. He was vaguely aware that the gentle breeze he'd noticed earlier had become a howling gale as the branches outside Lilith's love shack creaked and swayed violently, thrashing about in the wind. A sensation of rocking and swaying overcame him too, and he felt as if he was falling through space, through darkness, through time. A stray thought crossed his mind — maybe this was what was meant by the expression 'the earth moved' — that wonderful earth-shattering feeling that couples in love were supposed to experience during sex. He'd never experienced it prior of course and felt so gratified to now be the deserving recipient of this wondrous sensation — at last, he thought, at last, I am getting what I've deserved all along.

"Rrrrrrove," Lilith growled in his ear, "my love of the ages; my destiny."

Her breath in his face was now a hiss; her teeth, fangs; her kisses, bites; and her formerly silky soft hands now raked across his body like claws, tearing his flesh apart. Rove was more than happy — there was nothing he liked more than a bit of S & M. Lilith seemed to be one step ahead of him on every count, the epitome of perfection in a woman. But she had become very furry, he thought, and seemed to have shrunk in size. She was on his face now, and as much as he enjoyed being the recipient of oral sex, he hated a fur-burger — the pleasure/input ratio in this instance was always skewed in the woman's favour, which went against his every, naturally selfish, inclination. And Lilith was so very furry 'down there' that he began to struggle for breath, his mouth and nose completely blocked by hair. It crossed his mind that he would suggest she get a Brazilian before any further romantic trysts.

"Lilith, stop, you're suffocating me!" he managed to cry out between muffled sobs.

Early the next morning, Rove turned up at the local medical clinic looking as if he'd suffered a near death experience. Covered in bites and scratches, he claimed he'd been attacked by a giant feral cat, and that the bruises which covered every inch of his battered body had come about during his escape — a grove of apple trees had shed their fruit on him as he'd run through an orchard, almost like a stoning, he said. He could not explain what had happened to his crown jewels — they had disappeared without a trace. After the doctor sedated Rove and placed him in a straitjacket, he promptly booked him for psychiatric evaluation at the nearest mental health unit.

Back at Apple Tree Cottage, Lilith sat in the conservatory with Claw perched comfortably on her lap, kneading her curvaceous thighs through the folds of her sheer midnight-blue gown, his purring vibrating so loudly into the stratosphere that no unwelcome visitor dared trespass on the grounds of Apple Tree Cottage. He had that morning signed papers ceding his entire business — including all its holdings, staff, intellectual property and inventory — over to Lilith, in what others might term a 'hostile takeover'. But he was extremely satisfied with what he thought was a deal made in heaven.

"My dear boy," Lilith said as she stroked his beautiful silky black coat and tickled his ears, "I think it's time to make apple sauce and apple jelly seeing as we've had such a bumper crop this year. Totally out of season of course, but this is Apple Tree Cottage, after all! And how about apple crumble and clotted cream for dinner? Then we can talk about compensation for your annual leave, which was so rudely cut short..."

Claw II looked up into Lilith's face and narrowed his eyes in blissful deference, oozing with utmost devotion and obeisance. He'd never imagined he'd work for a woman, but in this instance, he was more than happy to concede to the far higher intelligence of a true Queen of the Night.

Jeannie, Jerome, the Publican and Pope John Paul Too

Jeannie and Jerome walked into my pub late one sultry Sunday afternoon. Heads turned as they do when strangers rock up unexpectedly in a small town, but she made straight for the bar as if she was on home turf, confident as. Her companion brought up the rear, a few shuffling steps behind her. She ordered a triple brandy and Coke; he wanted a handle of Old Dark.

"I'm driving," she said, as she flicked me a twenty-dollar note. A strange remark, I thought, since she'd be consuming more than twice the amount of alcohol he would. It's part of a bar manager's job description to size up your customers, monitor their rate of consumption and assess their state of mind. This was a new career for me and I was still being super conscientious.

The couple took their drinks to a picnic table on the deck where I had a clear view of them through the open French doors. I was intrigued; they made an odd pair. The guy was sallow-faced with sandy-coloured hair cropped at the collar Prince Valiant style. His hand moved often to his brow to push back a lock that had fallen across it. He was tall but didn't seem to fit his rakishly thin frame. In contrast, the woman was short and curvy and clearly a fair bit older than him, though her face was unlined. Her silver-streaked hair and large brown eyes formed the perfect chiaroscuro. When I'd served her at the bar, I noticed she had a disarming crooked smile which she used both effectively and often.

A hush fell over the room as the six o'clock TV One News jingle sounded from the wall-mounted TV. The Sale of Liquor Act dictates that entertainment — or if you abstract that, any form of distraction — should always be provided for your customers, to take the focus off alcohol consumption. Even gambling qualifies, I thought, as I glanced over to the bank of pokies in the pub's discreet gaming alcove. Sometimes, we also got in live acts. The night before, we'd had an Elvis impersonator who'd recently moved into the area. His amazing show had kept the punters going till the wee hours. It was always great for the takings when the local community scrubbed up and turned out.

But all eyes were now on the main news of the day: *The death of Pope John Paul II in the early hours of this morning has united over a billion Catholics around the world in an immense outpouring of grief which is expected to result in a pilgrimage of unprecedented proportions of the faithful to Rome.* I'd heard it all before so decided to take a smoko and asked my offsider, Stacey, to cover for me. I grabbed a Woody from the chiller and headed out back, flopping into a plastic garden chair and swinging my legs up onto a dustbin. Believe me, the best thing about the hospitality business is the downtime.

I had rolled up, had a few puffs, and was just beginning to relax when the door burst open, and the woman with the crooked-smile came to a standstill beside me. I leapt up, startled. The yard at the back of the pub was a staff only area. She stuttered an excuse; said she was looking for somewhere to be alone. Her eyes were swollen and mascara streaked down her cheeks. Jeez, there's something about a blubbering woman that always stumps me. I did the polite thing and offered her a seat. She sat down and stared absentmindedly at the ground for a few moments, then started rummaging around in her bag.

"Hey, can I get you anything?" I asked. After all, this was the woman who'd ordered a triple brandy and Coke a short while before. It never ceased to amaze me how soon the heavy drinkers needed a top up.

"Um… no, I'm good, thanks."

I sat down again and inhaled deeply on my cigarette. I was determined to have a few more drags before making a hasty retreat. "Having a bad day, huh?" I asked.

"Yeah. One of the worst." She'd pulled a rosary from her bag and now fingered it bead for bead, moving it between her hands.

"That bad, huh?"

"Well, you see," she sniffed, "it's just that…" She was rolling one of the beads so forcefully between her fingertips they'd turned white. "He's *dying*."

"Hey, you must have missed the news," I said. "He died last night." Now, of all things, I was thinking, I'd have to counsel a devout Catholic through the Pope's death, on top of a hell weekend of dealing with the local yokels and their need to anaesthetise themselves at the end of the working week. She turned to face me but looked right through me. I shifted in my seat. "You know, the Pope," I continued.

"Oh… yeah," she said. Her eyes dropped to the rosary. "I was actually talking about the guy I'm with. Jerome."

"Right. Jeez, sorry, my mistake. I mean, a lot of Catholics are pretty upset right now. When I saw the rosary, I just sort of assumed, you know… Eh, what is it they say about assumption? That it's the mother of all fucked-up thinking."

There was an extended silence. The woman looked worldly, but maybe she objected to me effing and blinding. Or maybe she objected to my pathetic attempt at pop psychology.

"He's quite *young*, though, isn't he?" I went on, hoping to steer the conversation back to her chosen topic. It's always *all* about the customer, isn't it?

A longer extended silence. I started looking forward to that quick exit. "Hey, what would I know anyway?" I continued. "Look, it's pretty busy this evening. I'd better get back behind the bar."

She turned to face me again and her features softened. I could tell there was no way I was getting out of this that easily. I started feeling panicky, trapped like an insect in a jar, rapidly using up the available air supply. I'd already broken the unwritten rule — I'd crossed the professional line between publican and punter. And I knew there was no going back.

"That's okay," she said. "How were you to know? He *is* young, too young, only thirty-two. It's his birthday tomorrow. But I guess thirty-three's an unlucky number, eh?" She dropped the rosary into her lap.

I wondered what she meant. I mean, her son? Younger brother? Her *boyfriend*? Whoever he was, he didn't look that good, for sure. Maybe he *was* super sick or something, but I wasn't a fucking doctor, was I? And why was thirty-three an unlucky number? Suddenly a light bulb lit up in my brain and it clicked. The death of Jesus Christ by crucifixion at age thirty-three. As if I could ever forget. All those years at Sacred Heart College had made sure of that.

"What are you saying?" I blurted out. Even though I didn't really want to know.

Fresh mascara-stained tears rolled down her cheeks. "That he may not make it through the night."

"He's that ill, is he?"

"It's very near the end," she said wistfully. "I know. I can sense it. It's as if there's a kind of shadow hanging over him, like... like a dark presence."

It occurred to me she'd probably watched way too many zombie movies. "Jeez, if it's that bad, why isn't he in a hospital or something?" I asked.

"He was being looked after at the West Auckland Hospice but last week he just got up and walked out, told them he wanted to do things his way, insisted on driving even though he could hardly walk. Next thing we'd bought a tent and some gear and were heading north. After a while I asked him where we were going and he turned to me, grinning, and said, 'To the end of the road'.

"Soon, I had to force him to let me take the wheel. He gets real sleepy after he's popped his morphine tabs. But it's stressful driving when he's writhing and groaning in the seat beside me. Northland's got great scenery, yeah? But there's not much else going for it, eh."

Her face suddenly blossomed into the crooked smile thing. I could see now what the attraction was; why Jerome was with her. She might have been older than him but what the heck? There was something really appealing about her — her voice, mannerisms and looks sucked you right in, alright.

I took a few slugs of my drink while she continued her sob story: "We've been on the road tiki-touring around, like it's the best holiday either of us has ever had. But I can't seem to get through to him..." She sighed, sank back down into her chair and stared at the rosary, then started working it again, bead for bead, bead for bead.

"I guess what upsets me most," she went on, "is he's kind of shut himself off, doesn't want to know, believes he's unworthy. But that's the whole point, isn't it?" She looked up at me again. "We're all human. Fallible. Sinners. That's why we need the saving grace of His forgiveness. Right?"

Bible bashing now! Jeez, what next? Religion's the biggest con of all time; a man-made construct used as a form of mind control. Worse still, the Catholics had a monopoly on it. Centuries of wars, pillage, extortion, rape, all in the name of Christ. It sickened me to the bone. But this strange woman was so sincere, so endearing, I found myself beginning to sympathise.

"That's a big call," was all I said.

In the following silence, it hit me with a large dose of irony that this complete stranger had just randomly confided her deepest fears to me. I started feeling like a newly ordained priest trying to find words of comfort for a believer facing a tragedy. Or maybe I should be dishing out a penance; the couple weren't married. But this was no ordinary confessional — we were sitting in the back yard of a pub with no screen between us.

But the way she kept looking at me, with all that gushy-goo-gaa softness, I knew I was going to have to come up with *something*. I was, however, no seasoned adept at Catholic hocus pocus, even though I should have known it like the back of my hand. There was no way I was going to resort to that centuries-old artifice, distorted by power and graft and grift and greed. The easiest thing to do was to default to hospitality mode — my saving grace. It went with the territory, you know. Upselling and all that.

"Look," I said, "the unit down by the water's edge is vacant. Why don't you guys stay over? You could probably both do with a break from the road. We do a mean roast dinner on Sunday nights."

She stopped working the rosary and laid its worn wooden cross across the palm of her hand. She was quiet for a moment, and closed her eyes as if in prayer. When she opened them, she looked at me once again, flashing her cute, crooked smile.

"Yeah, good idea," she said. "Thanks. I'd better also get back." She put the rosary away, wiped the messy black tears from her cheeks with her sleeve, then got up. "My name's Jeannie, by the way."

Back behind the bar, I noticed the newcomers had moved inside and ordered a meal. They were talking animatedly and I could only guess what the conversation was about, although I sensed it had something to do with what Jeannie had shared with me. Good luck to her. Jerome didn't appear convinced, though.

As the evening softened into night, they selected a few slow numbers on the jukebox and held each other close on the dance floor, Jeannie helping Jerome stay upright. The other patrons and the staff couldn't help staring, all of us fascinated by their strangeness and their strange attachment.

At the end of the set Jeannie returned to their table and Jerome ambled awkwardly over to the bar. "Hey. Jeannie said I should talk to you about the accommodation."

"Sure, I'll just get the register, and grab the keys."

When I returned, Jerome was leaning on the bar counter with his back to me, watching Jeannie smiling at him from across the room.

"You seem really smitten, mate," I said, hoping to lure him into conversation. I'm not usually so personal with customers, preferring to maintain a professional detachment. Otherwise, you end up being a counsellor, mediator, or worse, a convenient line of credit towards the oblivion of inebriation. But since I'd already been forced across the line by Jeannie, I figured, what the hell. I was keen to hear Jerome's side of the story.

"Yup," he said, "you're right about that, man." He turned to face me, and grinned, full and wide. It was probably the way he'd looked at Jeannie in the car when they'd left the city. "Hey, how about a nightcap, man? A neat whisky is what the doctor ordered tonight." Leaning in close, across the counter, he reached up to push an errant lock of hair out of his face. The angry scar of a prior injury marked his temple.

"Sure," I said as I poured each of us a nip of the best. Johnnie Walker Black Label. He downed his in one gulp. I followed suit, and refilled our glasses.

"Cheers, man," he said. His eyes bored into me. "You know, before Jeannie, I'd never looked at a dark woman before, let alone an older chick. No way. It was always blonde on blonde for me, the younger the better. But you know what? Blondes are interchangeable. Clones. Cardboard-cut-out dolls."

"Oh yeah?" Up close I could see how dull Jerome's complexion was, how his eyes were sunken in their sockets, and how his shrunken gums barely held his teeth in position. He was so thin that given half a chance he could have fallen through his own backside.

He went on: "Jeannie is something else, man. She slipped into my life when I was hung up on other stuff. Next thing, she'd wormed her way into my heart; reeled me in, hook, line and sinker. Ever had a woman do that to you?"

"Now that you mention it..." I was thinking about Mercedes, the woman who had caused the operatic unlocking of my own constricted heart and turned me into a lovesick puppy, then unceremoniously dumped me, pushing me to place I was at now. Running this godforsaken pub in the wopwops.

Jerome laughed at the expression on my face. "I guess she got right under your skin before you even realised what was happening. It scared the hell out of me at first. Jeannie is so sure of herself. Cold, like ice; hot, like fire. And when you're flapping around like a big girl's blouse, you're not fit to handle the heat or the cold. Know what I mean?" I nodded. I knew what he meant alright. And I didn't particularly enjoy being reminded.

Jerome laughed again, then threw back the contents of his glass. I'll never forget the sound of his laugh: it was the guffaw of a terminally-ill man at a critical juncture on his personal journey between stupidity and wisdom. But I knew full well that the defining moment — that instant of longed for and much needed clarity which jolts you out of your comfort zone like a slap in the face — often comes when the time to take advantage of it is fast running out.

He leaned in even closer and lowered his voice. "When we first started rooting, I told her it meant nothing to me. She did her sweet smiley thing, and all she said was, 'So what? All that matters is, it means everything to me.' That woman is all about what she wants to give, not what she needs to take," he said, pointing his finger at me. "She helped me face what I see in the mirror each morning, man."

I nodded. "Good on you, mate," was all I could think of saying by way of reply. Jeannie was using sign language from across the room indicating it was time I wrapped things up. Jerome and I did the business and said goodnight.

Within a half hour all the other patrons had cleared out, returning to their individual destinies, subdued by the prospect of another week of responsibility after a long weekend of forgetting. After Stacey knocked off and headed home, I locked up and strolled down to the beach. I like to stretch my legs after a long shift; it helps me wind down before hitting the sack.

It was a clear, balmy night. The moon was half full and the tide was high. I rolled up, lit up, and walked along the beachside path beneath a row of pōhutukawa trees. The darkness and the quiet felt good: no piped music, no shrill voices, no empty handles being banged on the bar counter demanding refilling, no scraping of chairs when a drunken argument or domestic broke out.

As I navigated a bend, I heard voices and noticed movement in the water. Jeannie and Jerome were naked, waist-deep, and she was holding him in her arms while uttering an incantation. Jerome repeated each phrase after her.

"I believe in one God, the Father Almighty... And in one Lord Jesus Christ, the only begotten Son of God, born of the Father, God of God, Light of Light, True God of True God, begotten, not made, consubstantial with the Father. . .who was crucified, suffered and was buried. On the third day, He rose again, according to the Scriptures. I believe in the Holy Ghost, the Lord, the Giver of life and one holy, catholic, and apostolic Church." There was a short pause, then Jeannie gave the blessing: "In the name of the Father, the Son and the Holy Ghost, I baptise you now, and wash away all your sins. Christ's death on the cross means He has taken on the sins of the world, absolving you of yours. You are now free, a new man; reborn, remade in His imagery; eternally forgiven, eternally saved."

The water bubbled around Jerome and a shadow rose out of his head, blacker than the sky, blotting out the stars. I shivered despite the balminess of the night, hairs rising on my arms and the back of my neck. The shadow grew larger and larger and I saw the silhouettes of clawed hands flailing at its edges. Suddenly Jeannie let Jerome go and there was a lot of splashing about in the water. For a moment I thought he was drowning, but he soon surfaced, spluttering.

"Happy now, my sweet?" he called to her across the water.

"I'm ecstatic!" she shouted, her laughter peeling out like church bells. Then they moved back towards each other and embraced.

I stood there, absolutely stunned for a few moments, an incidental witness but as much a part of this human drama unfolding in the backblocks of Northland as Jeannie and Jerome were. For the first time since I was seven years old, when Sister Teresa Angelica had slapped me across the face for stealing lollies from the jar she kept on her desk to reward good behaviour, a knot formed in my throat. I turned away to retrace my steps back to the pub, but needed to use the security night lights to guide me, I was that choked up. It was as if something had been unlocked in me, and groping my way up that slippery slope in the dark, late that Indian summer Sunday night, my sight blurred by tears and my throat constricted with emotion, it occurred to me that despite all of life's disappointments, detours and dead ends, for all the wishing and the wanting and not getting and the growing older and more cynical, there comes a time when you are forced to give up and let go, to accept things just the way they are, and to make the best of them the only way you know how. With a little help from your friends. If you are lucky enough to have a few...

By the time I reached my flat above the tavern, an exhilaration I hadn't felt in a long time was beginning to flood through me. It felt good to know that salvation was not only for the lucky and the strong, the pious and the good. It occurred to me that night that when we stop believing in something bigger and better than our mundane, disheartening reality, we are left with only our paltry, useless, damaged selves in a wanting world in which redemption doesn't exist. But Jeannie had offered Jerome a deliverance that was possible *despite* himself. Jeannie still believed in miracles. And I couldn't help admiring her for that. Jerome was one helluva lucky man, really.

I fell into a chair and flicked on the TV. BBC's all night news coverage lit up the screen, and once again the subject was Pope John Paul II: *In his youth, he was a member of an experimental theatre group and published a collection of poetry. As Pope, he was known as something of a showman and embraced the media, encouraging extensive press coverage of his travels and religious activities, never missing a photo opportunity. One of his favourite sayings was...* I was bored stiff and soon dozed off.

As it turned out, Jerome's thirty-third birthday was another fine day. I tended to my usual Monday morning chores, tidying the chillers, taking stock, placing orders and doing paperwork, while Stacey got stuck into the big post-weekend cleanup. While I worked, I got to thinking about Jeannie and Jerome. And Pope John Paul too. He was apparently a self-confessed media junkie who'd quip with a twinkle in his eye, every time he went on camera, "If it isn't on TV, it never happened..."

Yeah, right, I thought, as I opened the doors to the first punters of the day: the dishevelled occupants of a lewdly-liveried camper van who had freedom-camped overnight on my property, and our most dedicated and loyal customer, the local barfly, who spent more time at the pub than he did at home. Ah well, where would you be in this business without your customers? Besides, the barfly's wife was known to be an unbearable nag. And in New Zealand, we are always hospitable to tourists. They're our life blood, other than farming exports!

Jeannie and Jerome emerged from their cabin around midday and called in to the tavern to settle up. They seemed in high spirits and I watched as they crunched across the gravel to their car, Jeannie waving animatedly goodbye as Jerome got in behind the wheel. As their car spun out of the parking lot, I saw that Jeannie had hung her rosary from the rear-view mirror and its worn wooden cross was swinging in a wide arc between them.

Asian Cigarettes

ESOL EXERCISE

ESOL Tutor's Instructions to English Language Students:
Write a short piece about something that happened to you yesterday after class. Don't worry about your spelling, grammar, or punctuation, just write whatever you can, using the English words and structures you already know. Aim for about 200 words.

I sit in courtyard at Brooklyn Bar on Queen Street, in Auckland, City of Sails.

I drink beer. I play Pokémon on my Samsung.

You stand by my table. I look up.

You smile. You say, do you mind?

I say, no, it is okay.

You sit down. You look at me. You say, you look sad.

I say, what means sad?

You make face like something is wrong.

I smile. I say, yes, I am this… sad.

You say, why?

I say, I no like this place. I shake my head. My friends and everything I like is at my home.

You say, you must be Japanese.

I say, how you know this?

You say, I am English teacher. I tutor many Asian students.

I say, you are clever.

You say, no, experienced.

I say, what means this?

You say, it means to have lived a lot, learned a lot.

I say, ah. I smile. You smile.

I say, my parents they send me to New Zealand for learning English.

You say, you have come to the right place.

I laugh. You laugh. You drink your beer. I drink my beer.

You smoke your New Zealand cigarette. I smoke my Asian cigarette.

You take your Samsung from your bag.

I say, what game you play?

TRANSIT LOUNGE

Maehoghada at Wellington International Airport. I'm stranded here for the night in the new terminal — Kiwis call it "the Giant Pumpkin" — with some of Tolkien's mythical creatures for company. Wind and wild weather have delayed my connection to Christchurch till the morning and the few remaining *won* in my wallet won't cover the cost of a hotel room let alone a taxi ride anywhere, so this is my accommodation for the night. It feels good to have my feet on the ground again though, having flown non-stop from South Korea. The app on my phone says the English translation of *Maehoghada* is 'witching hour'. I Google this term, then check back with my Korean dictionary to verify the meaning. *Wa!* Witches exist in both languages. Interesting.

My digs for the night? Not so interesting. I'm slumped on one of those moulded plastic chairs that are bolted to the floor in long rows in airports and other public spaces. The ones with hard, angular armrests so you can't lie down. It could be worse, I guess — I've slept in some pretty strange places: in a toilet stall at Seoul Central Station when there was an electricity outage and the trains weren't running. On the beach at Taylors Mistake when the German tourists I'd been hanging out with disappeared after I fell asleep in the sun.

Despite the late hour, I feel pretty wired: sleep-deprived, jet lagged, eyes glued wide open, high on ephedrine. I take ephedrine for my sinus headaches. They started when I first came to live in New Zealand as a foreign student. The doctor said something about pollen; something about there being so much vegetation here — trees and stuff — the air is saturated with pollen dust. In Seoul there's very little vegetation and mostly only steel and glass and concrete, so I'd never had a problem before.

My parents get the ephedrine for me on the black market. It's from China and super cheap. And stronger than anything you can get in New Zealand. I carry a small bottle of pills in my pocket with a doctor's letter when I travel, but the bulk of them, Eomma packs into the lining of my suitcase. Korean mothers always pack their son's cases, no matter what age we are. I also bring in a couple of cartons of ESSE cigarettes, but I declare them and pay the customs duty. That way, the customs officers think you've declared all your contraband and don't bother to search your bags. I would go to jail, for sure, if they found the cache of pills. But I take the risk because I really need the medicine: it dries up my nose, fires up my synapses, and keeps me alert and awake so I can study for twenty hours a day.

I am studying medicine in New Zealand, and when I qualify as a surgeon, I'll get a green card and go and live in Seattle and open an appearance medicine clinic there and get rich. When I get rich, I'll sponsor my parents and sisters to come and live in the States also.

That is the plan, anyway. It's my parents' dream. They talk about it all the time. I wanted to be a writer — maybe a journalist, or an author. My college ESOL teacher, Mrs B, told me my command of language was outstanding, and always encouraged me. She said she'd never had a student with such a brilliant command of the English language. Even her English speaking ones! But my parents have chosen my career for me. And as a son, a Korean son — as my parent's only son — it is my duty to fulfil their dream. This is the Korean way.

But it's super expensive to study overseas, and a doctor's degree takes many years, too many years. Plus I attended college here in New Zealand as a foreign student for five years also. So, when I need money, I sell ephedrine tablets to Kiwis. They crush the pills and cook them and smoke them and go crazy, like witches at witching hour. Kiwis are undisciplined. And many are fat, and also lazy. Spoiled! Yet they believe we Asian kids are spoiled. *Wa!* They're so funny to watch, especially when they get high. They play loud music and party hard and fuck each other silly. We Asians are much more self-controlled.

But how am I going to pass the time tonight? My medical study books are packed in my suitcase and I have nothing to read. It's so late, all the shops and restaurants and kiosks in the terminal are closed, and it's hushed and quiet. There's not much action in the Giant Pumpkin tonight, only a few other passengers in the same situation as me. Complicit. In transit.

Suddenly here's a loud bang. *Wa!* A gunshot? I spin around, scared stiff. Until the Christchurch Massacre last year, I'd always felt safe in New Zealand. Now I dance on pins and needles all the time. Well, that's what my *halmeoni* — my grandma — says I do, because I'm jumpy as shit.

Whew! Okay, no problem. Just a service door banging open as a cleaner shuffles into the hall, pushing a bucket and mop in front of her. She crosses the concourse then pauses in front of the huge cantilevered windows overlooking the runway. In her white shift she looks ghostly, suspended in space between this dimly-lit interior and its shimmering reflection in the massive panels of glass behind her. Dunking her mop into the bucket, she swirls it around in the sudsy water, then smacks it onto the tiled floor, swish, thunk, splash.

Bracing herself, she takes a deep breath, arches her body, extends her neck. Then she sets off, moving down the long empty rows of chairs, pushing the bucket before her, mopping as she goes — straight, turn, straight, cross, straight, turn, straight, cross — a dancer twirling across an empty stage, a skater skimming across a frozen lake.

In the row behind me a high-pitched voice begins counting. I turn to see a doll-like girl dressed in a frilly old-fashioned dress with white tights and button up shoes, just like the outfits my sisters wear to church in Seoul. Her hair is parted on the crown and plaited at the sides of her head with ribbons, like Elsa in *Frozen*, a movie my sisters watch over and over. She moves down the row of chairs, arm raised, index finger pointed like a magic wand. Or, perhaps, a sword. She is counting the seats, articulating the numbers carefully in Queen's English: 'one' is *won*, 'two' is *tuu*, 'three' is *thhrrreee*.

With each utterance, she bows slightly towards the seat in front of her, her head tipping forward, her chin touching her chest. The rag doll hanging from the crook of her arm is listening as intently as I am, her head cocked and a look of enquiry on her face. The girl is practising the art of semaphore in Story Book Land, numbering the Knights of the Round Table, charging them with grave responsibility, urging them to deeds of great daring. This story is very popular in Korea and many Korean children play this game.

A middle-aged woman sits diagonally across the aisle from me, stockinged legs placed side by side, feet in sensible shoes, handbag open on her lap. Rummaging through its contents, she pulls from deep within it a makeup bag and a pack of travel tissues. Flicking a powder compact open, she tilts her face this way and that, examining her features in its tiny mirror. Then she reaches for a tube of lipstick: *Ruby Woo*, by MAC. I recognise it — my girlfriend back home uses the same brand and colour. After removing the cap, she winds up the rose-red wand until it protrudes from its protective gold case. Following her reflection in the mirror, she paints a red line across the place where her mouth should be.

Viewing her reflection once more, she turns her head side-on and face-on, tilting her chin up and down. She clicks her tongue, annoyed, frustrated, and raises her tired eyes to the vaulted ceiling in the common gesture of despair. She sighs, pulls a tissue from the pack, and begins to rub the lipstick off.

Once again, she paints the place where her lips should be, a slash of red, a gash. Once more, the mirror is extended. Wide-eyed now, incredulous, she sees the red lines blur and break up as the hole her lips should frame opens in surprise. I see what she sees: the impossibility of making herself beautiful — beautiful enough for the imaginary lover who waits for her at our future-forward destination.

The cleaning woman is moving in ever decreasing circles now, closer and closer to where I slouch in my seat, her shadowy form gaining sharpness and definition as she turns and twirls towards me, executing a perfect figure of eight. I see the bulging varicose veins beneath the hem of her shift, the bunions peeping out of their self-made holes in her canvas shoes, the way the silver hairs on her upper lip glint as they catch the light, sparkling like tinsel on a Christmas tree. I rise. I stretch. I move towards her. We make eye contact. We greet each other with a smile. We bow.

Then she skates right into my arms, allowing me to pull her into my embrace. I spin her around and we set off as a pair. *I am the perfect floor mop*, I whisper in her ear. *And you, dear lady, you are the world's most accomplished dancer.*

Wa! The domed roof above us cracks open, like a dinosaur birthing out of its shell; the floor beneath our feet gives way like breaking ice. We waltz out into the night sky with the wind propelling us upwards, as the airport terminal recedes into the distance below. From the sky it looks like an elliptical, atomic-powered UFO banking into land on the earth's surface. Not even vaguely like a giant pumpkin!

Suddenly I crash land back into my seat. The counting exercise behind me is increasing in speed and volume. The Knights of the Round Table are numerous and they must be counted; all of them. The girl continues up the row, faster now, shrill, her arms tracing through the air like a Korean fan dancer. *Won, tuu, thhrree, you will never catch me; four, five, sex, numbers are not complex; seven, eight, nyne, we ascend the helicline; ten, eleven, twelve, into your true nature I will delve.*

I turn back to see the loveless woman now trying different coloured lipsticks. As each one fails, she breaks it off its stem and throws it to the floor. A pile of crumpled tissues is growing at her feet. The woman's face is crisscrossed with pink and orange and red and purple slashes; none are right. Her hands, holding the mirror, tremble; her arms shake. The mirror clouds over with condensation. Her knee begins to jerk up and down and her tights catch on the rough edge of the plastic seat. I watch as a ladder runs down her leg and across her foot, where it disappears into her shoe.

I stand and cross the distance between us, stopping right in front of her. She follows her line of sight from the chaos on the floor, up my legs and torso, to my face. Her misty grey eyes are blank, glazed. I cock my head and half smile at her, willing myself inside her mind.

Your reflection is an illusion, I say. *Give this vain exercise up for good. Okay?* I bend and take her face in my hands. *May I kiss your many-real-bleeding-beautiful-ravaged-multiple mouths?*

She relaxes her shoulders now, relieved. Her mouth opens to reveal a row of perfect white teeth as her plump peach-coloured lips frame the grateful words, *Thank you.*

I gather her discarded tissues in my arms and throw them high, like juggling balls, into the air above my head. Each rumpled tissue sails upwards into the vaulted ceiling space of the transit lounge, then slows its speed as it completes its notional arc, floating gently down through the viscous, artificial air. The woman watches, her head tracking the motion of each ball like a cat watching a long game of table tennis.

Wa! White flags rain down upon us, white flags streaked with red crosses. Paper planets with red rings. Bleeding-heart doves. Confetti.

QUEEN STREET CADDIE

Late one wet and windy night, after a long day at a workshop in the central city, I stop by an ethnic food court on Queen Street. After placing my order at the counter, I choose a table and sit down. A discarded newspaper lies open across the Formica table top. The headline jumps out at me: '*GOLF CRAZY*', followed by the sub, '*Number of golf clubs per capita in New Zealand second only to Scotland*'. It occurs to me that for golf enthusiasts, this might be a compelling reason to immigrate to New Zealand. Is this fun fact about the number of golf courses in New Zealand perhaps the reason why many of my foreign students take golf lessons every afternoon after school?

Leaning back in my seat, I begin to take in my surroundings. Being a consummate people watcher, food courts rate highly on my list of ideal locations, almost up there with airports, malls, bus and train stations. Nothing much to see here tonight, though. The place is almost deserted.

Built environments fascinate me too, as much as people do. Looking around, I notice how each of the seven or eight different food outlets here are decorated and signposted to reflect their national cuisine. Crudely painted ethnic scenes surround the kiosks and each is adorned, on their walls and counter tops, with various culture-specific ornaments: the universal signifying tropes of different nationalities.

I find myself wondering whether the countries represented here — China, India, Japan, Indonesia, Turkey, Korea and others — have golf courses in their countries. Do they even play the game? I imagine people from these nations scrunching up their faces in incomprehension when they realise that golf involves smacking a small, hard, white ball down long stretches of grassed fairway and around manicured lawns into a flagged hole, to score the least number of points. The game would probably seem pointless to them, not to mention the waste of space and the water required to keep the greens green.

In the hazy reflection of a grimy wall mirror I catch sight of a young girl who is sitting on the counter of the Chinese food kiosk. Perhaps she doesn't know that sitting on a table is tapu. I change seats, so I can observe her more easily. The people-watching gene in my personal make-up is rather entrenched, I admit, though I do try not to stare. But her attitude and posture are intriguing. She's slightly built as Asians often are, and wearing a washed-out grey school tunic cinched at the waist by a sash, over a grubby white collared shirt. Her Mary-Jane school shoes are scuffed and worn, and her frilled bobby socks pool in folds around her ankles as if their elastic has gone slack from repeated laundering. I reckon she's about ten or eleven years old.

I examine her face and demeanor carefully. The round, high-cheeked, generic bone structure of Chinese children, with their hooded almond eyes and bow-shaped lips, flat facial profiles and small, neat, button noses are particularly attractive to me. She wears a centre parting in her hair which allows it to fall into a shiny black fringe and shoulder-length bob. Sitting desultorily on the countertop, her arms are rigid and her hands press against the serving bench on either side of her torso, her legs swinging backwards and forwards and her heels banging against the front of the counter, thud, thud, thud. Boredom and disdain flicker in her eyes, discontent evident in the sulking pout of her mouth. I find it interesting that a face so unmarked by experience, so youthful and innocent, can convey such complex emotions.

I ponder her fate. As it's probably too late for a school child to be out and about on a weekday night, I can only surmise she's attached in some familial way to the operators of the Chinese food outlet. Yet the stall is unmanned and appears to have been shut down for the night. Where is her family? Why is she here all alone? Waiting. For what? I wonder if I should I approach her to enquire is she is okay. I wonder how good her English is and whether she'll understand me.

The smell of roast lamb kebab distracts me as a smiling service person delivers my meal. I haven't eaten anything since early in the day and need to fortify myself for my long drive home, so I tuck in, momentarily distracted.

Suddenly a swift movement crosses my peripheral vision. I glance up to see the girl hopping smartly off the counter. She stands to attention in front of it now, staring across the room. The door to the food court has swung open, then closed, and a balding middle-aged man is striding across the food court towards the girl, muttering what sounds like a minimally restrained reprimand in Chinese. An unlit cigarette hangs from the corner of his mouth. The girl flinches, but quickly regains her composure, rearranging her demeanour into its former look of disdain and ennui.

The man is hefting a large golf bag bulging with woods, irons, wedges and putters. Perhaps he is 'golf crazy' and practices at the indoor driving range nearby, preparing for the day when he might be able to afford time off from his fast-food business to visit a few of the country's three hundred and ninety golf courses. Perhaps this is the reason that motivated him to come and live in New Zealand. Or perhaps it's one of his reasons. Perhaps he is hopeful that his 'daughter' or 'granddaughter' will start to play when she is old enough to wield the clubs, and that she will work herself up the ladder to become an internationally rated golf player, like Lydia Ko. Everyone has their own version of heaven, I guess.

When he reaches the girl, he leans his golf bag against the counter, and, motioning towards it, utters what sounds like an order. The girl steps forward like an automaton, almost clicking her heels to attention. Then she slips an arm through the bag's strap and heaves it over her shoulder. Buckled forward under its weight now, she starts hobbling towards the door. The man follows, urging the girl with flailing arms to get a move on and muttering under his breath. Then he leans forward and gives her a small push.

My heart lurches. I need to do something, say something. My mind is screaming, *That's no way to treat a child!* Little white balls start bouncing around in my head and beating and banging against the inside of my skull like the balls in the Lotto Draw gravity-pick machine on TV. I try to stand up but find I'm rooted to the spot. My mouth opens but no sound comes out. I raise my arms in the air, but the few other customers in the food court are oblivious, minding their own business.

I need to tell the man we do not treat children like that here, in *this* country, keeping them up till all hours when they have school tomorrow, verbally and physically abusing them; that in the West, children are not treated like slaves but as cherished members of their families, that they are protected by human rights and the values of a fair and just society, that even if they are only just *girls*, they are treasured.

But the door of the food court has opened and closed with a great gush of wet air, and when I finally get up the gumption to follow the strange pair, the man and the girl are gone, lost in the throng of moviegoers exiting the cinema next door, obscured in the darkness by a curtain of slanting rain.

Too Much of Nothing

Maungaturoto is not a dead-end town; a geographical characteristic that is often in a place's favour in terms of its potential for growth, for when you reach the end of the line it's often easier to stay put than face a return journey. But no, Maunga — as it's affectionately known to the locals — is actually on the way to somewhere else. Most travellers pass through the village in a blur, looking neither left nor right, slowing only to observe the urban speed limit.

The railway tracks that slash through the settlement, heading southwest from Whangārei to Dargaville on the Kaipara, are a rusted reminder of a different future. The few streets that comprise the township appear to have been randomly carved upon the undulating landscape and meet in a tangled spaghetti junction at its centre. The main road winds along an exposed ridge that drops away behind the few stores and sagging houses which hug its verges, where untidy back yards descend steeply into gorse-choked gullies. Dust blows in eddies round sharply-angled corners, and the signs above the few shop fronts rattle a feeble welcome as stray cats creep from their hoardings to beg. On any given day, aside from the few cars always parked up outside the Maungaturoto Tavern, the streets appear almost deserted. Travellers could be forgiven for believing they were passing through an abandoned film set somewhere in the wopwops of Nevada.

But this is Northland, New Zealand. A kilometre to the east of Maungaturoto, on the flat expanse of a small lowland valley which runs beside the potholed Highway 12, a scrapyard squats in splendour, bordered at the back by a curving line of dusty willows drooping wistfully over a semi-dried-up stream. In the centre of the yard is a huge, block-shaped, modernist red barn which serves as an office and storeroom, surrounded on all sides by piles of car, tractor and truck wrecks, between which waist-high grass and colourful flowering weeds, like black-eyed Susan and morning glory, grow in abandon at this time of year. It's February — suicide month — and the heat and glare of the sun refracting through the north-facing windows of the building are debilitating. Not a breath of freshness stirs the air and the silence is palpable, save for a few blowflies butting themselves against the grimy, closed windows.

Slumped on a grubby stool behind the counter, Frank waits dejectedly, drumming his grease-encrusted fingertips on the countertop. Glancing up once again at the large wall clock that dominates his life with its interminably slow ticking towards five o'clock, he reaches for the dirty rag he keeps under the counter and wipes the sweat from his forehead and the back of his neck, then continues his finger drumming, in time with the buzzing blowflies.

Suddenly his face animates, contorting with pleasure — it's a quarter to! He leaps up, grabs a plastic fly swat encrusted with the remains of dead bodies from a nail on the wall, and attacks the blowflies. They fall to the sill, joining others of their kind decomposing there in a crust of dust. Then Frank locks the cash register and pops the key in his pocket. No need to cash up; there hasn't been a customer all day. Bright and chirpy as a box of birds now and whistling a merry tune, he goes outside and strides across the yard to retrieve his huge wheeled sign from the roadside — MAUNGATUROTO CAR WRECKERS

AND SCRAP METALS: ONE MAN'S JUNK; ANOTHER MAN'S TREASURE — wrangling it back across the yard and into the barn, where he stores it for the night. He can't afford to have hoons deface his sign or make off with it. After securing the door of the premises with a padlock, he leaps up into the cab of his battered tow truck, and starts it up with a roar.

Five minutes later, the truck hisses and squeaks to a halt outside the Maungaturoto Hotel & Tavern. Frank parks in his usual spot, just off the main road, where he advertises his tow services to passersby. The barman's greeting is always the same: "A man could set his watch by you, mate! Beer o'clock it is!" Hendry rings the old ship's bell hanging in the bar and announces in a singsong voice, "Happy Hour, Happy People!" Then he turns back to Frank. "Two for the price of one then, mate, as per usual?"

Frank retires with his handles of Speights Old Dark to the lattice-framed veranda of the hundred-year-old pub which faces onto the metal parking lot. He downs his first beer in a couple of gulps, then reaches for the pack of cigarettes he keeps stashed securely in his shirt pocket, lighter always tucked into the box when it's a couple of ciggies down. He only allows himself a few smokes in the evenings now; five to be exact. His doctor has recently put the hard word on him.

As he sucks on his first cancer stick of the day and glugs his second beer, he feels reasonably content and begins to relax. Audrey shuffles by on her way home from work at the local newsagents, a package of fresh takeout tucked under her arm for tea. Frank waves a cursory greeting. "Enjoy your fush and chups, Audrey! Or is it Chinese tonight?" The owner of the dairy across the road comes out with a stack of flattened cardboard boxes to throw into the skip in the alley beside his shop. A couple of skeletal kittens poke their heads out from beneath the hoardings, and Frank watches bemused as Ravi chases them away, hissing, "You vermin, get lost! Or else I'll make a fookin' good curry out of you!"

A modified car throbs into the service station next door and a couple of lowlifes leap out, yanking their low riders up. One pumps gas while the other goes into the servo shop. Forty seconds later, he exits at speed, carrying a load of snacks and energy drinks. The pair leap back into their car, the driver fires the supercharged ignition, and they tear off, looking neither left nor right as they exit the forecourt onto the main road, souped-up twin exhausts flaming at the rear of their vehicle, black smoke pumping into the stratosphere. The owner of the petrol station, a balding Turk with a physique like a spinning top, runs out of the shop with arms flailing, shouting, "Hey! HEY! I have video surveillance, you fuckers! I will track you down and make you pay! PAY! This world was not only made for you!" Frank sympathises; this is a regular occurrence. Ali needs to update his systems and operate on prepay like they do in the cities now if he wants to avoid this.

Frank knows he's fortunate that, in his line of business, he doesn't have to deal with hit-and-run customers. In fact, he doesn't get many customers at all; it's been a long, slow week. TGIF. Thank God it's Friday. Not that his weekends offer much to look forward to. He keeps the yard open on Saturdays to service tiki-tourers and any passing weekend trade, but business is slow enough that he's able to sit for hours at a stretch in front of Sky Sports in his flat above the shed with his friend Johnnie Walker for company, and a couple of packs of crisps and store-bought dips to ease the liquor down. He only ever raises himself from his sticky white plastic 'Graceland' couch if a customer toots their arrival down below. But this is a rare occurrence, rarer than on weekdays, when he keeps a conscientious vigil behind the counter, if only to keep up appearances.

By Sundays, though, Johnnie is done for and Frank is usually suffering from a hell hangover. His devoutly Puritan Scottish mother and grandmother would have turned in their graves, but their remedies for a bender still served him well: a large bowl of Scotch oats drowning in thick cream and a pinch of salt thrown over your shoulder into the eyes of the devil. At least he was partly faithful to one of their many Biblical injunctions: *Man will work for six days straight, but on the seventh he will desist and rest, and read the Lord's book.*

The Lord's book didn't actually get much of an airing at Frank's. Opera was his religion. Lying prone on his couch with a toxic headache, he'd reach for the Hi-Fi remote (which lived on his matching 'Graceland' white-vinyl-padded, smoky-glass-topped, coffee table) and with the press of a single button, he'd set his five-disc CD player, stacked with Pavarotti, on random play. The soaring, pulsing, throbbing, yowling sounds of opera always seemed to purge him of all his misgivings about ending up in this dead-end business in this godforsaken town with no wife and kids to keep him company, and nothing to look forward to, excepting getting plastered every weekend. He would spend hours on the couch every Sunday, still three sheets to the wind and in a bath of sweat, with the melodious and gut-wrenching sounds of Turandot, Aida and La Bohème washing over him — drowning him in waves of emotion — until he recovered sufficiently to take a shower and put himself to bed, to recover his strength for the week ahead.

Having returned to the bar for another round tonight, Frank is sucking on his third cigarette of the evening and wondering what's happened to his drinking buddies: Bert and his crew — Number 8, Gunna, Rod Burner and Ten Speed. Milking must have run late; town seems even quieter than usual. Apart from a few voices inside the pub, the only sound is the throaty purr of a V8 approaching from the west, cruising way above the speed limit.

A few moments later the vehicle in question swings dangerously wide around the nearest corner, then skids and slides to a halt in a cloud of dust in front of the tavern. Frank notes the make and colour — it's an older model Commodore Club Sport, burgundy or brown, he can't tell which, the vehicle is that dirty. *If this joker carries on driving like a bloody cowboy, there might be a tow job for me tonight,* he muses.

Next minute, the passenger door swings open and he hears raised voices over the distorted techno music pumping from the boot of the vehicle. The longhaired male driver is leaning across the female passenger, yelling, "Unbuckle, bitch! And get a move on!" The woman struggles with the seatbelt and as soon as it releases, the driver pushes her out of the car and she falls awkwardly to the ground.

"What about my bag?" she shouts.

"Get it yourself!"

The woman stumbles to her feet, raking away with a bloodied hand the hair that has fallen across her face, and approaches the boot, while the driver revs the engine. The boot pops open, activated by a switch from inside, and she lurches towards it, grabbing a battered holdall from its depths moments before the car pulls violently away, spraying metal in all directions and sashaying back onto the road. The woman stands there in shock for a few seconds, then shakes her head and shouts after the Commodore as it gathers speed around the next corner, "Well fuck you too, Jerome!" Then she turns and stumbles towards the tavern, the spokes of her high-heeled sandals catching in the gravel.

When Frank returns to the bar for another round a short while later, the mystery woman is perched on a stool and slumped over the bar counter, stuffing peanuts into her mouth as if she hasn't seen food for days. Hendry, the barman, makes googly eyes at Frank, as if to say, "Shout the lady a drink, Frank, come on."

"The same again Hendry, thanks," Frank says. Then he adds, hesitatingly, "And what about you, Miss, can I get you something?"

The newcomer is circling her head around as if releasing the tension in her neck. At first, she ignores Frank and he's about to walk away when she suddenly turns to face him and makes disarming eye contact. "Yup, okay," she says. Turning back to Hendry, she adds, "Make it a triple."

"Yes, ma'am. So, what'll it be?"

"Vodka, lime and lemonade. Lots of ice."

Frank detects a resigned nonchalance in her voice, an attitude he is long accustomed to in his treatment by women. But when Hendry winks at him, it makes him feel braver.

"Okay. Cut the beers. Make that two, please, Hendry, two triples... of... what she said." Hendry's surprised. Frank only drinks beer at the pub; his spirits' purchases extend solely to his standard weekly off-sales order of top shelf on a Friday night which he takes home with him, hugging it to his chest like a girlfriend. "Triples it is," he grins, amused.

"So, what brings you to Maungaturoto?" Frank asks the woman.

"What's it to you?" she asks, mumbling through a mouthful of peanuts.

"No reason. Just haven't seen you about is all."

The woman stops throwing peanuts down her throat and turns to face Frank. She is cross-eyed like Karen Black, the actress. In fact, everything about her is Karen Black — her big hair, strawberry blonde and teased up into a high crown, her fitted stovepipe jeans, the yellow wet-look top hugging her pointy breasts, her curvy black eyeliner and shocking pink lipstick, and those fire-truck-red, super-high-heeled, strappy sandals.

"Well, if you really want to know, I didn't exactly pick it out of a 'tourist brochure'," she says, doing the air quote thing with her fingers, and laughing in a brittle way.

Frank feels encouraged. "Yes," he pauses, searching for something meaningful to say. "It's not exactly the sort of place a person would choose to visit, is it?"

She leans back on the barstool and swivels around to face him. "Oh, it's not *that* bad, I guess. I've lived in dumps all my life. You know, 'familiar territory'." She laughs.

"Join the club," he says, noting that she'd used air quotes again. "Well, I'm Frank," he continues. "How do you do? And this is Hendry..."

She waves his hand away. "Mercedes." Her fringe has fallen forward, and she flicks it away with a grazed hand. Frank notices that her temple and cheekbone are badly bruised.

"That's pretty grand," he says. "How did you end up with such an exotic name?"

"It's a long story. Sure you really want to hear it?"

"Yeah. Why not?"

"Okay. If you must. I warn you, though, it's boring — not the stuff movies are made of." She takes a large swig of her drink, more than half of it, Frank notes. "Mum was white trash and lived in a caravan park in the back blocks of Golden Bay. She wore kaftans and flowers in her hair, went everywhere barefoot, and smoked a bent pipe. Sometimes with a fill of tobacco. Sometimes marijuana. She drove a beat-up, psychedelic Kombi with a string of shells hanging from the rearview mirror. It had one of those old tape players; you know, the ones that chew up all your Doors and Moody Blues tapes. Well they chewed up Mum's. She would spend hours — days! — with a pencil, trying to rewind them.

"That clapped out old heap of nuts and bolts and diesel-spewing fumes only stayed on the road because Mum's long list of loser boyfriends successively worked on it in return for board and lodging and Mum's other 'favours'. Not really sure what those were because she was an awful cook! Haha. I guess in her mind, keeping us in transport made up for the fact her boyfriends usually had nothing else to offer. Anyway, she named all of us kids after cars, as if we'd somehow channel them into being for her! Yeah, true story! My sisters are Jaguar and Porsche. Porsche pronounced with an 'ay' at the end, the Italian way. And my brother's Rover. Rove for short. Our baby sister 'Mini'. She died of whooping cough."

"Sorry to hear you lost a sibling," Frank says. "I don't have any. Or any other family either."

"And I have too many," Mercedes answers. Then she fixes Frank with her disarming squinty gaze. "Funny how names often tell heaps about a person, don't you think?"

Frank is stumped and looks at her questioningly.

Mercedes laughs. "If I'm going to get through this, I'm gonna need a refill." She flicks her bangs off her face again. Frank nods at Hendry and Hendry starts mixing her another vodka sour while she continues: "In my brother's case, Mum couldn't have been more accurate with her selection of name." She pauses and takes another large swig of her second drink, then stands up and starts rummaging through her holdall, pulling a battered tambourine from its depths. "Hey, guys, do you know that old ballad? 'The Gypsy Rover'?"

Frank and Hendry shake their heads. No.

Mercedes smiles. "I always think of it as my brother's 'signature tune'," she says, as she does the air quote thing again and moves a few steps away from the bar. She runs her hands down the front of her curvy jean-clad thighs and flicks her hair away from her forehead. The other punters in the bar turn to watch. New blood is a more compelling subject than commiserating endlessly about the goddamn drought, the price of fertiliser, and how successive governments neglect the farming community.

Mercedes begins to sing in a husky lilting voice, while tapping the tambourine against her thigh:

The gypsy rover came over the hill
Down through the valley so shady
He whistled and he sang till the green woods rang
And he won the heart of a lady
Ah-dee-do-ah-de-do-dah-day
Ah-dee-do-ah-dee-day-ee
He whistled and he sang till the green woods rang
And he won the heart of a lady

When she finishes, she takes a bow and returns to her bar stool. The small audience claps, and there are a couple of wolf whistles, *'yeah right'*s, and *'go girl'*s.

Mercedes turns back to Frank: "My brother, Rove, is a scoundrel and a serial womaniser who roves all over the country breaking women's hearts. But who's to blame him? It's not as if he ever had a decent 'male role model' when we were growing up. We don't know who our father is, or even whether he's the same person. 'Go figure.'"

"I blame the DPB," grunts Frank. "If single mums didn't get extra payments for each kid, they wouldn't be so loose with their... well you know what I mean... That was lovely," he pivots. "Are you a professional?"

"I wish," she replies. "I've done a lot of singing, though. A lot of 'singing for my supper'." She flashes those cool, crossed eyes at him.

Frank ventures another question. "So, getting back to your name... Mercedes. Aside from the car, being German and all, the name is actually Spanish, isn't it? Any Spanish in the family line?"

"Maybe. I wouldn't be surprised. Mum wasn't exactly committed to maintaining the purity of our 'Anglo-Saxon bloodline'. She used to say that, down there in Golden Bay, you could travel the entire world without ever leaving the beach front. *Especially* if you were the owner of a Kombi camper van."

Mercedes stays on in Maunga. It isn't as if she has anywhere else to go. Frank offers her his bedroom and sleeps on the 'Graceland' couch, sweating profusely on the white plastic upholstery, empty Pavarotti

CD covers pricking into his back from their hiding places between the white vinyl cushions. He never asks Mercedes about the bloke in the Holden and she ventures no explanation, but he offers her his first aid kit so she can sort out her cuts and grazes and bruises. And when she asks him about the lounge furniture and matching coffee table he tells her that the salesman at Harvey Norman said it was an exact replica of the suite Elvis and Priscilla had in their living room at Graceland. Mercedes was super impressed.

When Frank wakes on Saturday morning he hardly recognises the flat. Mercedes has unpacked her holdall, and her transistor radio is on the kitchen bench broadcasting Big River, the local radio station. Quite ironic, really — Northland was experiencing the worst drought in living memory and the river at the back of Frank's property was barely producing a trickle. The sizzle of bacon frying in the pan and the sound of coffee bubbling in the percolator spike Frank's appetite. A good feed will sort him out after all the alcohol he consumed last night. Mercedes has opened all the windows, and the sweet-sour smell of silage curing in the neighbouring paddocks drifts through the flat. It occurs to Frank how much he loves the scent. He wonders why he's never noticed it before.

"How do you like your eggs, Frank?" Mercedes asks him. "Over easy?"

He nods. Whatever way they come will be perfect as far as he's concerned. As perfect as Mercedes is in every way.

She's laid a green and white checked cloth over the grimy kitchen table and filled a jam jar with wildflowers. As he eats his big fried breakfast, she reminisces about her childhood in Golden Bay. One of her mother's loser boyfriends had a guitar and she'd picked up a few chords and riffs, and some old fella down there that she'd been pretty fond of had given her lessons on the piano. She'd gapped it in her mid-teens, hitching to Picton and catching the ferry to Wellington, where she stayed at the Y and busked on Cuba Street. She's been on the road ever since, singing in bars and restaurants, performing at country and western jamborees, winning prizes at folk festivals, hoping someone somewhere — a promoter or producer — will warm up to her, give her a break. Offer her a recording contract. Maybe.

At around ten that morning, the phone starts ringing off the hook. Every man and his dog need some or other part or piece of scrap today. Frank strolls the yard with his customers, fulfilling their requirements. Mercedes hangs in the office, rocking babies to sleep in her arms and chatting to the womenfolk who've accompanied their partners today, having heard about the newcomer and the dramatic way she'd arrived in Maunga. Mercedes shares recipes, remedies, and ideas on remodelling, and the local women think she's The Oracle.

Toothless and floral faced, Gunna hops from car wreck to car wreck. "You getting any, man?" he asks Frank, wiggling his forefinger in the air.

Balding Ten Speed chimes in. "Yeah, she's one hot babe, mate," he says, waving a Toyota Ute silencer in front of him. "Must be my lucky day. I've been looking for one of these for ages."

Bert pipes up. "You've landed with your bum in the butter this time, eh?"

Frank shrugs. He and Mercedes had been pretty plastered by the time they'd got back to his flat last night. He could have perhaps gone there but wasn't convinced she was keen enough. Despite his emotional loneliness and need for human connection, Frank prides himself on being a gentleman. He would never take advantage of an intoxicated woman.

Weeks pass and soon the morning mists of early autumn come down upon Maungaturoto and the land begins to cool once more. The world, both human and animal, comes alive again, as temperatures drop to more comfortable levels. And the rains come at last — drenching torrents that saturate the parched earth, filling water tanks and dams and old baths which serve as cattle troughs in paddocks; torrential downpours drumming on tin roofs and gushing down streets, causing people to run from their cars for cover with newspapers clutched over their heads and squelch through mud to get to their front doors. Day after day, as winter sets in, it rains, the water gushing downhill, following the contours of the land, flowing into the dried-up creeks and streams, spilling into the waterways that feed the big rivers of Northland, washing away the sweat, dust, grease and grime of all

Frank's summers, bringing the promise of newness.

Maungaturoto Car Wreckers & Scrap Metals hasn't been this busy in years, and Frank's weeks pass in a blur of business as he attends to local and regional walk-ins, and fulfils telephone orders that he ships out by courier to other parts of the country. The recession is a blessing in disguise; people are repairing instead of replacing their cars and tractors. Because Frank has stockpiled for years, he is easily able to service his newly thrifty customers.

Mercedes earns well too. Hendry organises a PA system for the pub and she sings and plays the old honky-tonk there on Friday and Saturday nights. She's that popular, she draws large crowds, and often the car park out front is chokka. Hendry can afford to employ a decent chef at last and increase the selection of meals on offer. During the week, Mercedes reads tarot cards in a small room behind the office which she's decorated like an Aladdin's Cave with sarongs, Buddha effigies, incense, and whatnot. Everyone who crosses her path feels lighter and happier; everything she does shines with the effort she puts into it. And to Frank it seems as if she carries all the magic of the world within herself and in her battered holdall — her tinkling laugh, her vivaciousness, her resourcefulness. Not to mention her mesmerizing, squinty, cobalt eyes.

Deep into winter Frank senses a shift in Mercedes' attitude towards him, in the way she speaks to him and looks at him, in the way she takes care of him and expresses concern about him. He isn't a bad looking man, with a full head of thick, wiry, brown hair and a good physique. Even if his lamb chop sideburns are rather old fashioned and his habitual dress choice of khaki shirt and short shorts give his age away somewhat, the local womenfolk consider him a good catch, and people have often wondered why he's still single. Even Frank doesn't understand why. Probably because he's never met the right person. Living in the wopwops did narrow the possibilities somewhat.

One Sunday when the weather was fair, Mercedes prepared a picnic and she and Frank walked across the paddocks to the stream at the back of the property. She loved Frank up on the picnic rug among the remains of their meal, with the scent of crushed spearmint in her golden hair and the taste of red wine on her lips, beneath the weeping willows, with the river flowing vigorously past them, red and yellow and gold with fallen leaves.

"Call me Mercy," she whispered to Frank as he bent over her, lost in her alluring, liquid cornflower-coloured eyes. "Call me Mercy."

Time passed, and soon it was February again: suicide month. A day dawned when Mercedes' magic had run out. She woke up tetchy; her sparkle had fizzled out. Everything was wrong. Nothing was good enough. When Frank slipped upstairs at lunchtime, the flat looked as if she'd never been there; the checked tablecloth had disappeared, the transistor radio was silent, the couch was a mess of Pavarotti CD covers. Mercedes was quiet, unlike her usual ebullient self. Frank chucked a sandwich together and ate it without speaking, not wanting to precipitate anything. A parping car outside called him away.

When he returned to the office a while later, Mercedes was sitting there, her holdall packed and standing by the door.

"Are you leaving?" Frank said. He placed his hands on her shoulders, but she jerked away.

"You didn't think I was gonna stay forever, did you?"

"I didn't think about it much, Mercy."

"Well, maybe you should have."

"But you just turned up here, out of the blue, and when you stayed on, I ... I thought..."

"Oh, you stupid man."

Frank winced, and flustered now, he reached compulsively for the greasy rag beneath the counter. Mercedes watched him with contempt as he began to raise it to his face.

"Mercy, I don't understand what's happening," he said.

"Frank, you've been more than kind, but this isn't the life I want."

"I thought you were happy ... I thought *we* were happy."

"You really didn't believe I'd want to spend the rest of my life in this shithole with you, Frank? Surely?"

Her words stopped him mid-action and he froze to the spot. A couple of blowflies began to buzz against the windows, the sound distracting him. The rag fell from his hands as he moved out of long habit to grab the fly swatter and bash them to death. But something made him hesitate, and he replaced the swatter on its nail and backtracked to the nearest window. His fingers shook as he fumbled with the latch, but suddenly, he released the catch and the window gasped open, setting the flies free.

Frank leaned on the sill, taking in deep gulps of air. In the silence behind him he heard Mercedes mutter again, "You stupid, stupid man." Then, the striking of a match as she lit another cigarette, and the sound of liquid connecting with ice as she sloshed a generous dollop of vodka into her glass.

"I... I don't think I'll be able to go on without you, Mercy." He wrung his hands, strains of opera playing through his mind, odd snatches of lyrics and music. "I can't go back to how it was before you came."

She glanced up at him and her squinty, watery eyes seemed to Frank to be the very essence of her, of her rare beauty. He had never wanted her as much as he did now, in the moments he was losing her.

"You're pathetic, Frank. You should have got out of this dump years ago, before you turned into a fossil like that heap of rusting junk in your yard." She gulped her drink and flicked her ash dramatically on the floor. "You should never have bought a white lounge suite either, you stupid idiot! What were you thinking? It's impossible to clean, for God's sakes! And don't call me Mercy!"

"You said you liked retro stuff; that the Graceland suite was... cool."

"I lied."

"Why did you stay, then? Why did you get close to me?"

"Why do you think? I was marking time. It's not as if I had any other options, did I?"

"But why did you do all of this? For what?" He looked around at the tidy office, the freshly swept floor she was now defacing with ash, the vase full of dahlias she'd grown that summer in flower beds along the roadside.

"Don't you know anything about women, Frank?"

Frank wasn't sure what she was getting at and kept quiet.

"Do you want me to spell it out? State the obvious?" She swigged her drink and flicked her ash on the floor again. "I was using you."

A thought suddenly occurred to Frank. She was hurting him to make things easier for herself. She didn't mean what she was saying. She couldn't possibly, after what they'd come to mean to each other.

"I'm shifting to Auckland, Frank. Leaving on the four o'clock bus. No more living in dumps, no more singing for my supper, no more road running. It's time for me to grow up, get a proper job. I've been kidding myself I'll ever make it as a singer..." Frank noticed Mercedes didn't use air quotes anymore.

A car tooted outside. Mercedes killed her cigarette in the ashtray and stood up. She ran her hands down the front of her thighs, composing herself. "That'll be my taxi," she said.

Frank noticed she was wearing the same strappy red high-heeled sandals and tight jeans she'd arrived in, almost exactly a year ago. He staggered past her to the door and out into the yard — he needed to see the taxi for himself, to understand that what was happening was real. Perhaps she would give him a few minutes to take it all in and get himself together before they said goodbye. He so wanted to find a way to make it easier for both of them, a way he could set this bird free so she would fly back to him one day soon.

But she walked right past him without a second glance, pulling her wheeled holdall behind her. She threw her bag onto the back seat of the taxi, then hopped in and fastened her seat belt. Her door slammed shut and Frank watched, stunned, as the 'Rolla spun out of the driveway spraying metal in every direction. Mercedes didn't even look back.

Piles of car wrecks loomed up in front of Frank, dwarfing him. He stumbled across the yard and fell against the bonnet of an old Hillman Classic, hanging his head in despair. It seemed to him as if the living world had ended, as if softness, light and colour had drained away. All that remained was cold hard steel. He'd had too much of nothing for far too long, in the land where rust never sleeps. He needed to do something different, get amongst the living, make big changes, reinvent his life. Reinvent himself.

In the black void of his pain-numbed mind a stray thought began to form. He remembered seeing an advert in the Northland Gazette for a pub and motel outfit on the east coast that had come up for lease. He'd picked up a few tips about the hospitality business from Hendry over the years and had a clean record so would be eligible for a bar manager's licence. Maybe, if he could talk her into it, Mercedes would come back, provide the entertainment, add her sparkle to the place.

He decided to follow her taxi to the bus stop and talk to her, offer her an alternative. He would flash up the tow truck. Maybe there would be someone out there on the highway who needed a tow, whose car had broken down. He could kill two birds with one stone.

There was a rumbling overhead and Frank looked up. A thunderstorm was brewing and great dark clouds were gathering over Maungaturoto. The sky was cobalt like her eyes, with only a single streak of white remaining, squinting and glinting through a small crack in the massing clouds.

He strode across the yard to the roadside to fetch in his sign. When he got there, he changed his mind and went back to the shed, returning with a tin of red paint and a brush. He painted 'FOR SALE' in large red letters across the sign and moved it into a more prominent position on Highway 12 so that it could more easily be seen by passersby.

When he'd finished, he locked up and jumped into his tow truck, pulling up a few minutes later in front of the Maungaturoto Tavern where he parked in his usual spot.

"A man could set his watch by you, mate!" Hendry said when Frank walked into the pub.

"But I'm early today," Frank said. "It's only four o'clock."

"No matter," Hendry replied. "By the look of you, the earth has tilted on its axis, so, beer o'clock it is, formally and officially." He rang the old ship's bell, then turned to Frank. "Two for the price of one, as per usual?"

"Aren't you going to say, 'Happy Hour, Happy People'?" Frank asked.

"Now that wouldn't be appropriate, would it? Not today, mate," Hendry replied.

Ka Kite, Bro

A battered Harley Davidson burns full throttle down a quiet suburban street in the small Northland service town of Wellsford, then chops down a few gears, slowing as it passes the black-walled compound of the Head Hunters' gang pad. The pillion passenger raises her arm high in the air, flipping the sign of the bird. Then the rider drops the bike onto its side, anticipating a sharp curve in the road ahead. His passenger leans with him into the camber, her arms folded around his middle. As the bike exits the corner, the rider wraps the power on, urging the hog up a steep hill on the outskirts of the town. Switchbacks and hairpin bends slow its progress as it sashays to the left and the right, making its way to the top of the hill, where it skids and slides to a standstill on a sandy verge underneath a cell phone tower.

The passenger jumps free, pulls off her helmet, and allows her long chestnut hair to cascade down her back. "Yeeha!" she shouts. The leather-clad rider kicks the bike stand down, kills the ignition, and flashes a wide, wicked smile her way. They high-five, then turn together to look over the town spread out across the valley beneath them in the darkening winter evening.

Smoke drifts lazily from chimneys and the smell of fast-food hangs in the air. Across town, along the western skyline, the neon-lit silhouette of El Tapora Bar & Grill cuts the shapes of cacti and sombreros into the sunset, like a tavern in a Speights' advert. In the middle distance, Rodney Road pulses and throbs with the red and yellow lights of heavy long-weekend traffic. But deep in the hollow of the valley, where the railway tracks and shunting yards slash through the lower part of town near the gang pad, all is dark and still. In the gathering dusk, the run-down station buildings and derelict sheds seem to lean against each other like weary watchmen, dust blowing in eddies around their footings, the evening breeze fanning the flames of a small fire.

The bikers stand still, watching, waiting, hearts beating like thunder, breath streaming from their mouths smoke-like into the cold, thin athmosphere. A few moments later, their faces animate as the railway yards light up like a fairground, followed by an explosion which shoots debris high into the air, as a deafening boom ricochets across the valley. The teens watch as the fire spreads rapidly, tearing through the derelict buildings alongside the tracks. Almost immediately sirens start sounding across the valley, four long eerie wails, low to high pitched, calling the emergency services to action.

The girl turns to embrace her companion. "You're so hot, bro. This is the best job we've ever pulled." The youth clings to the girl, allowing her long hair to fall around his shoulders like a cloak of feathers, warm and comforting. Her hair crackles with static as his palm smooths it down her back.

She pushes him away. "We better make tracks, eh."

"I thought you said we'd be able to stay in Wellsford for a while. With Aunty Vai?"

"Yeah, but that was before we heard Dad was back, right? Why we're doing this, remember?"

"I know, Kitty, but I'm tired of running. And I can't handle it when we have to split up."

"Me too. This will be the last time, though. I promise."

The lad shrugs his shoulders. "If you say so."

"I'll cut through the stock yards to Aunty's on foot, get her to drive me up north. You take the bike and head south to the cuzzie-bros in Huntly. Lay low for a few days. I'll message you when the heat dies down."

"There'll be cops everywhere, Kitty! It's Queen's fucking Birthday weekend!"

"Stick to the back roads, Tae. You'll be sweet. Just keep it together, eh?"

"Yeah, okay. What you said. Shit, you know I'll do anything for you."

"Good one." She slaps the boy rider on his back and ruffles his hair. "We'll be together again soon, yeah?" She turns to walk away, raising her arm to wave goodbye. "Ka kite, bro," she says.

It's late, and Kitty and Tae have been sent to bed. They don't usually have a strict bedtime, even though they're only seven years old, but their mother has visitors tonight. They're lying side by side on the divan they share in the back room of the house, listening to the rhythm of the rain drumming on the tin roof. Kitty feels drowsy, but Mum has told her she'll call her and if she doesn't come straight away, she'll get what's coming to her. Kitty has a plan, though, and she's prayed and prayed her plan will work. Aunty Vai told her that if you pray long and hard enough for something, the Lord steps in, because you've proven your faith. And even if things don't work out exactly as you might want them to, things always *change*...

Tae is also thinking about Aunty Vai, and how, when they'd been staying at hers at Christmas, she'd had lamb chops and saussies and sweet corn on the barbie, potato salad with chopped boiled eggs dripping with mayonnaise, and Pam's fizzies in all colours of the rainbow. Later, she brought out this huge trifle in a big bowl, with sponge cake and boysenberry jelly, thick yellow custard, and a whipped cream topping covered in hundreds-and-thousands. He ate so much he felt like a beach ball and all he could do afterwards was roll around the place for a few hours. That night he felt crook as, and spewed his guts out, and spent a long time on the dunny with the hot squits. But it had been worth it.

It's not like that here at Mum's. They never get a good feed. Since Mum got back custody of them, it's been boil-ups, fish heads and tap water. Mum's a bad woman. Aunty Vai had told them the house fire that happened when they were babies was her fault. "Your Mum was drunk and stoned and passed out with a lit cigarette between her fingers. Nek minute the couch was on fire and she ran outside and got the hose and started spraying water through the ranch slider. But the blaze spread so bloody fast, you kiddies could have burned to death in your cot in the back bedroom. Lucky a neighbour called 111 and the fire truck showed up real quick," Aunty Vai had said.

Tae's eyes are closing now and when Kitty sees him drifting off, she digs him in the ribs. Then she grabs him by the shoulders and shakes him awake. She keeps talking about the matches, making him tell her over and over again where she's hidden them in a hole in the side of the mattress, and what he's supposed to do with them when Mum calls her.

She pulls a worn photograph out from underneath the pillow. He knows it well. A smiling young couple dressed in fancy gear are posing in front of a house truck with a circus poster pasted on its side. "Check this out, bro!" Kitty tears the photo in half down the middle, carefully separating the two subjects. She hands Tae the piece with the smiling, red-haired man. "Put that in your pocket, and look after it." The other half depicts a petite dark woman in a sparkly leotard with a feathered headdress. Kitty tears it into small pieces and strews them across the wooden floor. "That'll make good kindling, like the kapok mattress will."

Suddenly the back-lit shape of their mother fills the doorway, her shadow falling across the floor. She leans against the door frame, bathrobed and beckoning, a lit cigarette hanging from her mouth. One side of her face and neck is disfigured by burn scars. "What's going on here?" she says, in a husky voice. "I thought I told you kids to go to bed?"

"Can't sleep, Mum," says Tae. "My puku is growling."

"You're always hungry, boy, like you got worms. Not to worry, Uncle Ray's got a big bag of lollies for you kids. If you do what he says, mind, girl. He wants you to come and see him now."

Tae sits up. "Yippee!"

"Not you, boy. *Kaitirea.* If you're a good boy and go to sleep, you can have your treats in the morning."

"Aw, Mum!"

"Do as you're told, or else! Right bloody girl's blouse, you are, just like your father."

Kitty glances nervously between her mother and her brother. "I'll sort him out, Mum, no worries." She encourages Tae to lie down and pulls the covers over him.

"Hurry up, girl. Ray's given me a bag of dak to sell. If you're both good kids we can get some pukka kai from the Four Square and hit up the op shop for blankets and a heater." As their mother's jaw moves up and down, the curved lines of the moko on her chin flicker behind the smoke of her cigarette. She turns away and the children hear her footsteps echoing up the hall.

Kitty hugs Tae to her chest and he leans in, comforted, his mind drifting, his body slackening, relishing the feeling of her hair and how it folds around him soft and feathery, full of static electricity. But when Kitty feels him cleaving to her, she pushes him away and shakes him so hard it feels like all the bones in his hollow little body are rattling.

"Listen up, bro, get a grip," she hisses in his ear. She holds his face in her hands now, forcing him to make eye contact. "Start counting now, yeah? Count to a hundred, like I taught you. Slowly. One. Breathe. Two. Breathe. Right? When you reach a hundred, just do it! No mucking around! And when you get the fire going, get yourself out of here quick smart, eh? But don't forget to grab the bag of clothes I packed before you jump out the window! If you get this right, you'll be shoving those lollies down your throat long before morning, I promise you!"

"But, Kitty, what about Mum? What if..."

Kitty cuts him off: "Don't worry, bro, nothing bad's gonna happen.

The fire truck will get here in time, like it did when we were babies. Uncle Ray is getting super creepy, making me sit on his lap and running his hands up and down my legs. Last time he even tried to kiss me. As for Mum, she needs a bloody wakeup call! It's illegal to sell cannabis, I heard them say so on the TV!"

"What's *illegal* mean?" whispers Tae, probing Kitty's face for an explanation with big eyes.

"It means you can get into trouble with the po-po, you could end up in jail! We've already lost Dad. Soon we'll be two parents short of a happy family. We've got to get out of here and get back to Aunty Vai's."

"Okay, Kitty, I'll do what you said."

"Good boy. I'll meet you over by the water tank soon as. Like we planned. Ka kite, bro," she says as she gets up to leave the room.

Early Tuesday morning after Queen's Birthday weekend, an unmarked police car slows to a halt outside Wellsford Police Station. Detective Constable Darren Wood steps from the vehicle dodging the large puddles caused by recent heavy rain. He activates the electronic car alarm, makes sure his police radio earpiece is in place, then reaches up to check his handgun is still securely positioned in its holster under his left armpit. He'd booked out a weapon that morning having been told there was a suspected gang connection to the case he'd been sent up from Auckland to investigate.

What a fucking dump he thinks, as he walks towards the single-story prefab building that passes for a cop shop in Wellsford, stepping gingerly over the uneven footpath and noting the pathetic looking flowerbed along the front wall, a mess of knee-high grass and drowned weeds. Soon he is seated at a desk in an interview room inside with a view over the filthy back yard of the take-away outlet next door, a large mug of black coffee steaming in his hands, eyeballing the local cops who huddle around the desk in a deferential circle.

"Okay, boys, what you got?"

Matt, the Officer-in-Charge, clears his throat. "Our main suspects are Kaitirea and Taero Rawhiti, a.k.a. Kitty and Tae McQueen. They're siblings, twins actually, unidentical, a boy and a girl, aged sixteen."

"Right. Have you got a description of them?"

"She's a looker," says Tom, the rookie cop, "all legs and arse. I'd give it to her anytime." He wiggles his index finger in the air.

"Shuddup, Tom! This is serious stuff." Matt glares at the new boot, then turns back to Detective Wood.

"We evicted them from the Wellsford Tavern recently so got a good look at them then. The girl's tall, about 5'10", a light skinned Māori with very long, reddish-brown hair, and blue-as-blue eyes, like the Highland sky."

Detective Wood screws up his face.

"Um... I'm of Scottish descent, sir. It's a common expression there."

"Okay, okay. What about the male suspect?"

"Wiry dark hair usually pulled back in a short ponytail or man-bun. Darker skin than the girl, and smaller — as short and stocky as she is tall and lean. Dumber too. She's the talker. He doesn't say much. A distinguishing feature is the huge tattoo which covers his entire back. A flaming torch, apparently, according to a couple of the local yokels he showed it off to."

"Right," says Detective Wood, "So, what do we have on them?"

"As detailed on the rap sheet, they've been suspects in various petty arson incidents up in the far north, but because they're juveniles and their targets have always been low-key, they've pretty much gotten away with their pyromaniacal spree up till now."

"Mmm. So, they have a history of youth offending. Frankly, I'm not surprised. There's always a backstory of petty crime when kids get involved in big shit like this. Anything in particular which throws light on their latest misdemeanour?"

"Well," says Matt, "the house they were living in, in Kaitaia, when they were seven years old, burned down. At the time, fire investigators put the blaze down to old wiring, rat infestation, that sort of thing. It was a rundown old shack out in the wopwops, apparently."

"Right. Any casualties?"

"Their mother and an uncle died in the blaze, but the twins escaped or were rescued. No one really knows. They've been indigent ever since, passed around the whānau. Apparently, a large quantity of cannabis was found in the freezer after the fire. It was believed at the time the mother had gang connections and was operating a tinny house."

"Beats working as a cleaner or waiting tables for bottom dollar, doesn't it? The benefit is pathetic; people can't live off of it. The reason why people in this predicament are always having to do something dodgy to make ends meet. What about the father? Let me guess — he's a lowlife who shot through, abandoning the family when the going got tough."

"From what we've been able to piece together he took off when the twins were babies or maybe even before they were born. We're still waiting for CYFS to check their records. The fact it's been a holiday weekend hasn't helped."

"We'll probably find CYFS have got a file an inch thick on these delinquents. Right now, though, we need to focus on tracking them down and bringing them in for questioning. So, this is the biggest job they've pulled to date?"

"Yeah. As far as we know."

"But what makes you think *they* did it? Why have you identified *them* as our main suspects? I still haven't heard any actual evidence that will lead to a prosecution."

"They always leave a calling card — they tag a wall or building near the arson site with the word 'MAHUIKA' in red paint. This time they tagged the wall of the local gang pad. Their head honcho has already been up here to lay a complaint, sounding off about wayward youth and indiscriminate vandalism. Bit rich if you ask me."

"Okay, okay. We all know these bloody gangs are a law unto themselves. Don't get me started. Successive governments continue to ignore the problem while we're expected to keep the streets safe and sort out the damage they do."

"Too right." Matt nods in agreement.

"'MAHUIKA', you say? What does it mean? Anybody bothered to find out?"

There's a protracted silence as the local cops search each other's faces for the required information. The detective waits but when nothing is forthcoming, he slams his fist down on the desk, spilling coffee everywhere.

"What the frigging hell? Don't you know this is what goes down in a report as 'gross incompetence'? For fuck's sakes, get me the local iwi on the phone right now!"

The cleaner who has been mopping the corridor outside the interview room pokes her head through the door. "Excuse me, Matt, I might be able to help you with that. I think it means 'Goddess of Fire'." She waddles into the interrogation room, a broad smile on her ruddy face.

"Oh yeah? Was wondering where you were, Vai. I need you to get Detective Wood here another cup of coffee. And bring a cloth. There's been a bit of an accident."

The detective cuts in, standing up. "Hello and pleased to meet you. Vai, is it? I've come up to investigate the explosion at the railway station on Sunday night. Seems you might be able to throw light on this... Māori terminology. Would save us a lot of trouble."

"Yes, Vai, you've seen the tagging, eh?" chimed in Matt.

"Yup. Sarita has been learning about Māori mythology at school and told me Mahuika means, 'Goddess of Fire'. Or 'Queen of Fire'. She's surprised I didn't know. Says we should get up to speed with our own culture and history — that it's been supressed by the pākehā for far too long."

"That's a great help, Vai, thanks," says Matt. "Could you get that refill for the detective now please?"

Detective Wood sits down again and leans back in his chair, stretching his arms out in front of himself and cracking his knuckles.

"Ouch", says Tom, wincing. Matt glares at him again. Why had *he* of all people had the misfortune of ending up with this imbecile trainee cop when Tom could have been posted anywhere from Cape Reinga to Bluff?

Wood sighs. "Anything else I should know?" he asks.

Matt shrugs. "The kids apparently survived a house fire when they were toddlers. There is a suggestion their father was with the crew that rescued them on that occasion. We won't know the full story until we get the CYFS' file, but it seems their mother lost custody of them for a while after that. There's also a rumour circulating that the parents were in the circus back in the day, doing a fire breathing act and stunts with burning poi. Apparently Mum got into trouble and there was a nasty accident."

"Right, now we're getting somewhere; a picture is starting to emerge. But what's these kids' motivation? Why the fascination with arson? Unresolved childhood trauma? Or old-fashioned teenage delinquency? Attention seeking, because they've been abused and neglected? All of the above? And why have they now resorted to blowing up government property?

Once again, an uneasy silence fills the room. Tom puts his foot in it, voicing what they're all thinking: "Um... we thought that's what you came up from Auckland to find out, sir."

Detective Wood feels his patience running out. These fucking country bumpkin cops are a city detective's worst nightmare. He could be at home right now, trying to patch up things with his wife, if it wasn't for this stupid callout. She's mentioned the D-word and threatened to take him to the cleaners, all because of one little indiscretion. The thought of losing his kids brings on a visceral response and he lives with a constant knot in his stomach, probably the beginnings of an ulcer. Nine times out of ten the mother gets custody of the kids, even if she's a no-hoper and a good-for-nothing slag. Not that Layla is anything like that. Bugger! It's because she's so bloody perfect and makes him feel inadequate that he'd had the frikking affair in the first place.

But this is not the time to demonstrate any personal weakness. He needs to focus on the job at hand, show leadership, put his personal problems on the back burner for now. Especially if he wants to get back to Auckland by the weekend. The All Blacks are playing a test against South Africa. The only time he ever has any fun is down at the local rugby club where he and his mates get together to watch the match on the big screen.

"Right," he says, "I guess it's time to call in a criminal psychologist. I'll get on to it." He stands up and navigates past the desk, lurching towards the middle of the huddle, pointing at Matt: "You! Put out an APB on these kids immediately; I want all units in the north trying to track them down. And make it high alert!"

"Yes, sir."

"As for the rest of you bungling idiots," he continues, his accusing finger sweeping now from side to side, "get out onto the streets and talk to anybody and everybody who might have had anything to do with these juveniles. I want to know who their connections are, where they were staying, and anything else you come up with. Oh, and book me a motel room. Looks like I'm gonna be here for a couple of days."

Kitty and Tae lie in their cot in a back bedroom, their tiny bodies curled around each other like koru. A candle burns on the dresser, its flickering light a welcome focus in the darkness. From time to time, they hear their mother cackling in the front room, the sound of strange voices and the clink of glasses. Thick smoke sucks through the open door curving around them where they lie, accompanied by the sweet smell of marijuana. They breathe it in knowing that soon they'll feel warm and hazy and will drift away into the oblivion of fantastical dream-like visions, able to forget for a while that this caged space with its damp mattress and thin coverlet has been their whole world for as long as they can remember.

Later, they awaken to the sound of hissing and spitting. A bright haze glows and flickers up and down the walls and an intense heat fills the room. They pull themselves up and cling to the side of their cot as flames lick towards them across the wooden floor. Tae turns to Kitty, terrified and screaming, and she holds him tightly, her hair shrouding him like a protective cloak, shielding him from the smoke and heat haze. The synthetic net curtains hanging across the window catch fire and dissolve in a puff of smoke. Kitty thinks she sees her mother's face in the remaining singed coils — her haunted eyes, her neck scarred and twisted like thick rope, the moko on her chin that flickers, flame-like, when she speaks.

"Mama, Mama!" she calls. But no-one is there.

Soon the noxious fumes overcome the toddlers and they fall back into their cot, coughing and struggling to breathe. The sound of breaking glass reaches them and then a hand is shaking them. They hear a man talking, saying they must hurry, that he will carry them out to safety.

"Come on, jump into my arms! Aye'll tae the wee one first," he says in a strange, lilting accent. Tae clings to Kitty and won't let go of her. She peels him off and pushes him into the man's arms.

"It's our Daddy, Tae! The fireman! Come to save us," she says. As the fireman disappears into the smoky haze she calls out after her brother, "Don't worry, he'll come back for me! Ka kite, bro."

"All rise." A hush falls over the courtroom as the judge enters and takes his place behind the bench. "Youth Court, North Auckland; Judge Andrew Becroft, Principal Youth Court Judge presiding. You may be seated."

A loud scraping of chairs. Kitty and Tae sit next to each other in the dock, behind the police prosecutor. Kitty is confident and relaxed, but Tae seems agitated and keeps fiddling, his forehead crinkled up in greasy folds. He knows that after their court appearance he and Kitty will be separated again and he can't hack it. To the twins' right, their social worker confers with a male colleague. On their left, the youth advocate rustles and rearranges his papers, and beyond him, the CYFS appointed youth justice coordinator yawns absentmindedly. The seats reserved for family members behind the dock remain vacant.

The Court Taker begins speaking again: "We are gathered here today to hear sentence in the case of Kaitirea and Taero Rawhiti who have been charged with committing an indictable offence; namely the wilful destruction of government property by arson at Wellsford Railway Station, on Sunday 4th June 2017. The court has heard the prosecution's case and considered all the evidence presented by it. The court has also heard the case for the defence and has given due consideration to the expert witness reports submitted by it to the court. Judge Becroft to now pass sentence."

The judge asks the young people to rise and addresses them: "Kaitirea and Taero, I wish to impress upon you the seriousness of the crime you have committed, and, notwithstanding the extenuating circumstances with which this court has been presented, to which it's given due consideration, and despite the fact that no one was injured in the explosion you wilfully planned and executed, I find you both guilty of the above-mentioned charges, and am recommending you be remanded under supervision, and held in residential custody, separately, under the legal guardianship of Child Youth and Family Services, until such time as you have been rehabilitated. You will both undergo counselling, and arrangements will be made for you to each complete a satisfactory period of community work, of no less than three hundred hours, in reparation for your crime."

Tae's face crumples like a baby's. He hangs his head, biting his bottom lip as his eyes cloud with tears. Kitty slings her arm around his shoulders.

"All rise," says the Court Taker. "Court is now adjourned."

There's a flurry of activity; papers are gathered together and briefcases snapped shut. Kitty and Tae hear their names being called and turn to see Aunty Vai smiling at them from the family bench. There's a man standing beside her; the man in their treasured photograph, only he's a lot older-looking now. A badge glints on the breast of his starched formal uniform — the eight-pointed star and silver ferns of the New Zealand Fire Service. He looks shyly at the twins, then begins to move hesitantly towards them.

Kitty grins and turns to her brother: "What did I say, Tae? I told you so, didn't I? I told you everything was gonna be sweet, eh?"

The twins embrace and Kitty's hair falls around Tae's shoulders, like a cloak of feathers, the korowai of their brave Māori ancestors. But Tae pulls away and stands straight and tall, a warrior who has returned home after a long, hard journey, a boy no more.

"Good one Sis. Ka kiti."

México/Retablo

Qué haría yo sin lo absurdo y lo fugaz?
What would I do without the absurd and the fleeting?
— Frida Kahlo

My dearest Frida,

I have exciting news — I'm coming to visit at last! Your imaginary friend was never just a figment of your deepest longings and existential loneliness; I really do exist, my dear! I'm coming to México to experience your view of the world — the sound of a hummingbird's wings aflutter, the scent of soft Iztaccíhuatl snow falling through silent air, the weight of handwoven cloth and its drag on the body, the brightness of a cruel sun in the naked eye, the tang of bittersweet *limón* syrup sipped through crushed ice.

We share so much: the horror of a loved one's betrayal, the gift of a kind father's blessing, the curse of a cold, hard, steel rail, the ability to survive in a world of darkness and light where goodness is fleeting and the fantastical is real. I long to feel, as you did, the brush of a monkey's plush pelt against my cheek and its small simian hand folded in mine. I long to see blood beading on the surface of my skin as a keen blade reveals the living pink flesh that lies hidden beneath. You will show me how to disguise my scars, how to transform the ugly bits and broken pieces of me into art. You will teach me the artifice of immortalising everything, good and bad, through the saturation of colour, the thrill of sensation, the obstinacy of endurance, the ashes of passion, in order to catharise my sorrows.

At the Floating Gardens of Xochimilco we shall drift in a barge without care, you reclining beside me in all your living glory. We'll talk without ceasing, your face reflecting the confidences I share, your sweet Spanish sibilances echoing in my ear, your mouth speaking words of wisdom that take wing and scatter into the sultry air. We'll drink El Jimador tequila till our mouths are raw from sucking on salt and lemon. And to soothe our blistering tongues, we'll pluck sprigs of purple mint from the riverbanks, and chew them until our lips are bruised livid.

Back at La Casa Azul, we shall link arms and walk side by side in the courtyard, turning in unison together at the end of the path like synchronised swimmers. When we stop to admire your huge cacti collection, we'll speak of how they throw spiky, spiny shadows against the adobe walls. And when we pause under the orange tree, we'll say how we both adore the heady scent of orange blossom as it drifts through the air, intoxicating our senses.

And when our skin is shining with perspiration and sweat prickles through the coarse fabric that binds our bodies, when the matted hair in our armpits is damp and salty like sea sponges and, between our thighs, bare skin chafes against bare skin, we shall retreat indoors to the cool dark of your chamber. There, we'll remove our crowns of camellia flowers and disrobe, dropping our bright cotton skirts and beribboned *huipils* to the floor. Will top and tail on your canopied bed, me in my discount store underwear, you in your painted plaster corset. We'll smoke Te Amo cigarillos and blow rings, guessing the significance of their portents. We'll tickle each other with paintbrushes and tattoo our bodies with crayons; cryptic messages understood only by us. You will arch your brows and tilt your head and make eye contact and point to the pillow which cradles your head at night with its embroidered inscription that reads, 'do not forget me my love', and I will nod in acquiescence. When I come to rest in your loving arms and my lids slide closed to sleep and dream, you'll tattoo a pair of charcoal eyes on my lids like Xolotl's, the Aztec god who wept so much, his eyes fell out of their sockets.

When dusk falls, and coolness flows into the valley, from the wall of mountains surrounding us, we'll rise and dress, donning heavy Tehuantepec-style gowns and carved bone earrings, and we'll hang chains of Mexican medallions from our necks which will tinkle and jingle with every move we make. We'll comb frangipani oil through our hair and pile it up on our crowns in coils, to decorate it with flowers and ribbons. We'll paint our nails blood-red and pat rouge on our lips and cheeks to match. We'll darken our brows with kohl, joining them together across our foreheads to swoop like fork-tailed swallows across our waking minds. Winking at me in your dressing table mirror, you'll spread your arms wide and say, "Feet? What need have we of feet when we have wings?"

Your gaze will remind me how you always make direct contact with the viewer, enabling them to see right inside your wild, uneasy heart.

We shall dine in the courtyard of La Casa Azul beneath your beloved magnolia tree, its pink blooms folded closed in the gathering dark like barren wombs. While we eat *quesadillas* with *ensalada de nopales*, mariachi players will sway and croon in the shadows, plucking and thrumming their *vihuelas*, drumming out the rhythms of their songs on their sound boxes — the stomping feet of all the dead marching into Hell.

When night falls around us like black velvet, soft and close, your servant will light torches on the balconies, to keep the wolves away till dawn. In those bright circles of light we'll allow the shadows of our former selves to live again as silhouettes in the fire-strike on the adobe walls. And when we have worn ourselves out with laughing and dancing, we collapse into our chairs to rest, we'll throw *rebozo* peasant shawls around our shoulders to stop the chill that comes down from Anáhuac after midnight, and drink rich, sweet *café-solo* in the navel of the moon.

On this Day of the Dead, you will teach me how to feel again, dear Frida, how to feel more than just pain.

Jet engines hum as I doze fitfully at 40,000 feet, hurtling through the stratosphere towards you at five hundred miles an hour, reducing the space between us in seeming slow motion. My journal falls closed on my lap and my pen drops to the floor, rolling away as the plane tilts, to be lost forever. The voice of the pilot wakes me: "Ladies and gentlemen, on our left, to the east and south, the Mountains of the Sleeping Lady. We are now beginning our descent into the Valley of México. Estimated time of arrival at México City: 11.45 AM. The weather is clear and warm: ground temperature 36 degrees, wind south-easterly 6-7 knots, humidity 76 percent, visibility poor."

The magical city of your birth and death stretches in every direction beneath us Frida, a vast expanse of slums stretching to the foothills, the cityscape rendered hazy through a pall of smog. As the plane descends, through the porthole giant, smoking, refuse dumps come into view, crawling with ragged people and bone-thin dogs, then rows and rows of identical condos — cheap government housing projects crisscrossed by narrow streets of asphalt, no green of grass or tree in sight — giving way gradually to industrial and urban sprawl: chimney stacks, vast used car graveyards, excavation craters plumbing the depths of the earth populated by towering construction cranes, a matrix of tangled streets choked with emission-exuding traffic crawling to and from the heart of the city, where steel and glass towers pierce the sky. You wouldn't recognize it, Frida.

As the plane's landing gear hits the tarmac there is a collective held breath in the cabin. Then, the chatter of passengers starts up again as we taxi down the runway.

I sit quietly, thinking about Davey, about how I need to let him know I've arrived safely.

Two years ago, the unthinkable had happened; something I am still unable to easily speak of. After the tragedy, shock and grief and anger pushed me onto a runaway train with a one-way ticket to the Land of Hopelessness. The only other passenger travelling that route made sure he got into my compartment and sat right next to me. His name was Grim Death-wish. Over the course of our hellish journey, we became exceptionally well acquainted.

My husband had been a cop. A detective at Auckland Central. The police service counsels close family about the dangers of the job, preparing you for the worst. But this was not a work-related accident so I probably didn't receive sufficient support at the time. Or maybe grief has its own timeline and counselling would have made no difference. Darren and I were having marital problems so I blamed him for the accident, even though an investigation found a drunk driver had crossed the centre line, forcing Darren off the road, causing him to hit the barrier. My children had been strapped into their seats in the back, no doubt singing songs and chanting rhymes as they usually did in the car.

The coroner told me to take solace: it would have been all over for them in a matter of seconds.

Yeah right. A matter of seconds which would ruin the rest of my life. All sense of purpose and meaning leached from my life when the three blameless faces of my precious children stopped being the first and last things I laid eyes on each day.

Soon, my grief and anger turned inwards. Believe me, it doesn't take much to hurt yourself.

First, you become a serious alcoholic. When you are suffering, deeply grieving, questioning everything, one drink leads to the next and the next until your feelings are so numbed down you are able at last to switch off. Second, you stop eating. It doesn't take much to stop eating because grief steals your appetite and what little need you have for sustenance is assuaged by the calories in the copious amounts of alcohol you're imbibing. Third, you cruise the city streets at night and hook up with unknown, dangerous men and play cat and mouse with them.

It doesn't take much to pick up a prospect because the bars and clubs are full of men who are like trained hunters. When they spot easy prey they move in like a coordinated task force, quickly and efficiently. You don't care what they do to you after you've passed out, and don't want to know what they did to you when you wake up later in a hospital bed. You scream at the doctors and nurses and police officers and tell them to fuck off and leave you alone and stop asking questions.

It doesn't take much, believe me. Because your pain is your only friend right now.

My father, desperate to help, booked me into rehab and paid for it. My family didn't realise these facilities for the fucked up only make you more desperate and depressed than you were in the first place. And when the grossly damaged people you're locked up with help you go out of your way to hurt yourself some more, you do. Maybe a lot more. Because they're not only fellow addicts, they're also enablers.

No one gets it, do they, Frida? That hurting yourself is easy. Living is the hard part.

Like you, I drank because I wanted to drown my sorrows. But my sorrows soon learned how to swim, just like you said yours did. And when they'd learned how to swim, they soon turned into sharks, intent on a feeding frenzy. The liquid oblivion in which I was trying to drown my sorrows was soon shot through with the blood that seeps and flows from raw, gaping wounds. We both know, dear Frida, injuries can only be sterilised and sewn up and patched over. Sometimes they heal. Sometimes they don't. The scars they leave, however, are permanent.

You cannot ever recover from what this life throws at you and what it takes away from you.

The doctors and therapists tried every known psychotropic drug on me until eventually they found one that calmed me, and for the first time in eighteen months, I stopped crying. They tried every known therapy on me too and gradually I started responding to the therapist, nodding in acknowledgement and acceptance when she fed me her platitudes.

In due course, they told me I was getting better. "Recovering." Recovering? Maybe in their estimation. I knew I'd just been dumbed down, numbed by Big Pharma, rendered 'functional'. Drugs had now taken the place of alcohol to assuage my grief.

The awful reality of the central tragedy of my life continued to cut across my being like a grossly infected wound for which there is no remedy, no cure. To say it would heal was a lie. To say you could get over it if you put your mind to it — that time heals all ills — was prevarication, was denial.

By this stage, I'd heard so many lies I didn't know what the truth was anymore. The only thing I knew for sure was, there was nothing more important to me than my woundedness. I wanted to hang on to it, cleave it to myself. Because it was mine, because it belonged to *me*. It was the big, bright badge of courage I kept polished to a high sheen and wore on my breast, as you did yours, Frida. It was the tattoo across my forehead that read, 'walking wounded'.

Like you, Frida, after your accident, I never wore dull clothing ever again. Underneath the aura of functionality, our wounds were able to suppurate away quietly and discreetly like boils under poultices, hidden beneath the cover of our bright, beautiful clothing and adornments.

This was when I began to paint flowers and birds, like you did, Frida, to keep them alive for ever. To stop them from dying. To celebrate all the colours in the world.

The day came when I told the doctors and therapists at rehab what they wanted to hear. That I was better. "Recovered." And I watched as blossoms flowered across their faces and they heaved great sighs of relief, believing they had 'fixed' me.

When they discharged me, Davey came to pick me up. We'd grown up together as neighbours and had been college crushes, a long time before. He'd always rued the day I'd married Darren Wood when he was on his OE, and after the funeral he reappeared on the scene, visiting me at rehab and bringing me paints and paper and charcoals and pastels, encouraging me to start drawing and painting again; to pick up the career I'd dropped because after I'd married and the babies were born in quick succession, I'd had to give it away.

"So, what now, Layla?" he asked as he drove me to my parents' home.

"I don't know. Get a job, I guess. Find a place of my own. Go through the motions…"

"Go to Mexico."

I looked at him askance. "Oh yeah? Why?"

"You'll find out why when you get there. And throw away that Paxil and Demerol and all those other meds you're on. You've got to learn to live again, Layla. Without them." He told me he'd come into an inheritance and would pay for the trip; thought it'd do me good. He knew how much I admired you, Frida; knew that studying you and your art was the one sure thing that had kept me going since the tragedy. And he loved me, wanted to see me *truly* better. Healed.

Soon after the plane hits the tarmac at Guadalajara Airport, we taxi pass the grandstands the authorities have erected alongside the runway for the poor to visit for entertainment. The welcoming party moves me: large groups of schoolchildren in bright matching uniforms, arms waving, hair blown back; officials shouting instructions through loudhailers; peddlers touting candy floss, balloons, canned drinks and bags of *churros*; tourists with cameras; random groups of rubberneckers and eyeballers. As the aircraft deploys reverse thrust and the sound of its engines rises to a crescendo, the spectators clamp their hands over their ears and their mouths open wide, hundreds of eyes following the progress of as the plane as it slows, executes a wide turn in front of the grandstands, and approaches the terminal.

I catch a taxi to Coyoacán, the district you lived in on the outskirts of Mexico City. The route is perhaps not unlike your daily journey to and from college a hundred years ago, when the tram you were travelling in crashed, impaling you on a steel handrail. The sound of screeching brakes and screaming horns would have been forever etched on your memory as they now echo in mine, the weeping lament for the babies you'd never give birth to as real for you then as the tears I now cry for the children who are lost to me.

From that moment on, for both of us, all was irretrievably broken, never to be recovered. Only patched over, plastered over, painted over, decorated over, suffered over, endured over. Transformed into something else. Transformed into art.

When I reach the Caza Azul it's as you left it, so unlike the nondescript, suburban villa I'd lived in on the other side of the world in West Auckland. I stand in your garden drinking it all in: the air is heavy with the scent of *Dama-de-Noche*, the window frames are parakeet green, the walls electric blue, the floors are polished to a high gloss, incarnadine. Massive yuccas and elephant ears form a botanical backdrop to your collection of ceramic sculptures and Mexican paper-mâché figures, and a medley of mosaic covers walls and floors where broken crockery and bric-a-brac has been repurposed into art. Bold and bright and beautiful and garish and uncompromising and real. The heavily propped stage of your lived life.

The yard of our regulation grey state house had consisted of an unmown, weed-infested lawn bordered by a scraggly macrocarpa hedge. A rusty Windy-Dry twirled ceaselessly in the salty southerlies, pegged full of children's and baby's clothing. In the corner of the section were the ashes of a bonfire, where in a temper once over how my life as a wife and a mother had cheated me of other options, I had set fire to all my art materials and books. I never returned to the house after the tragedy. I couldn't face the dirty dishes, the floor littered with toys, the domestic debris. You'd have taken these everyday things, dear Frida, these artefacts of a life lived, and utterly transformed them, into enduring art. I walked away into another life without a single vestige of the past. I wasn't as strong as you were. Or as talented.

That is why I've come, Frida. I need your help. You will teach me how to live again.

My loved ones were laid to rest in plain pine boxes, quite unlike the ornamented catafalque that carried you in state on the day of your public funeral — an Aztec queen in full regalia — along the wide avenues of México City, bordered by throngs of people dressed in memorial black who waved palm fronds and sang traditional Mexican songs for you. At your cremation, it is rumoured that you sat bolt upright, arms outstretched, and said, "*Adios amigos,*" your burning hair a glorious golden wreath around your head, a halo of light.

My children's bodies lie wrecked and decomposing beneath the volcanic soil on a bare hillside at Waikumete cemetery, like the shells and bones buried in a midden. On the day of their funeral, we sang hymns for them, but there had never been an opportunity to say goodbye.

Frida, your essence is airborne and endures through the ages, flying high like the bright birds you painted — the squawking parakeets and huge macaws of the forest — rainbow coloured, blindingly bright under the sun, creatures of Mexican myth and legend, of the super réal, of the ethereal. Rain falls on my babies' graves two hundred days a year, the sound of it a keening dirge for the premature dead and their obscure, wasted lives. But on the odd calm, still day when I visit, tiny piwakawaka flit and squeak around their mounds, bringing me messages of solace from beyond the grave.

So, my dearest Frida,
When morning comes, let us meet outside of time and space where all those who have passed this way before now reside. We'll crown our heads with wreaths of bougainvillea: vermillion flowers crunchy like crepe paper, leaves desiccated with age, thorns like daggers to pierce our brows. And in the sun-drenched courtyard of your blue, blue house, with your pet chihuahuas at our feet, we shall drink sweet matcha with Trotsky and his wife,

and talk of revolution.

Revolutions of men. Revolutions of the human spirit.

We will keep you company as you sit in front of your easel recording your life, and you will tell us, "I paint myself because I am the subject I know best... the only subject I can really know and understand at all." And you will teach me how to paint in the *retablo* style, so that I too, like you, can celebrate my miraculous recovery from disaster, my return, my limping life — the continuation of a sort of life, a life of sorts. We'll build wings out of blood and bone and flesh and sinew and the feathers of dead birds, to enable us to fly in our dreams to those we have lost who live, still, in our hearts. We'll decorate bombs with flowers and ribbons and hug them tightly to our breasts at night, the sound of their endless ticking a reminder to keep what we love close, you and I.

And when a bold idea crosses your face and animates your features, Frida, you'll leap up and spin around like a young girl — in spite of the effort, despite the pain — your embroidered skirt twirling as it flies through the air like a kaleidoscope turning through mirrors of coloured glass. You'll clap your hands together like castanets, and your wooden foot — belled and beribboned and wearing its bright red boot — will stamp the ground flamenco style, raising a cloud of dust into the air.

Then you'll raise your shining black eyes to the burning sky, spread your arms wide, and shout, "So live. LIVE! Because *La Santa Muerte* dances around our beds at night, and, believe me, she is a far better dancer than we lowly playthings of the gods could ever be..."

The Apple of My Eye

"Bobby has been on my mind all morning, Officer. He hasn't called in to the shop for a couple of days and I kept reminding myself to look out for him. I was thinking that if he didn't turn up today, I'd call in at his flat and check in on him after work. If only I'd gone round sooner! Oh dear, incoming hot flush! Be still my beating heart! Forgive me, Officer, this is just such a shock…"

"Look, sorry about having to visit you at work, Audrey. Can someone get you a glass of water? As I said, this isn't a formal interview. We're just gathering information about Bobby's background right now. No charges have yet been laid."

"Right. Well, as you know, Bobby's my sister Deirdre's son. He's handicapped; no doubt that is obvious. Sorry, I guess I should use the term 'differently abled' — that's more PC nowadays, isn't it? Anyway, it's all Deirdre's fault! Although she never acknowledged it, she didn't take proper care of herself when she was pregnant. Just between you and me, she was a bit of a party animal in those days. Believe you me, we all put two and two together when Bobby was born with special needs. When the doctors said he was brain-damaged it came as no surprise. I still get cross as two sticks thinking about it…"

"Fair enough, Audrey. It's good of you to provide this detailed information. We need to hear anything that might be relevant to the case."

"Well, when Deirdre realised how bad things were, she went teetotal; transformed herself into a model parent. Literally. She made sure from the get-go Bobby got all the specialist help he needed, I will give her that. I watched from the side-lines as he struggled through his early life, grimacing through difficult exercise routines and communication drills, painstakingly learning the most basic of life skills, each small, hard-won gain taking its toll on him, every laboured inch a mile in anyone else's shoes. He did so well, Officer, really. Believe you me, we were all amazed by his progress, doctors included. As a young adult, he is now able, with IHC and WINZ support, to live independently."

"Yes, so he said. He's in a flat up the road from New World, isn't he?"

"That's right. He loves having his own place. But he still spends a lot of time at mine. And that's ok with me. You see, I loved him from the start — his crooked little smile and twinkly cross-eyes wormed their way into my heart from day one. I decided early on I'd do my part, be a good Aunty to him. But he's more like a son to me, really. I've never been able to have children of my own."

"So, you and Bobby are close, then?"

"Yes, thick as thieves. Bobby's good-for-nothing father shot through early, dropping Deirdre like a hot pie, leaving her holding the baby. Bobby's birth name is actually 'Rover', after his dad. I have no idea why his mother thought it appropriate to name him after that awful toe rag, really!

"I digress. Being a single parent is hard enough but being a single parent to a handicapped kid is nothing short of your worst nightmare, believe you me! Deirdre was forced to turn to family for help, it was that full-on looking after him. She wouldn't have coped without regular time out. Deirdre did all the hard graft, bathing and feeding and therapy, that sort of thing, while I was the one who did all the fun things with him, taking him to the play park and the beach, and when he got older, the zoo and the movies, and Rainbow's End for special birthdays. But the circus was his favourite. Of course, in those days they came to town every year. His favourite act was the fire eaters.

"My whole aim in life was to put a smile on that dear boy's face and a laugh in his belly. I had a formative influence on him, I'm sure; gave him a reason to live. Kids imprint, you know, even the retarded ones. When I helped him build his first Duplo castle at age ten, and saw the look on his face when he got it right, I knew he'd find the strength to rise above it all. Literally."

"Excuse me interrupting, Audrey. You said your nephew's birth name was Rover. Why is he known as Bobby?"

"I started calling him Bobby when he was little and it soon caught on. It suits him. Because he has such a bubbly personality. Because he bobs up and down when he walks. And it matches his surname! 'Bobby Kennedy' sounds more flash, doesn't it? What sort of a name is Rover anyway, I ask you? It's a car! Besides, his father didn't deserve the honour of having his son named after him, really. Even though Deirdre still holds a torch for that ne'er-do-well, even after all these years, God knows why."

"Right. So, having played a large part in his upbringing, you got to know Bobby pretty well. How would you describe Bobby's character?"

"He's an absolute sweetie, pure as the driven snow. Even though he's simple, he's always been good-natured. Always does what he's told. No arguments. No fuss. The apple of my eye, he is, that boy, the apple of my eye. In his mid-teens when they couldn't do any more for him at school, he started hanging around town every day, chatting to the storekeepers and shoppers, running errands for them and helping out. Everyone is very fond of him, even if it took them a while to get used to his weird little ways..."

"I believe he's quite the local personality. By the way, we found him in the bush down by the river — it's obvious he's been living rough for a couple of days and was soiled and hungry, and seemed very disoriented."

"Oh, my poor, wee, darling boy! What he must have been through!"

"Not to worry, he's safe and sound now, down at the police station, and having a good feed. We asked him what he'd like and he said KFC."

"Oh, he loves takeaways! Deirdre never let him have them, but they were our dirty little secret, if you know what I mean, Officer."

"Who doesn't love a takeaway now and again, Audrey? But do go on…you were telling me about his daily routine."

"Well, he usually calls in here most days, and if we aren't too busy with customers we shoot the breeze for a while, then get him to do a few jobs for us, things he can cope with, like dropping the mail off at the post office and emptying the rubbish bins. He turns up at ten o'clock on the dot every morning; you could set your watch by him! 'Come on, ladies,' he says, 'Time to get a load off your corns and bunions.' He pops the jug on for morning tea and always munches through a handful of bikkies from the tin. He has a very sweet tooth, you know.

"But I digress. Before coming here, he calls in at Unicorn Books and takes old Mr Willis's dog for a nice long walk. Mr Willis is getting beyond doing it himself, as you probably know. Bobby and Old Nick are a familiar sight around town — Bobby 'bobbing' up and down the sidewalk, dragging his bad leg behind him, always wearing that cowboy hat of his on the back of his head like a cartoon character, with Old Nick way out ahead of him, sort of pulling him along. You have to ask yourself who's taking who for a walk. Know what I mean?"

"I do, Audrey. I've seen them myself! So how does he spend the rest of his day? It could be important to the enquiry."

"Well, after he's called in here, he goes down to the service station where they get him to wash and valet the cars, and he sweeps out the workshop. In return for his couple of hours' help, the mechanics shout him a cut lunch, and the manager slips him a twenty, under the table. Oooh, maybe I shouldn't haven't told you that, Officer! Anyway, Bobby enjoys sharing a couple of jokes and a yarn or two with the other blokes, even if he doesn't always understand what they are saying. The lads are good to him, tolerant. Always make him feel like one of the boys.

"In the afternoons, he heads over to New World where he buys lollies and a pastry — usually an apple turnover — and a drink. He has his afternoon tea on a bench outside, then hangs around the car park offering to push people's trundlers for them and helping them pack their groceries into their boots. The mums always forgive the odd litre of spilt milk or bag of upended potatoes because Bobby makes their kids laugh. He has a rare gift, you know, and that gift is to be able to instantly pacify a niggly child. Literally. They are fascinated by him, not only by his appearance, but his magic tricks. Bob's your uncle, he can pull a toffee from behind a child's ear or a pineapple lump from their pocket like a pro! Lollies he's planted there himself, of course!"

"So, Bobby made himself useful around town? Even though he wasn't able to get a normal sort of job..."

"Exactly. Life on Elizabeth Street wouldn't have been the same without him coming and going. He loved being around others and everyone made him feel needed — *special*. He was even nominated for that 'Community Thank-You-Bouquet' thing the local paper runs once a month. You know the one I mean? He was happy as Larry when he got a big write-up in the paper with his photo beside it!"

"You and his Mum must've been very proud."

"I was proud as punch, although I've no idea what Deirdre thought, Officer. We haven't been on speaking terms for years, really. As I've gotten older, I've started resenting her more and more. The fact that *she's* Bobby's mother, and I'm not. Especially as I've done so much for him, and we've spent so much time together. I've always treated him like a son, even when he started nicking things. He's the apple of my eye, that boy, the apple of my eye."

"He was stealing from you?"

"Well, he's always had the run of my house, as I said, and he has a tendency to help himself to things without asking — bits and bobs, knickknacks, treats, that sort of thing. Matches. Oh, how he loved playing with matches! And if you asked him why he'd taken such and such, he'd just shrug and mutter 'little treasure', clinging to whatever it was for dear life. 'Little Treasure' is what I often called him, so I guess that's how he picked that term up in the first place. 'My Little Treasure,' I'd often say, when giving him a hug.

"But I digress. If he nicked anything big, like money or jewellery, and I scolded him, his face would crumple and he'd start weeping. Believe you me, I couldn't bear to see my Bobby cry and I'd give in; let him keep whatever it was. Until I could get it back off him without a scene, of course."

"Fair enough, Audrey. By the way, have you noticed any recent changes in his behaviour or demeanour?"

"Now you mention it, Officer, after he was awarded the Community Bouquet, he started asking me all these questions about the past; stuff he's never been interested in before. 'Aunty,' he'd say, getting a wistful, gleamy look in his eyes, 'How come I'm different, tell me, why aren't I like other folks?' and 'Why do people look at me funny when they don't know me?' and 'Aunty, why won't anyone give me a proper job? What's wrong with me?' He'd go on and on like a stuck record, literally!

"Well one day with his constant nagging and whatnot, I blurted it all out, told him everything. That it was all his mum's fault. I didn't think he'd understand. I mean, he doesn't really understand much at all!"

"Right. By the way, Audrey, when we found him, he was clutching a BBQ lighter and reeked of alcohol."

"Oh, God, no! Be still my beating heart! Who would have plied him with drink? And why would they? Did someone want to take advantage of him? The thought is too awful to contemplate..."

"It's too soon to tell. We're bringing in specialist services to assess his condition. When he's recovered, we'll interview him, and try and establish a timeline of events. Look, I'm sorry to have been the bearer of bad news today, Audrey. Hearing about your sister's death can't have been easy, despite the bad blood between you. Especially as this is probably going to be escalated into a murder investigation... The fire crew are doing a site investigation as we speak."

"You're not suggesting...? Oh, my poor, wee boy! Bobby must have been to hell and back, Officer."

"We're not assuming anything right now, Audrey. You ought to know, though, when we found him, he was hugging an empty bottle of sherry to his chest. He says he got it from you."

"Now you mention it, I've been wondering what happened to that plonk. Believe you me, I don't drink, never have, Officer. Only keep it for emergencies, you know. When Bobby gets worked up about something, I let him have a couple of toots; have done since he was a baby. As I said, he has a real sweet tooth — loves the stuff! Always under my supervision, of course. He's as pliant as a lamb afterwards. Putty in my hands. Literally. The apple of my eye, he is, that boy. The apple of my eye."

The Journey

She strides through the automatic doors of Christchurch International Airport into the new world. The bright antipodean glare blinds her and the smells of ozone and jet fuel and strange vegetation accost her senses. Squinting now and shading her eyes with a shaky hand, she scans the forecourt, locating a taxi rank across the road. Pausing between her past and her future she takes a deep breath, then begins to navigate the wide pedestrian crossing in front of the terminal, pushing an overloaded trolley ahead of her. It strains under its load, its wheels stubbornly resisting any change in direction, but she presses on.

Like the flotsam and jetsam surrounding a shipwreck, three children bob along beside her, their sizes and shapes distorted by various items of hand luggage: the assorted paraphernalia of international travel, the volume and disarray of which inevitably increases en route. The oldest child, a twelve-year-old boy, forges ahead, a skateboard tucked under his arm. The smaller of the two girls, barely school age, straggles absentmindedly behind the group, dragging a tired looking doll along the ground. The middle child, also a girl, hangs on to her mother's jacket, scowling and complaining.

Soon their luggage has been prised into a taxi-van and the family pile in, collapsing onto the seats. A mother, three children, four suitcases and the leavings of a life, all safely tucked away for now. The woman pulls a piece of paper with an address on it from her pocket and thrusts it into the driver's hand. She notes from his appearance and accent that he too is an immigrant, a stranger from a strange land.

"Good kids," she says as the taxi pulls away from the curb. "We've made it. Isn't this exciting? Our big adventure is…" She draws her children close; a mother hen gathering her chicks into the warm, dark place beneath her wings. Her voice trails away as the vehicle gathers speed, its motor humming up a few decibels. The children huddle together quietly, watching the unfamiliar landscape pass by through a blur of exhaustion. The woman pulls a large pair of dark glasses from her handbag and pushes them onto her face. They cut the glare, but also hide the uncertainty flickering in her watery eyes.

A few weeks later, the family are in Auckland now, and rain has been lashing the streets for days. She is not coping as well as she did when she first stepped on New Zealand soil. Downcast and clutching an empty jewellery box, she leaves an antique dealer in Greenlane and runs across the wet street dodging cars and puddles. The rainwater hitting her face mingles with her tears as she feels for the door handle of the Hilux van she'd bought from a German couple at Taylors Mistake, near Christchurch. Perhaps it was not only Taylor who'd made an error of judgement; perhaps she should have done more research and planning before relocating to the other side of the world with three children and four suitcases in tow.

She'd gotten the van for a song because the tourists were due to fly out the next day. It rattles along the road like a haunted hot box and she has to turn the heater on full when the engine overheats; a tip from a farmer near Kaikoura where she'd been forced to pull over, smoke pouring from the bonnet. He'd appeared out of nowhere on a quad bike with a sheepdog on the back. He'd said she was sure to get a job up in the Big Smoke even though she'd been unsuccessful in Christchurch; New Zealand was short of teachers.

That was if they made it to Auckland in the first place. Near Rotorua they'd had a puncture. A handsome young Māori riding a Harley had pulled over to help. She'd been wary at first, intimidated by the Viking horn helmet and the Headhunters gang patch, but he'd been charming, a huge belly laugh shaking his frame when she'd cursed the state of the van. After he fitted the spare, he waved the family on their way saying, "Ka kite, anō!" "See you later!" It's a greeting that will later come to epitomise the Kiwi world view to her. In a country with a small population and only two degrees of separation, the likelihood of crossing paths with someone again is high.

When the family finally made it safely to Auckland, they'd christened the van, 'The Crusader', after the Canterbury rugby team, and out of sheer relief.

Now, she brushes her cheeks dry with a coat sleeve and heaves herself up into the driver's seat, hoping the row of children sitting behind her haven't noticed that she's teary. She needs to be strong for their sakes, because the implications of this international shift hang over them too, like the dark sky overhead, pregnant with rain. They sit quietly, glum and mute, knowing this is not the time to be fooling around or asking for something to eat.

Starting up the engine, she flicks on the wipers and inches the vehicle out into the stream of traffic, tracing her way back to the motorway. Moving on helps her push the rising tide of grief and hardship back down inside her, keeps her focused on the end goal even if she's not exactly sure what that might look like. The important thing is to keep putting one foot in front of the other, a platitude her father favoured. *Ah, well, it's no big deal*, she tells herself, *getting ripped off on this side of the world feels the same as it would anywhere else.*

She's good at self-talk — she knows she's not the first woman to have made such a journey with young children. And she won't be the last. Being forced to travel great distances to escape dire circumstances is nothing new: women and children are perennial casualties, the collateral damage of war, famine and pestilence. When she feels low, she forces herself to remember the destitute woman who had knocked on her *own* door a few years back, with two exhausted toddlers clinging to her skirts and a sick baby in her arms. She'd been desperate and starving, fleeing drought and crop failure, searching for a husband who had migrated to the city to seek work. He had never returned.

Her situation is quite different; she is not looking for a man but running from one, and she is not yet destitute. She has prospects, and an old friend, who lives further north, has offered to put them up until she finds work. She had helped that poor woman on her way with food and a small amount of money. But sometimes she still jerks awake at night with a stab of fear, wondering what became of that woman and her children, and whether it was wise to have left her own home in the first place. Courage is often based on ignorance, stupidity, or even false hope. *Is she, herself, guilty of any of these in choosing to move halfway across the world in search of a better life?*

She drives north, over the Harbour Bridge. The cityscape gradually gives way to suburbia, and soon the family are driving past lifestyle blocks and tumbledown smallholdings where vacant-eyed livestock stand mute in rain-drenched fields. From time to time, she glances at the purse she has tossed on the seat beside her with her now denuded jewellery box. Even though the purse is no longer empty, she knows what's in it won't get them very far. She glances at her hands on the steering wheel, feeling strangely underdressed now, as if an integral part of herself is missing. The wedding and engagement rings she'd pawned with a few other pieces of jewellery had been on her finger for so long, she'd lost count of the years. All that remains of them now is a pale band of indented skin where they formerly fitted, far too snugly, on her ring finger.

'Christchurch, the Anglican Parish of Warkworth': so reads the sign at the entrance of a modest weather board church, the sort that are endemic in ex-colonies and can be seen across this land, solitary and run-down in paddocks where they are used as livestock shelters, framed on hilltops by big sky where tourists snap selfies and visit public toilets, ignored on street corners where they continue their functional lives as banks, massage parlours, pharmacies and taverns, or nestling cosily alongside sports fields where they have been repurposed into village halls and are now used for flower shows or community dances, scouts or guides meetings, farmers' protests and funeral wakes.

That this church is still a functioning place of worship feels like a sign. She wants to believe that some great plan is unfolding, that her faith has actually led them here. Granted, Warkworth is not the pristine southern city she'd pinpointed on a map months ago when she decided she needed to flee and chose to immigrate to New Zealand. But it'll do.

She enters the church self-consciously and slips into a back pew, trying to pick up the threads of the sermon. "Faith has not always meant the same thing. In the medieval past, Christianity was sanctioned by the sword. The authority of the Holy Catholic Church was sacrosanct and the Church with wrath and fire brought the Word to the heathen of the empire, compelling them to believe and obey. The opposite of faith in those times was *heresy*, something so shocking, so deviant, it was punishable by death. But faced with the rise of science through the Renaissance and into modernity, *doubt* became the opposite of faith. Empiric evidence gradually became more important than blind belief. Mankind began to understand also, that there is no privileged, absolute standpoint for the assertion of truth; that all interpretations of reality are relative and contingent and contextual and evolving. Now, in our topsy turvy, fast-changing world it is *uncertainty* — the uncertainty we face at every level of our lives — that has replaced the heresy and doubt of old. It devolves to us to counter this uncertainty by projecting meaning onto reality, by asserting that the universe itself is ultimately meaningful, despite uncertainty, despite relativity."

The minister invites the congregation to approach a giant chainsaw-cut wooden cross which dominates the interior of the church, saying, "Any trouble which may be unspeakable, any grief which may be unanswerable, any fear which paralyses, any chaos which fails to be undone, nail it to the cross as Jesus was nailed." Others go forward, but she remains seated; transfixed, unmoving. Someone has pressed a rusty four-inch nail into her hand and it digs into the soft flesh of her palm. But she can't give it up just yet, needs to hang on to it for a while longer, needs it to remind herself of the crosses others bear, even though hers feels so heavy right now she can barely carry it.

She holds the nail tightly in her hand, a symbol of what must be endured, what must be overcome, what is worthwhile, what is enduring.

It's the middle of the night and she's sitting on the edge of her son's divan in the corner of the open-plan living room. The cottage they're living in only has two tiny bedrooms; she has one and the girls share the other. The boy's eyes are dark and moist, shining with angry tears. "Why did you bring us here, Mum? It's such a dump. And this rain? Will it ever stop? I want to go back to Africa! I want to go home!"

She tries to cradle her son in her arms but she can tell from the strength of his struggle his childhood is over. Yet he is too young to understand what she is running from and what she is searching for. He only knows that this present, the interstice between the past and the future, is all just too hard. He wants things to be the same as they were when he was growing up on the other side of the world, where he had a pet dog, and he played cricket and soccer, not rugby. Where the sun shone every day, where its warmth seeps into your bones. Where he had a mother *and* a father.

She promises her son that somehow, some way, she will make it all better. She tells him that although this feels like the end of something, it is also a beginning. As his shuddering and struggling subside, she rubs his back until sleep overcomes him. She sits for a long time late into the night, listening to the wind whipping the dense thicket of trees outside and the rain falling on the roof like Judgement Day. Her hair sticks to her head in swathes of sweat, her nightdress is soaked through. She feels as if her soul is waterlogged and will never dry out.

Will he ever forgive her? she wonders. *A boy needs a father, yes, but does he need a bad one?*

Her son had been born on a stormy night, just like this, on the other side of the world, in Cape Town. While she lay sobbing and thrashing on the hospital bed with him stuck in the birth canal his father had promised her he'd never make her cry again. A hundred years ago, even fifty years ago, she or her baby, or both of them, might not have survived. But forceps had pulled her baby free and they had been united in this life. The boy's father's words are forever etched on her mind, forming an often recurring internal echo, an earworm, a sad song stuck on repeat play. If only she could switch it off, consign it to oblivion. No matter. She has her children, and they are safe. They are forging a new life, a different life.

Late one Sunday afternoon, she drives the family to Scott's Landing to escape the confines of their cramped home and get some fresh air. Settlers came ashore here in the mid-19th century and established a farm and a homestead which still stands today. It reminds her of Belvidere in the Cape where her own ancestors had beached themselves on a wild shore, cleared a village green and built a church, where they had felled ancient trees and burned the tangled undergrowth of native forest to clear land for grazing and crops, imposing their will over generations on a hostile continent and climate, clashing with indigenous people from other parts of Africa who had migrated to the Cape also, making counter claims upon the land.

All of history, she muses, is one of dispersal and rearrangement, dissolution and reestablishment around the crux of survival. Each of us at any given time is actually treading water at one of the stations of the cross, where we find ourselves stuck at a uniquely personal point on our own journey, as we travel internally, externally, emotionally, and geographically, through time and space, to somewhere else, always in transit, always positioned somewhere on the continuum between loss and gain, gain and loss, order and chaos, chaos and order, dragging our crosses through each successive day towards Gethsemane.

Evening is approaching, and the rain has stopped at last. The sky is pellucid, streaked with remnants of pink, grey and violaceous cloud. The light has a luminous quality about it which makes everything seem both sharp and muted. It's deathly cold and strangely still; even the flow of the estuary seems motionless tonight, trapped at that point of stillness between the tides. Down on the beach the older children chase each other with crabs, the sound of their laughter muffled by the icy air. She and her youngest are boulder hopping at the point. The rules of the game are simple — don't land in the puddles or slip off the rocks. Stay connected. Don't lose the other's hand.

"Mummy, mummy, this makes me feel like a giant! These rocks are my mountains, the waters running and pooling here are my rivers and my lakes. See, my people live here." The girl's words fade away to an echo in the stillness as her mother peers strangely into her youngest's face. The child has already adopted the Kiwi accent and has made friends at school. Her mother is pleased about the bigness of being she is claiming for herself. The memory of another happy little girl returns to her. *Joy is well remembered,* she thinks, *but it is offset, always, by the sorrow of loss that pervades her being like mushrooms multiplying in the dark.*

The other children run across the sand to meet them. It's time to head home, to prepare for the week to come. They walk hand in hand, stunned by the cold, cheeks glowing red, breath streaming from their mouths and condensing in the icy air.

Christmas arrives and with it the long lazy days of the summer holidays. Here in this run-down old villa at Sandspit she has found a semblance of peace and serenity, with its many interconnected rooms sloping away on sinking pilings, and a birds-eye view of the changing colours and moods of the estuary. The name of the house, painted on a piece of wood and nailed to the front door, is 'WHATUKURA' — place of learning. There is an ancient orchard at the back with persimmons, mandarins and lemons surrounded by feijoa hedges, and in the garden beds at the front, old roses and lavender compete for colour and scent. A stream runs through a wooded gulley beside the house, downhill to the harbour. She has planted a branch from an attractive variegated-leaved shrub in a bucket of sand in the living room, and the children have decorated it with homemade baubles: magazine and newspaper cutouts of snowflakes and stockings and angels and Father Christmases which they've glued onto cardboard and hung with string.

During the day the children play out of doors with other neighbourhood kids, roaming the bush and beach. At night the family sleep with unbarred windows and unlocked doors while possums raid the outdoor rubbish bin and ruru coo in the gully. The nightlights of other houses twinkle across the water while the sky above glimmers with billions of stars.

On the other side of the world, in Johannesburg where the family had lived not so long ago, gunshots pop in the dark as sirens wail and police helicopters circle above, their searchlights arcing across the sky. Sometimes she misses that sprawling, industrial, giant of a city, situated on the high dry savannah of southern Africa — where mountains are mine dumps, and cold steel and concrete substitute for grass and trees, where the acid rain falling from smoke-filled skies dissipates in the polluted gutters and pot-holed streets of shame, where what needs rescuing are not hedgehogs crossing the road or fledglings that have fallen from their nests, but ragged street children who sniff glue to dull the pain and trauma of their daily lives, where the poor sleep on beds of cardboard in bus shelters and alleyways clutching their meagre possessions to their breasts — for after all, it was once home. But time will hopefully erase the worst of it from memory.

She is standing at the kitchen sink washing the lunch dishes and looking out into the garden. Her daughter is playing under the tramp, constructing a make-believe 'Barbie World' in the shade there. The Barbies are sunning themselves on doll-sized deck chairs while the girl arranges a miniature barbeque and throws tiny mock sausages on the grill. Then she adjusts the striped sun umbrella. "We don't want to get skin cancer, do we Ken?" she says.

The water in the Barbie pool glints invitingly and a doll-sized Lilo bobs up and down. "How about a swim before we eat?" The girl mouths Ken's words, turning him to face his companion. "I'll race you!" But he bumps into the barbeque and the sausages go flying. Disco Barbie comes to the rescue: "Don't worry about it, Ken. I'll sort it." The girl pushes the two dolls together in an embrace.

How easy it is to construct a perfect world when you're ten years old, her mother thinks.

A pair of woodpigeons swoop overhead, their wings beating the air as they return to their nest in the bush alongside the house. They mate for life, apparently. The shrilling of the cicadas is suddenly deafening, the glorious sunny day is somehow too brilliant, too beautiful.

One sultry afternoon, she is standing on the freshly mown lawn between her landlord and a plumber, looking from face to face as they contemplate the pipework that has collapsed overnight, leaving the house without a water supply. The men appear to be at a loss and she wonders whether she should offer them something to drink.

The magnolia tree growing beside the house is in full bloom. Looking up, she notices how its huge waxy-white flowers are fully opened to the sun, their erect pollen-laden stamens pointing heavenward like golden daggers in defiance of their large, limp, white petals which appear to be melting in the heat as they slip from their calyxes and float gently to the ground at her feet.

She turns back to the men, trying to focus on the problem at hand. Both are now staring at her and she blushes. She is standing in bare feet on the lush grass, her soft cotton dress framing her figure and falling to her knees where it sways, ever so slightly, as she inhales and exhales. Her hair burns bronze in the slanting sunlight, her mouth glints golden, the skin on her face, neck and arms glows warm and soft. Time stops, and she feels her power returning to her in a heated flush. *I am a woman. I am a mother. I am a teacher. I am making my way through this world,* she thinks. *I am healing.*

When she'd started teaching at the local school a pōwhiri had been held to welcome her and her family to Aotearoa. Māori women had sung a waiata, inviting her onto the marae, and a shiver had passed through her, hairs bristling at the back of her neck. Inside, a kaumātua had addressed her, telling her Aotearoa was glad her waka had washed up on these shores, that South Africa's loss would be New Zealand's gain. Her clenched hands had unfolded and the rusty nail had slipped through her fingers and fallen to the floor.

She is dreaming of Belvidere and an engagement ring which didn't fit very well, that had a habit of slipping from her finger. Five tiny pearls in a row, held in place by fragile, finely wrought, golden claws. She had chosen it herself. Chosen her own destiny. A May wedding solved the slippage problem; a gold wedding band now held the pearl engagement ring safely in its place. The birth of a long-awaited baby boy marked the passing of the first five years of her marriage. Two more babies soon followed, both girls, another five years adding up to ten.

By now her rings fitted too tightly, cutting into her flesh; a constant reminder of the ties that bound her, of the husband who repeatedly betrayed her. And from time to time, the tiny luminous pearls would fall from the engagement ring, slipping between their golden claws to be lost forever, down the sinkhole, in the soil of a garden bed, at the bottom of a shopping bag or the toy box. There was no way she could have possibly known, back then, that pearls mean tears.

In her dreams she often returns to Belvidere, the place of the white doves, far away, across the sea, where an old church and its graveyard stand alone between the bush and the ever-moving water; the place where all the sacred rituals of her life had played out: a marriage, three baptisms, and a reluctant goodbye.

She wakes suddenly, her mind stumbling through a haze of memories and misgivings. Lying silently in her bed, she hears the wind lashing the trees outside, breaking the dead wood free, and the relentless rain washing down, carrying every uncertain thing with it as it gushes into the gullies and creeks, following their ancient courses into the streams and rivers and estuaries and harbours of this land; down, down, down to the lowest point, to the nadir, until it flows out into the ocean deep. She thinks about how long ago and far away it all seems, how great the distance is, and how hard the road has been. Until, at last, she sinks into sleep once more, grateful that this day's journey is over.

Person, Woman, Man, Camera, TV.

Person

The young woman around whom this story revolves lost her real self in a rat-shitty room somewhere in the bowels of Auckland city. There was only one person in the world who could help her now — her mother. After a long, hot bus trip up north, followed by a thumbed ride with a creepy cow-cockie, she collapsed on her mother's doorstep, a wreck.

The kindness that greeted her was unexpected. Or maybe it was something she had forgotten; it'd been that long since she'd been home. She decided she would come clean, tell her mother everything.

Woman

For her mother, days bled into nights and nights morphed into days as her daughter's melt-down magnified, the fallout spreading like a mushroom cloud over their lives.

How had this happened? The girl had been a content and compliant child, while her siblings had been demanding, even difficult at times. Yet her older brother and sister had settled down into adult life with barely a wobble — they were successful professionals now, hitched to good partners, raising families of their own.

But their little sister's passage to adulthood had somehow veered off course. Her anchor had come adrift, allowing a strong current to drag her downstream into murky, dangerous waters.

Man

The girl's stepfather was also affected by her arrival and he ramped himself up into a state of heightened alertness, as if some external threat had loosed itself upon the world. When she'd turned up — her face raw with desperation, her wild dark hair flying — a nest of hungry fledglings had started squawking in his stomach. She wasn't his child; hell, he'd never even been a parent! Neither did he have any experience with this sort of thing. He felt like a new recruit with minimal training who's been helicoptered into a war zone and dropped into the field of battle with minimal backup.

Worse, the girl's mother was copping flak. It could only end badly.

Camera

The couple weren't spring chickens and they hadn't signed up for this. A peaceful retirement with an income from the sale of their produce had been the plan when they'd set themselves up on this modest lifestyle block north of Whangārei. Problem offspring hadn't factored into the equation.

They tiptoed around their own house like unwelcome guests, on tenterhooks, wary of upsetting the young woman. At night suspicious sounds woke them — low voices muffled by mist as summer heat gave way to autumn rain, the distant rumble of a car engine, wheels crunching on metal as it drove slowly away.

Was the girl high jinking it with hoons while they slept? They'd been young once; knew all the tricks.

"Surely her friends wouldn't drive all the way from Auckland in the middle of the night?" her mother wondered.

"Depends, I guess, love. On lots of things. I'll check out the security camera footage."

TV

Around the clock in the darkened lounge room, the TV blared as the young woman huddled under a blanket in her PJs, binge watching popular series in a sea of lolly wrappers, biscuit crumbs and spilled popcorn. News coverage was centred on the growing pandemic — where it had originated, how it had spread, who was to blame, what could be done — and the couple's sense of confusion about the girl's circumstances was exacerbated by foreboding about the bigger picture.

When her mother suggested changing the channel to get an update, the girl snatched the remote out of her hand.

"Who the fuck cares about the news?" she said. "We're all going to die anyway. If not from some deadly virus, there'll be a natural disaster, another world war, or a frigging climate catastrophe!"

The woman conceded. "I guess you're right, honey. There could be a meteor hurtling through space right now, on a direct collision path with earth..."

"That's just sick, Mum. No need to rub it in," the girl replied. She threw the remote onto the coffee table and flounced out of the room.

Person

As the days passed, the young woman shared bits of information about what had gone wrong back in Auckland. Her boyfriend had shot through and she couldn't afford the flat on her own so had shifted into a communal house in another suburb. Then her period was late.

"Everything was all messed up. I felt really conflicted about making the right decision. I never wanted to have an abortion," she said.

Her new flatmates partied a lot and the in-house grunge band — undiscovered as yet, but apparently destined for great things — provided the beats. Synthetic ecstasy was doing the rounds; it was cheap as chips in the city, the drug of choice of beneficiaries and the urban poor. Taking it when her hormones were all screwed up was a bad idea, and it wasn't long before she became addicted. The euphoric disconnection it induced in her dealt to her anxiety and wrecked self-esteem, made her life seem bigger, better, brighter. Made her feel like one of 'the guys'.

When she couldn't get a fix of the foul-smelling viscous chemical her body craved, she began to use alcohol to blunt its debilitating withdrawal symptoms. Alcohol helped her sleep when she was wired and wide-eyed at 2am, staring at the walls of her bedroom as they buckled and warped around her like melting ice cream. When the sound of the window banging on its broken latch thudded endlessly in her ears like a monotonous bass drumbeat. When the tatty curtain hanging across the night sky was the Angel of Death with wings outstretched, come to carry her away. When her pulse was racing, and her skin was crawling, and a little voice inside her head was telling her she would do anything to get hold of a vial of Liquid E. So she could at least die high.

"It's all my own fault," she said as her mother stroked her hair and crooned platitudes in her ear.

"Don't blame yourself, honey. We'll find a way through this."

She pushed her mother away. "Mum, you're *so* fucking naïve! This drug is impossible to get off — the withdrawals give you the screaming heebee jeebies — you can go into cardiac arrest! Look. Just. Fucking. Leave. Me. Alone. *PLEASE!*"

Woman

Every waking moment the young woman's mother scrutinised the accumulated evidence of the past in search of clues that might explain why her daughter had gone off the rails. Was it her parents' divorce when the girl had been just six years old that had pushed her off course? Was she stuck in a state of arrested development? Did she possess a fatal flaw?

Or was she cursed?

These questions simmered like magma beneath the surface of this unknown and hostile terrain as the girl's mother searched for safe passage through the bubbling sinkholes.

As time passed, the girl shared more: "Remember Tony Durbin, Mum?" Tony Durbin had been a builder in their former neighbourhood, the one where the woman had raised her children as a solo parent. "It wasn't just weed I was smoking back then. Tony gave me my first P pipe when I was fourteen."

Rage welled up inside the girl's mother — the rage of a wild animal with strong hard teeth, long sharp claws and an earsplitting roar. "I will kill that Tony Durbin, I will!" she cried, hot tears rolling down her cheeks as if anger had boiled her insides.

Her partner comforted her. "Two wrongs don't make a right, love," he said.

"I will kill that Tony Durbin, I will!" she told her son when she rang him with an update.

"I heard the cops were on to him, Mum. He might even be in jail by now."

"I will kill that Tony Durbin, I will!" she said when the girl's older sister phoned to commiserate.

"OMG, you're kidding me, Mum! Out little sis is the one who needs to wake up and smell the coffee —life is not just one big party!"

Man

Watching from the sidelines as the girl suffered withdrawal and screamed obscenities, slammed doors, broke a window, and woke in the wee hours sobbing, her stepfather didn't interfere but stood witness while the girl's mother incanted a prayer to counteract her hysteria. The dog and the cat kept out of the girl's way, slinking into the shadows when she left her room to forage for food. Or alcohol. Alcohol was the only thing that calmed her and kept her cravings for Fantasy at bay.

The man replaced the alcohol as soon as his partner asked him to. Even if it meant a last minute dash to the liquor store just before closing time. He swept up after the girl when she stubbed cigarette after cigarette out on the railing, discarding her butts across the deck. He picked up her empties and carried the recycling bin, overflowing with empty Cody's cans, to the kerb as fast as she got through them.

He felt as if he were playing a bit part in a horror movie — as if his reactions to the main storyline were a foil, intended to reflect just how much could go wrong in someone else's life.

At odd hours when the girl finally slept her mother got on the blower, seeking help. Later, she beckoned the man into the washhouse where they could speak privately. There was a two-month wait for an appointment with Drug & Alcohol Services. The girl couldn't be seen by the local doctors until she was registered as a patient; she needed to fill in a form and give permission for her health records to be transferred from Auckland. There would be a further delay enrolling her with the Ministry of Health. At Whangārei Hospital Emergency there was a 24-48 hour wait for supposed 'non-urgent' cases. They'd heard it was the busiest and most underequipped hospital in the country; now they knew this to be true.

All the advice was to seek help elsewhere. But where else?

Camera

The nightly disturbances continued, and the man couldn't quite put his finger on it. He started checking the security camera footage every day, but it was no help; the camera only captured the approach to the house, not the long driveway, or the orchards alongside it.

As if there wasn't already enough to worry about. It was avocado season and the crop was excellent that year. But it would require all hands on deck to harvest it. The girl mooched around the house looking as if she'd been haphazardly stitched together, like Frankenstein's monster, while her mother ran after her like a slave, micro-managing her every move, when both of them could have been put to work.

What's more, the old girl was showing signs of strain. She burned meals and hadn't done the laundry in weeks. He'd run out of fresh daks, socks and singlets a while back, and was beginning to feel like a grubby bushman in need of a scalding hot bath. Hell, she barely had time to brush her hair! It was starting to form dreads...

If she, too, cracked up, he feared he'd be on his own, dealing with not only one but two cot cases.

TV

The news, when the couple got a look in, centred on the pandemic. Rumours about the virus were rife; how it spread, its dire consequences. Parts of Asia were in lockdown, and the situation in Europe, the UK and the States was shockingly worrying: hospitals were overflowing with the sick and the death toll was rising daily.

"I always imagined that plagues only happened in Biblical times, or during the Dark Ages," the man said.

"I always imagined it was only other people's children who got into trouble," the woman said.

The girl not only had drug debts but owed rent. Her mother threw money at the problem as if freshly minted fifty-dollar bills were being harvested from the avocado trees. It all added up — not only the bills, but the fancy toiletries, cell phone top-ups, cigarettes and alcohol. Then there were the treats —magazines, crossword puzzles, chocolates — stuff to take her mind off things, her Mum said. Yeah, he couldn't help thinking, stuff you take to the hospital when someone's had a close shave. Or when they're on their way out.

Soon it was the young woman's birthday. The family rallied, arriving en masse for the occasion, wearing plastic smiles, pretending everything was A-Okay. You could have cut the atmosphere with a knife. Instead, they cut a red-velvet cake decorated with twenty candles, and grinned and rolled their eyes through the birthday song like dying horses. There was a lot of talk about the pandemic, but the girl's problems were taboo.

The day after, a special news bulletin interrupted regular programming. The PM stood solemnly on the podium in the theatrette at the Beehive, delivering a sombre speech to the nation: "Tens of thousands of people could die if community transmission of Covid-19 takes hold in New Zealand," she said, her face pinched and drawn with the seriousness of the situation. "A lockdown is our best chance to slow the spread of the virus and save lives. To give everyone time to prepare, we will move to level four within forty-eight hours, at midnight on 25th March. Thereafter, only essential services will be allowed to operate, and only essential workers will be allowed out of their homes. We are asking you to please stay at home in your family bubbles. Work from home if you're able to. All child and educational facilities will be closed. Support each other. Be kind."

The couple decided they needed to stock up on groceries and the man said he would go into town and face the queues. The girl offered to go with him.

"But it'll be bedlam out there!" the woman said.

The young woman replied in a whisper: "I've got to try and get some help, Mum. While I'm still able to."

Person

There was a long wait at A and E. The bright, white, fluorescent strip lighting hurt the young woman's eyes and she felt taut and strung out, like fishing line that's snagged up on something unforgiving and is about to snap. When she did, she leapt out of her chair, marched up to the counter and shrieked at the reception staff.

Her stepfather tried to cover his face with a magazine, but she turned on him next: "Well, aren't you going to stick up for me? These wait times are a bloody joke!" He didn't answer.

"Fuck this shit!" she said, storming out of the clinic. "I'm going back to Auckland!"

A nurse ran after her, calling her back. "It's your turn, sweetie! The doctor will see you now."

"Too fucking late!" she screamed.

Through the plate glass window everyone in the waiting room watched with bated breath as the girl attempted to make a phone call on her mobile while lighting a cigarette. Her cell flew out of her hand and crashed to the pavement. As she bent to pick it up, she realised she had a captive audience and pulled an ugly face.

The nurse patted the girl's shoulder, mouthing comforting words. After a couple of long drags on her ciggie, she stubbed it out and smoothed down her flying hair.

When she came back inside, she asked the man to accompany her into the doctor's room. "Please," she said. "I could do with your support." He could no longer pretend he wasn't involved.

In the consulting room, she slumped in a chair, eyes blazing, cheeks flushed, sweating and faint.

"Right," the doctor said, as if she dealt with drug addicts every day. "Tell me what's been going on and let's have a look at you." She prescribed high doses of Valium and dispensed advice about 'going cold turkey' and 'being brave'. "You're fortunate your family are supporting you through this," she said.

The man grimaced and shifted in his seat. "But we're floundering," he said. "And I'm not talking about catching fish." He wrung his cap in his hands.

The doctor nodded. "It's not going to be easy. The health system is overloaded. And underfunded. But I've heard the Salvation Army is good in this space ..."

The sedative helped calm the girl, but the intense cravings continued and a few days later she ran away, breaking lockdown rules and hitching a ride with a truckie back to Auckland where she hooked up with her connections and went on a bender. A week later she returned to her mother's house, looking like something the weather had blown in: an out-of-season hurricane, followed by a one-in-a-century flood.

"I'm so sorry, Mum," she said, hands clutching her toxic headache while she vomited into the toilet bowl. "I've put you at risk, broken our bubble."

Her mother wiped the girl's face with a wet flannel. "I will forgive you, but only if you commit to getting better."

At the Salvation Army offices a masked woman, who looked and spoke as if she was a member of the Brethren community, showed the girl into a cubicle, where a counsellor sat behind a Perspex screen decorated with sunflower stickers and pictures of puppies and kittens. The two women were close in age but couldn't have been more different, one in a bright floral frock with dangly earrings that swung in irritating circles as she spoke, the other dressed like a creature of the night, hunched in her chair with one leg slung over the other knee, staring at the floor and picking at the mud on the soles of her Doc Martens.

"In this place there is no judgement," the counsellor said. "You come as you are, we meet you there. We'll get together weekly, and work through things. But you can ring me anytime. Or text. The main thing is you need to *want* to get better. If you *want* to get better, I promise, you will."

Woman

The woman felt guilty about how much she'd neglected her partner since the girl had landed on them with all her problems. A recent hip replacement had slowed him down somewhat, and he'd become more and more sullen recently, keeping to himself.

She followed him one day, watching from the cover of the orchard as he headed into the bush beyond. What was he up to? When she lost sight of him, she leaned back against a tree trunk, dizzy with exhaustion. The gloom of green that surrounded her — the stately solemn silence of the tall, strong trees, their outstretched branches glistening with shiny deep-green leaves and laden with ripe fruit — was strangely peaceful and comforting. Dropping her head to her chest for a few moments, she noticed that the grass was knee high and avocados were rotting on the ground.

A few days later, she was absentmindedly stirring a pot of porridge early one morning when her daughter walked into the kitchen. The dog and the cat remained where they were, stretched out peacefully on the mat in front of the old wood stove. The girl stooped to pet and greet them.

"Need any help, Mum?" she asked.

"So nice of you to join us for breakfast, Honey. We usually don't see you till lunchtime."

"I'm feeling a lot better."

The woman's face screwed up. "Really?" She felt like collapsing to the floor in gratitude and relief but her daughter gave her a big hug, holding her upright.

The girl noticed for the first time how her mother had aged; how her body had become blowsy and shapeless, her face a roadmap of wrinkles. She was noticing a whole lot of stuff these days that she'd missed when she'd been an addict.

"We're going to get through this, Mum," she said as she ran her fingers through her mother's matted hair. "Let me wash and style your hair for you later. You could do with some pampering."

As they sat together at the kitchen table, the girl sipping a mug of hot tea while her mother ate, the girl talked about the Sallies counsellor.

"She told me three things that I'll carry with me to the grave. They're like the mental health secret to coping: first, that living well is the best revenge, second, that action is the antidote for depression, and third, that service is the cure for obsessive self-interest. I suddenly realised that it's about cultivating the right mindset. And that it's not all about me."

Man

Every morning when he went out into the orchard to harvest, there were fewer avos on the trees than he'd left behind the day before. Okay, he'd lost some because he couldn't pick them fast enough, but this was crazy and he felt like his head was being fucked with. Suddenly the reason hit him like a punch in the face; thieves were at work. Hell, this couldn't go on. He'd ring the security company asap to jack up an upgrade and have some new cameras installed, hooked up to a monitor in his office.

He cornered his partner in the hallway when the girl was in the shower: "What if it *is* her druggie friends stopping in here at all hours of the night?"

The woman shushed him. "We just need to cope with what's in front of our faces right now. No use pre-empting stuff."

"But what if it's her lowlife mates that're stealing my avocados?" he hissed.

He had already started preparing to spend more time at his hut, leaving the women to it. Now he had two reasons to do so: he wouldn't be disturbed when a haunting nightmare woke the girl at some ungodly hour, and he would be on the spot to scare the thieves off. If they returned. When they returned. One shot was all it would take.

That night as he slumped against the wood pile in the hut dozing under the cover of his oilskin, a car's headlights arced across the orchard, startling him awake. An old Holden ute creaked to a standstill nearby and the doors swung open. Two young men jumped out.

"Hey, grab those boxes off the back," one of them said.

"Yeah, bro," came the reply.

The lads crossed in front of the hut to enter the orchard. He'd seen them around: they played rugby at the local club, walked their dog in the reserve, hung with their mates in the car park at the Maunu shops. Before the lockdown. He decided to hold back a bit on the scare tactics. The PM had said to be kind. And hell, he was trying, wasn't he? Even if he sometimes felt he was over it.

"Hey yous!" he said, in his growliest voice, emerging from the hut, rifle held high.

The taller lad stopped mid-stride and stepped in front of the short, stout guy, as if to protect him. "Hope ya have no intentions of using that thing on us, man!" he said.

"We was just hungry, is all," the shorter lad mumbled. "Like — you've got loads of avos, Mister."

"This is my livelihood! Brings in the extra cash me and my missus need to supplement the Super."

The younger lad pushed forward, aggressive-like. "Well, we

ain't got no way of making moolah, Mister."

The moon came out from behind a cloud and the man did a double take. "Hey. Is your Mum Doreen? From down the motel?" he asked, peering from face to face.

"Yeah. She lost her job. You know, the 'rona and all. She was paid under the table so can't get the wage subsidy."

The older youth chimed in. "You'd think twenty years of loyalty would stand for something, eh? But no. They just let her go…"

"Still no excuse for skulking round other people's property in the middle of the night, thieving stuff," the man said.

"Yeah. Na. Fair enough. But it's so hard listening to Mum gasp and mutter when she sees how quick her savings are running out, eh."

"Mmm, I get the picture."

"We're studying automotive engineering at the Tech, right," the short, stout lad continued. "But distance learning sucks! No hands-on, all boring book work — theory. And there's only so much Fortnight you can play before you go spare, Mister."

"Mmm, I hear what ya saying. I get it. Listen up. You boys keen on some good hard yakka? You can have all the avos you want if you get stuck in. I've got to get this fruit off the trees, asap. And when I get the crop to market, there'll be more than enough money to go round."

"Fo' sure? Fo' sure?" The short, stout lad's face lit up.

"Yup. Long as youse behave yourselves round here. And we'll have to stick to the bubble rules. Luckily, food production is an essential service."

"Chur, bro! Mum'll be rapt, ay. Hates us hanging around home all day, under her feet. Says the fridge door is going to fall off, we open and close it that often. Hehe."

The man smiled. "Looks like Doreen's gonna get some much-deserved down time. Might even be able to watch her own choice of programme now too, and not have her TV stuck on PlayStation 24-7."

Camera

The avocado harvest was done and dusted and spring wasn't far away. Lockdown had boosted sales. Avocado was the perfect ingredient for boosting immunity, to smash on sourdough and add to salads and smoothies. There was even a vegan recipe for an avocado chocolate mousse doing the rounds. The man had taught the lads how to prune the trees to produce maximum fruit next season and he left them working in the orchard, painting the cuts with wound dressing to prevent microbial infection, and headed inside for a break.

Sitting at his desk sipping a coffee and catching up on some paperwork, the corner of his eye caught a flicker of movement across the new security camera monitor. The womenfolk were setting up a picnic in a sunny corner of the orchard. They threw a colourful cloth over an outdoor table and pulled up a few garden chairs, then started unpacking stuff from a basket — bread, a couple of tomatoes, a block of cheese, a jar of pickles, some beers. A pile of snarlers too, and tomato sauce. A pie of some sort. The smell of baked apple and cinnamon still wafted through the house...

Mother and daughter chatted and laughed while they worked. The woman's face shone, and her hair hung like a silver waterfall down her back, glinting in the sun. The girl was buzzing around arranging the food and plates, fizzing with ... what? He couldn't quite put his finger on it. He continued to watch them, continued to wonder. Yes, that's what it was: life. She was fizzing with the rediscovery of how precious her own life was. He hadn't known her mother as a young woman, but she'd probably been as full of it, and as beautiful, as her daughter was today.

Shortly, his partner called the lads over. Then she was speaking to them. He knew her well enough to know what she'd be saying: "You boys've worked real hard helping the old man out. Time for a treat. It's a beautiful day for it, yeah? Go and wash up, then come and tuck in."

The lads nodded and smiled. They'd be saying something

like, "Wow, cool. Thanks heaps, Aunty." Then he saw the older lad glance quickly at the girl. She cocked her head to one side and widened her eyes, as if to say, "Yeah, I fancy you too. Now, let's get this party started."

TV

New Zealand's first lockdown was over, and media coverage turned to the upcoming elections, in Aotearoa and in the US. It was the end of a busy week, and the girl, the woman, the man and the two lads were relaxing in the lounge room watching the news on TV, eating fish and chips, and drinking cider. Doreen was there too, having joined them for the evening. *'BUY LOCAL'* had become a thing during lockdown, and she'd been spending a lot of time at the homestead making preserves to sell at the street-side stall. The three women had also started up a free-range chook operation and the sale of fresh eggs at the gate was raking in the cash.

The international news came on and everyone stared as the camera captured President Trump side-on, his inimitable profile topped off by the ubiquitous, yellow-dyed comb-over that framed his flabby fake-tanned face. He was standing in the colonnade of the White House being interviewed about his annual cognitive assessment.

"So, it was thirty to thirty-five questions," he said. "The first questions are very easy. The last questions are much more difficult, like a memory question. It's, like, they'll go: 'Person. Woman. Man. Camera. TV.' Then they'll say, 'Could you repeat that?' So I said, 'Yeah'. So it's: 'Person. Woman. Man. Camera. TV.'"

Trump continued: "Okay, now he's asking you other questions, other questions, and then, ten minutes, fifteen minutes, twenty minutes later he says, 'Remember that question, not the first question, but the tenth question? Give us that again. Can you do that again?' And you go: 'Person. Woman. Man. Camera. TV.' If you get it in the right order, you get extra points. They said nobody gets it in order. It's actually not that easy. But for me it was easy, real easy."

Everyone in the room exchanged funny faces.

"What the…? Play that again!" said the man.

The girl picked up the Sky remote and rewound the clip. "Look at the interviewer's face! He's absolutely fucking dumbfounded," she said.

The younger of the two lads laughed: "The Orange Clown. At it again. Hehe."

"Yes," the woman replied. "He's talking himself up, as usual, like the narcissistic buffoon he is."

"He's a very stable genius, apparently," Doreen chimed in. "According to himself that is!"

Everyone cracked up.

"More like a certifiable nutter," the older lad said.

The man looked around the circle of animated faces. The scene they'd just witnessed was beyond ridiculous — it was bizarre, it was absurd. What Trump had said today would go down in the history books, would be added to the canon, would feature in documentaries and films and critical analyses and doctoral dissertations far into the future, would become engraved on the collective psyche for posterity. Just like Lincoln's "Do I not destroy my enemies when I make them my friends?", and Martin Luther King's "I have a dream", and JFK's "Ask not what your country can do for you, but what you can do for your country."

What Trump had said today would probably soon be the continuous background loop or inane refrain on some nondescript band's latest electronic hit: "Person. Woman. Man. Camera. TV. Person. Woman. Man. Camera. TV. Person. Woman. Man. Camera. TV."

Hell, you just couldn't make this stuff up. No matter how hard you tried.

Lucked Out

The ditch Jake lay in, flat on his back under a dense thicket of privet, was damp and cool. He realised later this was a small mercy: if he hadn't forced himself to crawl towards it earlier, hadn't pulled himself over its rock-strewn grassy verge and allowed himself to roll down into its murky depths, if he'd stayed out in the open paddock where he'd landed, beaten up and broken, sunstroke and dehydration would surely have overcome him. An extended heat wave was scorching through the countryside, and that day's high, according to Big River Radio, was forecasting a high of thirty-two degrees.

Jake reckoned it was probably close to that now; not a good time to think of moving on. But these thoughts were hypothetical; he was incapable of moving. He felt like a helpless insect trapped inside a glass jar, lying subdued on the deceptive translucent bottom, resigned, at last, to its fate, having abandoned its frantic efforts to escape. In between conscious moments, he dozed, plagued by fitful distorted dreams during which, with flailing limbs, he gasped for air and water, sinking, always sinking, down, down, down, into the unknown depths of an unknown territory; a submerged land animal slowly suffocating to death in a strange underwater world.

He drifted in and out of consciousness for the longest time, the immense effort of having dragged his battered body across the rough ground, together with the pain of his injuries, stilling him to his core. Sometimes, forcing his gummy lids apart for a few moments, he watched the nebulous cumulus clouds high above him forming and dispersing, circling and weaving, in the vast, sunlit sky. Yet everything else was still and strangely quiet, save for the sound of his own blood whooshing loudly in his ears and the irregular thumping of his hard-beating heart.

After several hours had passed, Jake began to regain a state of increased awareness. He felt how the back of his shirt and trousers now cleaved to his body like a second reptilian skin; how the foetid wetness in the ditch beneath him had soaked through his clothing and deep into his bones. A deep chill shuddered through his torso. In his sudden returning fear, he gasped for a few wretched breaths, and the sulphurous stench of the rotting muck in which he lay flared in his nostrils and stuck in his throat. Then he began to sneeze, his body wracking with every outburst. Privet was his worst nightmare; he had always succumbed to it and knew only too well what would follow. Hives. He tried to raise himself onto an elbow, but his strength failed him, and he fell back again, shivering and feverish.

Time passed, interminably slowly, in super slow motion. Later, the ghost of a breeze sprang up. The world was gradually coming alive again as the earth began to cool, recovering from the intense heat of the day. Cicadas started up a rasping song. Blowflies began to dive-bomb Jake, swarming annoying loudly around his damp, sweaty clothing and bloodied face. He twitched from side to side to try and evade their landing attempts. It occurred to him again that he should be making tracks, but remembering his earlier vain attempt, he chose for the moment not to move, not to act; just to let the dying day pass slowly by.

When a couple of fork-tailed swallows started playing around the privet hedge, twittering and chattering cheerfully to each other as they swooped and hawked back and forth for insects, the words of a song his mother used to sing when he was a wee bairn came to him. Finding them infinitely comforting, he licked his lips with a parched tongue and whispered them to himself:

It's the time of the year
See, the swallows are here
Hush little one, there is nothing to fear
Be of good cheer, Mother is near

More time passed, and Jake fell from consciousness again. He dreamed his mother was holding him on her lap, rocking him in her arms, and singing to him, wiping the sweat and dirt from his face and neck with a rough terry cloth. Sometimes, when he was upset or agitated about something, she'd lock her arms around him so tightly he couldn't escape her embrace, and, rocking him back and forth, she'd say, "No worries, Boyo, I'll hold you *tight, tight, tight*, until *you* can hold *yourself* again." He would squirm and struggle and grizzle, pushing against her with all his childish might, but gradually his struggling would subside till at last he'd give up, and come to rest in her arms. He soon learned that if he did, if he gave up, she'd let him go — set him free — and he'd hop smartly off her lap, the indignity of it all over.

Other sounds began to crowd in on Jake's dream memories now — cattle lowing, cowbells tinkling, someone whistling and calling out. He startled awake to find a little dog panting above him and licking his face. He struggled up onto his elbow, lifting his other arm to brush the dog away. The dog whirled around him yelping, then zoomed in again for another scratchy pass across his face.

"Hey, hey, buddy, cut that out!" Jake said, dragging a blood-soaked sleeve across his forehead and managing to raise himself a little more. The spry fox terrier sat down beside him and started animatedly wagging its tail, watching to see what this stranger would do next. A curious smile appeared on the dog's visage as it curled back its upper lip and cocked its head to one side.

Jake wasn't yet out of danger and needed to be on the alert. A dog usually meant humans were nearby; this was no feral canine. He raised his head and looked over the edge of the ditch, taking in his surroundings properly for the first time that day. What appeared to be a stand of dappled saplings swaying in the evening breeze swam into view, but as his focus sharpened, he realised a small herd of thin cattle was shuffling by, their legs and bodies throwing shadows into the slanting light.

A girl's voice called out, followed by a shrill whistle. "Titch, Titch, where the hell are ya, ya stupid mutt? It's gittin' late and we've still to drive the cows back for milkin'. You know Maw'll be on my case ag'n for dawdlin' and takin' so long. C'mon, boy — git ya butt back over here now! C'mon! I'll give ya a nice juicy bone for ya tea when we git home…"

Jake could make out a pair of thin, bare legs, pale and freckled, moving towards him now in sharp relief against the dark legs of the cattle as they lumbered by. The foxy leapt out of the ditch and ran towards the girl, then turned full circle on four paws and started back towards Jake, jumping up and down, barking and yapping excitedly.

"What ya got, boy? A dead bird … or m'be a rabbit hole? Let's take a look-see, and then m'be we can git on…" she said.

The next minute they were upon him and the girl cried out, "My, my, what have we here, then?" She petted the dog's head, saying, "Shush, shush, Titch; yer makin' an awful goddam racket!"

She peered down at Jake, giving him the once over, and he squinted back up at her, propped still on one elbow. "Ya look like ya've been in the wars, don't ya, Mister?"

She was a slip of a girl, though tall for her age which he guessed was probably about fourteen or fifteen. Bare-legged and bare-footed, she wore a washed-out cotton sundress a couple of sizes too small for her. Before he could reply, she spoke again, turning to address the little barking dog who was hopping up and down beside her: "Wait till Maw sees what we bringin' home tonight, Titch!"

Her hair was magnificent; he'd never seen anything quite like it. It hung down her back to way below her waistline and was unbrushed and unkempt, like unbundled straw. When she hopped down into the ditch, it fell forwards, together with her bowl-cut bangs, to frame her sweetheart-shaped face like a curtain of blinding sunshine.

"Ya don't look like you're gonna get very far tonight, Mister!" she said. "Here, let me help you up." She bent down to give him an arm.

Jake gathered his sapping energy together in a tight ball and grasped her tiny wrist. The girl strained to raise him; beads of sweat broke out on her upper lip, and she swung her hair away and behind her back with a twist of her neck. As the little terrier continued to yap and prance in encouragement, gradually, with the girl's help, he raised himself upright.

After the great effort it had cost him, he staggered, teetering, almost falling back into the muck where he'd felt a modicum of safety not that long before, content to let time pass, content to allow his troubles to fade and morph in cloud-patterns. But the girl stabilised him, then took his face in her hands and in a slow steady voice, as if talking to a half-wit who needed things spelled out, she said, "I'm... not... gonna... leave... you... here... to... die... tonight, Mister!" She kept at him, pushing and pulling him up and out of the ditch, until he lurched into the race. As he stood there swaying, she slapped his cheek, hard and strong. The impact startled him, stung him out of his deathly reverie.

"Not a bad specimen of the male species, aren't ya, then?" she said, looking him up and down. Holding onto his arm, she brushed crud and straw from his shoulders and back, then turned and pointed.

"Now, listen here good and proper, Mister!" she said. "If ya can summon the strength to walk — which I suggest you do if you have any handle left on life itself, mind — follow this here track back to the road. Then head north till ya come to the sign 'Skulls Farm'. If ya turn in thar, ya'll see the house. You can wash up by the tank. Watch out for Granpaw though; he don't like no strangers." She laughed and called Titch to her. "Come on, boy, back to work. Let's git these 'ere girls down the race and in ta the milking shed 'fore their udders burst!"

Then she slapped Jake hard on his back and gave him a firm push in the right direction. "Off ya go then. That way!" She pointed. "Keep going straight, ok? Until ya see the road; then head north, like I said." Jake hesitated, still unsteady on his feet. "And ya better get going afore I box ya! Go on, now! On yer bike! It's not far; will only take you about twenty minutes!" She turned again to the dog. "Looks like we gonna be taking care of him for a while, don't it, Titch?" she said.

As Jake trudged along the race like a sleepwalker, the thought of the road up ahead heading true north to Skulls Farm seemed to be a compass of sorts that kept him putting one foot in front of the other. The hives had started, and it was hard for him not to scratch the rising angry red welts on his arms and face which were adding to his misery. As he plodded along, he tried to distract himself by going over the chain of events that had landed him in this mess.

He knew he was lucky to be alive; hang, he was lucky to be upright, let alone walking. And the girl had been helpful. But it dawned on him that he had been so unprepared for what had taken place that he had nothing with him, no gear, no cash. He thought of his savings book lying safely in the top drawer of his tallboy at his flat back in Whangārei. He had a couple of grand saved that would have helped him on his way, but he realised it would be a while before he would be fit enough to go back for it. And it would be bloody risky now too.

When he'd left home a few years earlier to seek his fortune, Mum had said he should buckle down and get over his wild ways; move on from the teenage delinquency that had earned him a bad reputation and police attention in their small country town.

"Make good, Boyo," she'd said. And he had. He hadn't expected things to be easy; all he'd ever hoped for was for Lady Luck to see him through with a little bit of the good stuff. He'd do the rest, he'd decided; pull up his socks, cut his own track, mind his own business, avoid trouble. Make Mum proud.

He'd been a good kid until his mid-teens when he'd started hating school. He found it demeaning having to squeeze his large frame into the confined space between the desk and its fixed bench seat, and he would fidget and wriggle all day, longing for the bell to ring. He also found it infinitely tedious listening to the teachers rabbit on and on about theoretical stuff that had no bearing on his daily reality. And he felt ridiculous wearing the ubiquitous shirt-and-shorts uniform of the schoolboy — he looked like a man, sounded like a man, could work like a man. He was deeply frustrated and busting to break free and get out into the real world.

All he'd ever done before, after he'd grown out of getting under his mother's feet, was deliver milk, mow lawns, bale hay, and sweep floors at the local grocery store. But he'd heard about the labourer selections outside the county offices in Whangārei and how darn easy it was these days for a keen youngster to get a good paying job in the construction industry. He'd packed his rucksack, stuffed the coin he'd put aside over his teenage years into his pocket, and headed north. He was immediately picked out of the line-up and hired by an outfit called South Pacific Projects.

He took to this, his first proper job, like a duck to water, relishing being out of doors in all weathers and physically active. He also enjoyed working alongside other blokes; the camaraderie of men was something he'd been starved of growing up with a single mother. Granted, it wasn't her fault that Dad had gone AWOL in Vietnam and never returned home, but he was full of envy for boys who went camping and trout fishing or duck hunting with their dads on weekends, or played cricket with them in their backyards of an evening.

The other workers showed him the ropes, explaining what

was expected, and Jake enjoyed the friendly ribbing that he, as a newcomer, was subjected to, and the macho banter that was commonplace on a construction site. At night, at the working men's hostel where he and other single blokes had been billeted, he slept like the dead, properly tired out for the first time ever. The grub there was great; Ma Mahoney, who ran the canteen, reckoned Jake needed feeding up and was always plying 'seconds' and 'thirds' on him. As the months passed, he felt himself filling out and beefing up, properly fitting into his large frame at last.

It was the early eighties, and the country was booming under the rollout of Prime Minister Muldoon's government's THINK BIG campaign, intended to boost economic growth. Large projects were under way; the oil refinery at Marsden Point was looking to expand and the construction of a larger port at Whangārei Heads which could accommodate oceangoing cargo vessels was mooted. Jake found himself in the right place at the right time. A young blood; well-built, well raised. Work ready. Life ready. If you showed up on time, did what was asked of you and put in the hard yards, it wasn't long before you got a hand up. Best of all was the way SPP's owner took a shine to Jake from the start, offering the lad every opportunity.

Gerven Millen had truckloads of family money behind him and was on a mission to change the world by changing the local landscape. After completing a few medium-scale construction projects, his company was now poised for the big time, having secured the contract to build Whangārei's first ever shopping mall.

Gerv wore khaki safari suits, large square steel-rimmed glasses, white slip-on brothel creepers, and a comb-over. This was a shoulder-length-long piece of wavy hair on the right side of his head that he glued over the top of his bald pate with Brylcreem, tucking it behind his left ear to secure it. But even a light breeze could be troublesome; it was invariably windy here at the coast. When the comb-over malfunctioned, Gerv resembled a character from Mad Magazine, and people nudged each other, pointing to it and tittering. He had even, on occasion, suffered the indignity of having the long piece of hair sucked out of his car window when he'd cracked it open a few inches to discard a cigarette butt. This comb-over issue was the bane of his life and the reason why an essential piece of his attire was the comb he kept tucked down the side of one of his long socks, to sort out the problem quickly and efficiently when it arose.

Within a couple of years Jake had moved up the ranks on the mall site, having earned the tickets required to operate heavy machinery. His pay had gone up commensurate with his new skills, and he was running a couple of teams, managing their workflow and performance. The other blokes liked Jake even though he was younger than many of them; he was practical and fair, gave praise where praise was due, but didn't take any shit either. The boss was impressed. Jake covered all the bases. Jake got things done. And Jake was the go-to guy when things didn't go according to plan and needed sorting out, which was par for the course on a complex construction site.

Jake soon found he had loads of dosh over each week after he'd paid his living expenses and wired his mum some money. Gerv introduced Jake to the manager at BNZ and Jake walked out with a savings book with a big, fat balance in it and a line of credit which got him into his first set of wheels. He'd learned to drive back on his uncle's farm in the Waikato, so getting his licence proved a mere formality. The greatest day of his life was the day he drove out of the Easy Driver car dealership on Herekino Street in a two-year-old electric blue Toyota Levin GT-V. He felt like a million dollars and knew it was only the beginning of things and believed he just couldn't put a foot wrong.

Towards the end of Jake's fifth year with the company, Gerv was gearing up to tender on the construction work required for the refinery expansion. This was to be the biggest project S.P.P. had ever undertaken. Gerv needed dependable people around him who he could reliably delegate to, a team of go-getters in the upper echelons of his company who could manage particular aspects of large jobs, so he could spread the responsibility around. Soon he was inviting Jake into his office on a regular basis and involving him in discussions about the project. They decided to contract a team of specialist quantity surveyors to do the complicated costings while S.P.P. concentrated on manpower and materials requirements, and worked on producing a timeline for the roll out of work. Gerv told Jake that after Christmas they'd fly out to the site in his helicopter so they could perform a recce from the air.

Millen's Robinson R22 was hangared at the company's storage depot in the industrial area along Old Port Road. Jake had spent a lot of time polishing the black beast when he'd first started working for Gerv, so was well acquainted with it. Gerv was always skiting about the R22, running through its specs and configurations, talking up its performance and abilities, and Jake was a willing audience, in absolute awe of the machine. Gerv would sometimes drive out to the depot with Jake on the pretext of checking in with the storeman or some other business, but these visits always ended with Gerv saying, "Come on, Jake, let's check on The Bird."

Jake admired the way Gerv had given the machine a pet name. He'd also given names to his fleet of private vehicles, which included an olive-green British import BMW Cabriolet that he'd named "Barracuda", and a classic red Mercedes Sports he'd had shipped in from Germany, that he called "Hot Stuff". On the odd occasion when Gerv took Hot Stuff out for a spin and Jake was lucky enough to ride along, Gerv would look at Jake wistfully and say, "You know, Jake, the dealer told me the Beatles used to drive around in this baby when they were playing in Hamburg back in the early sixties. I wonder how many birds they screwed on the back seat, eh?" Jake had listened with rapt attention. He'd been impressed. Very impressed.

The talk around the company was that Jake was rapidly becoming Gerv's protégée, his right-hand man, his sidekick. It was only a short leap of the imagination from that to, "Jake is being moulded into the boss's surrogate son." After all, Gerv only had one child, a daughter, and one day he would need someone to pass the baton to, to run S.P.P. This gossip gave Jake even more reason to work hard and do well. And it wasn't beyond the scope of *his* imagination that he, too, might one day be able to learn how to pilot the R22.

Jake eventually reached the road to Skulls Farm. As he trudged along, he hoped it wasn't much further; he was dehydrated, in pain, on the verge of collapse. The fact that he had nothing with him gnawed at the fringes of his mind like a dog worries a bone: he would now be dependent upon the kindness of strangers. The girl had seemed pretty feral; wild and unkempt, a bit of a hillbilly. Who knew what awaited him at the farmhouse? What her family might be like?

"Fuckit!" he yelled. If only he had some money with him. But it wasn't as if he'd actually planned this trip, had he? "Fuckit! Fuckit! Fuckit!" he shouted now, screaming out to the vacant sky and the parched earth in anger and frustration.

Suddenly, it dawned on him that he'd been framed. He felt it in his bones.

But why? By whom? He was a good grafter; kept his head down and his bum up. The boss' blue-eyed boy. Perhaps he had an enemy; someone who was jealous of him and the way Gerv favoured him. Someone who resented his quick ascendancy up the company hierarchy. Maybe this person had concocted some bullshit about Jake, so bad that Gerv had lost it before even researching the facts? Or maybe someone higher up the chain had fucked up a job and he, still the junior-project-manager-in-training, had been made the fall guy? He knew Gerv had a temper and had witnessed him exercising it on others; he was ruthless if crossed, everybody knew that. But the way he'd treated Jake was beyond the pale...What could possibly have justified it?

Hang on a minute. A stray thought began to form in Jake's mind. Could it have been Gerv's daughter, Samantha? But why would she have landed him in it? He thought she *liked* him; her behaviour certainly indicated that was the case. When he'd turned up early at the work Christmas do at the hangar to discover her prepping the food and whatnot before the guests arrived, she'd come on pretty strong. Jake didn't have much experience with women, but he'd seen enough girlie calendars hanging in site offices and behind hostel doors to have gotten a pretty good idea of what cut it as far as female good looks were concerned. Sam was a North Shore princess, private school educated. Sam was cool as a cucumber; butter wouldn't melt. Sam was sixteen going on twenty-six. Sam was sex on legs, a cute blonde bombshell. Sam's waist was tiny, her boobs more than a handful each, and the generous curves of her hips and backside the stuff of wet dreams.

And Sam couldn't take "NO" for an answer. Throughout the Christmas shindig, she never once let up on the hot rash attention she plied on Jake, and he'd been hard pressed to avoid her. He'd felt his skin beginning to prickle and had started sneezing uncontrollably as if an allergic reaction was coming on, but there was no privet at the depot as far as he knew; this was an industrial, urban landscape. Of course, he didn't want to be rude either, so he humoured her — she was the boss' daughter, after all. Later, when a good time had been had by all and the guests started drifting off, Gerv had left Jake and Samantha to tidy up so he could go and visit his squeeze at the Lotus Massage Parlour downtown. It was not a very well-kept secret that Gerv had frequented the place for years, ever since his wife had walked out on him.

"Now you take care of Samantha, hear? Get my little princess home safe and sound and tucked up in bed by midnight, Jake. We don't want her carriage turning into a pumpkin, now, do we?" he'd instructed Jake on leaving.

A good hour later, Jake was still trying to get the girl to get into his car. And the only one who'd turned into a pumpkin was him. He'd given it to her good and proper, bending her over the Christmas buffet table between the leftover glazed ham and wilted silly-season salads, raising her legs in the air and holding her ankles one in each hand, just like he steadied the handles of a live pneumatic drill when breaking up concrete.

The black Robinson R22 stood majestically beside them with her name, 'SAMANTHA', blazoned across its livery as if she was a hot dame from the Vietnam era. Jake had been admiring the shiny black fuselage as it towered over them, its high-sheen polycarbonate body curving past them to meet its tail rotor system, but was distracted from the business at hand when he noticed some streaks of dirt marring the almost-mirror image it produced. He was busy making a mental note to polish The Bird at his earliest opportunity, when he realised the image he was seeing reflected back at him was of Sam writhing and squirming and squealing on the buffet table beneath him. As a result, he'd got his rocks off rather more quickly than he would otherwise have liked.

Jake eventually got Sam home safely and soon she returned to her mother in Auckland. Gerv was relieved he didn't have to shoulder the responsibility of the girl anymore and shared his concerns with Jake over beers one Friday evening: "Thank God the holidays are over and Samantha has gone back home, son. It's the first time her mother has allowed her to come and stay with me since the divorce. I knew if anyone messed with her, I'd never get to see her again. I adore that little cupcake more than my life is worth. More even than that cute Asian doll down at the massage parlour who's currently tugging on my heart strings..."

Tugging on more than his heart strings, Jake thought, but he said nothing. What could he say? Jake's experience with women was limited, amounting to a few fumbled gropes at the pub on a Saturday night when, after the game, someone punched in a selection of slow songs on the juke box. He sensed somehow that Sam had suckered him, that he'd be for the high jump if Gerv ever found out what had happened. He decided to stay mum but intended to make good, even if it meant he'd have to marry her down the track. Hopefully there'd be no blowback and things would carry on as before. He was confident that there was lots of time to sort this out the right way; hang, the girl hadn't even graduated college yet. In the meantime, as Jake fantasised about next year's Christmas do, wondering whether he'd be treated to a repeat performance by Samantha alongside The Bird, he'd concentrate on consolidating his position of importance and indispensability in the company, and make sure he was in a position to make her a good husband down the track.

When, shortly into the new year, Gerv told Jake they were helicoptering out to the refinery site, Jake was incredibly excited. During the flight, Gerv seemed unnatually quiet, not his usual puffed up garrulous self, but Jake was distracted by the scenery — Whangārei Harbour was certainly a sight to see from the air — and he figured Gerv was concentrating on piloting.

When they'd been in the air for about ten minutes, Gerv said, "Time for some fun, eh? Loops and nose dives. You ain't lived till you've experienced the thrill of what a helicopter can do in the air!"

Jake was surprised; he wasn't aware that helicopters were capable of performing aerobatics. When The Bird started spinning through the air, his head began to reel and he told Gerv it was making him feel crook.

Gerv turned to look at Jack and suddenly his demeanour completely switched, like a gear change from cruise to reverse in a split second. He screwed his face up, his pupils retracted to needle points, and he lifted his upper lip into a snarl, baring his teeth. "That'll serve you bloody right, you fucking arsehole!" he shouted.

Jake was taken aback. They had always rubbed along pretty well, he thought, and he wondered what was going on. Next thing, totally unexpectedly, Gerv let go of the controls and launched into a frenzied attack on Jake. He'd been a welterweight boxer as a youngster — he was short and stocky and hard as an ox — and soon landed a few left jabs and right uppercuts which found their mark on the sides of Jake's head and upper body. Jake had been so surprised by the attack, he hadn't even thought to defend himself, let alone fight back. And when a further blow to his temple left him thoroughly dazed, Gerv leant over him, pinning Jake's arms down, and unbuckled his seatbelt harness.

The next few minutes were hellish. Gerv grabbed the controls again and executed a few tight loops and erratic manoeuvres. Jake found he was bouncing around the walls and the ceiling of the cockpit, retching from the depths of his stomach. In the confusion, he managed to grab hold of a strop, and hung from it, in mid-air, as the helicopter veered vertically downwards, nose-diving through space. When Jake saw the ground rushing up to meet The Bird at 300 km per hour, Ma Mahoney's big breakfast ended up all over Gerv's head and shoulders. He spun around and looked up at Jake with a face full of venom and hatred. "You bloody cunt!" he yelled.

Then he pulled The Bird up hard. Jake lost hold of the strop he was hanging from and fell back into his seat where the G-force pinned him down with such immense pressure, he was paralysed. The skin on his face was sucked down also, like a reverse facelift. Gerv suddenly wrenched forward on the stick, flinging the machine into a steep descent again, and Jake's body flew upwards once more, hitting the ceiling. As the ground fast approached, Gerv pulled back hard and slowed the machine to a hover a few metres above the ground. Jake landed awkwardly across his seat. Gerv reached over him, slid the passenger door open and pushed and kicked Jake until he fell out of the cabin. Jake's last glimpse of Gerv was of his comb-over flying like a flag in the turbulent air from the rotors, having parted company with his bald pate. Jake knew that losing control of his comb-over would have made Gerv as mad as a snake. It was the one thing in his life that he didn't have complete control over.

As Jake fell through the air, he believed it was all over, Rover. He knew the shiny rotary blades of The Bird were spinning at 450 revolutions a minute. Gerv had told him so when he'd first introduced Jake to the machine, boasting about how powerful it was, how amazingly manoeuvrable, how fast and fuel efficient. Each of those blades was handling a centrifugal force in excess of four tonne; a force that could rip one of the blades out of the rotary hub at any moment and cut Jake up into hundreds of pieces of meat. Bugger dying of sunstroke and dehydration; he might have ended up as hawk tucker, lying strewn out across that paddock in little pieces of flesh and bone.

He realised now, it was a miracle he'd survived being pushed out of a helicopter a few metres above ground. That was something. Hang, that was everything. Lady Luck hadn't deserted him quite yet.

He needed time to rest and recover, to figure things out, make a plan. Maybe he'd go back, explain what had happened and what his intentions were, sort things. As far as he was concerned, he was an innocent man, the victim not the perpetrator. And it was partly Gerv's fault anyway; he should have taken Samantha home himself. He was responsible for her, after all, and answerable to her mother. Or had Samantha engineered the whole thing? Jake remembered how, about thirty seconds after Gerv had left the party, Samantha had started rubbing up against him, kissing him and nibbling his neck, grabbing his arms and wrapping them around her torso, placing his hands on her buttocks and pushing her pointy tits against his chest, and he'd said, "What the hell?" and she'd said, "Hell, what?" and he'd said, "Your Dad said I had to take you home," and she'd said, "Daddy's not *my* boss; Daddy doesn't call the shots on me," and he'd said, "But it's late," and she'd said, "I turn into a vixen on the stroke of midnight," and he'd said, "That's an hour away," and she'd said, "I'm warming up to it."

And when she'd said that Jake knew he was a goner.

Gerv would hardly forgive him though when he found out his little 'princess' was no longer a virgin. Probably hadn't been for quite some time, judging by the way she'd behaved. Life wasn't fair, Jake thought, it wasn't fucking fair. Just when he thought he was finally getting somewhere and could write home and tell Mum all about it, make her proud, he'd been served a curved ball. That would have been bad enough, but the bloody bat was also warped.

When Jake reached the sign, 'Skulls Farm', hanging askew at the side of the road on crooked posts and crowned with a bovine skull, he turned into the driveway. The homestead loomed up ahead of him, a short distance from the road. A gracious Victorian villa, rundown but still impressive, surrounded by the usual wide, raised veranda, and shaded by mature oak trees. A mass of colourful dahlias bloomed along the front of the house, bordered by a concrete path that provided access to wide steps leading up to an imposing front door. Sash windows gaped open and muslin drapes sucked outwards in the evening breeze. Jake immediately warmed to the place — it vaguely reminded him of his childhood home: a working man's cottage constructed during the same era. This house was far less kempt than his mother's had been, but infinitely more grand.

He shuffled down the driveway towards the water tank hulking against the side of the house and opened the tap, scooping large handfuls of water into his mouth and splashing his face, neck and arms. There was a clearing here, and although the slanting sun still burned hot on his back, the feel and taste of the water was a blessing. Glancing down now, he saw how fresh blood had darkened his sleeve, spreading like red ink through blotting paper. But in the same moment, he felt resolve welling up inside of himself, coursing through his veins like the ever-moving sap which, cell by infinitesimal cell, nurtured the huge trees towering overhead. Yeah, he thought, he'd give Lady Luck another chance. He needed succour: water, food, sleep, medical assistance. No harm, was there? He could always cut loose at any sign of danger.

Suddenly a shadow fell across him. He straightened up as best he could and turned. An old man stood behind him, legs wide apart, hands resting on his hips.

"What the hell do ya fink yer doin'?" the old geezer barked, his eyes narrowing to slits, as he looked Jake over.

Jake shut the tap off and pulled himself upright to show respect. "The young girl said I should call in here…"

"Right," came the reply. The old man's arms jerked up like

a marionette's, his hands coming to rest on the braces holding up his old-fashioned button-up serge trousers. He tucked his thumbs beneath the braces, pulled them away from his chest then let them go, allowing them to snap back into position over his grubby checked shirt. He stared hard at Jake, moving his head from side to side while shrugging his shoulders, as if slacking off the tension in his neck.

"Well, well. As a rule, I don't take kindly to strangers turning up here unannounced. By the look of you, though, I'm guessing you come bearing some tales a' derring-do. And I do enjoy a good yarn. Can't see no harm in havin' a bit of male company aroun' here every now and agin'. Keeps my girls on their toes, ya know, and gives me a break from their gabblin' on and on 'bout nothin' but the work needs doin' roun' here..."

"I'd appreciate your help, sir," said Jake.

"Come with me," the old man continued, beckoning with a finger.

The two men moved around the side of the house, up the front steps, and onto the veranda. The old chap motioned for Jake to take a seat in a wicker chair and did the same. Shortly he fumbled in his shirt pocket and pulled out a wad of chewing tobacco, broke off a bit, and held it out to Jake.

"Here then... fancy a bit of baccy? So, what name do they call you by, sonny?"

"Name's Jake, sir. Jake Lazarus."

"And what brings you to these parts, eh?"

"Just passing through..."

"One of those, ay?" the old man cut in. "Well, well. We've had a few of 'em before; nothin' but trouble, I say. Ya be sure ta mind yer manners, young man, else I'll drive ya off the place with me shotgun, no questions asked!"

"I don't mean no harm, sir. Just need to sort myself out, get back on my feet. I can make it up to you, for sure. Maybe do a bit of work around here, or something."

"Maybe. But there ain't nothin' roun' here for free, young man. And don't ya ever forget it!"

Jake nodded and they sat in silence for a while, chewing on their tobacco. A few scraggly chooks rounded the corner of the house, scratching for pickings in the dirt. A large rooster led the group, jerking his head from side to side, checking that the coast was clear. The old man suddenly sat up very straight and motioned for Jake to be quiet. He watched the chickens intently, squinting as if it improved his vision and craning forward, the chords in his neck tense and protruding. Jake noticed that he was sucking his cheeks vigorously in and out; then he spat a stream of tobacco juice from his mouth, hitting the rooster bull's eye. The bird squawked loudly, causing all the chooks to scatter as raucous laughter filled the air. Jake realised now why the Bantam cock's white plumage was covered in dirty yellow-brown spots — this was obviously a regular sport of the old man's.

"Got ya, ya prick!" he shouted. "That'll teach ya to wake an old man up every bloody morning at sparrow-fart. Hehe." His laughter ended in a wracking paroxysm of coughing and he pointed a shaky bent finger at a bottle on a table nearby.

"Pass... that there... (cough, cough, cough) ... whisky over here... (cough)...quick smart, son. I believe... (cough, cough) ... it's time for my medication."

Jake passed the bottle and the old man pulled the cork with his teeth. Then he took a great swig, swallowed noisily, cleared the phlegm from his throat, spat again, and started laughing — the kind of laugh that would make a baby burst into frightened tears.

Jake smiled. He rather liked the old fellow, sensing he was more human than he'd at first appeared. He relaxed into the wobbly wicker chair he was sitting in, leaning back against a worn tapestry cushion, resting his head against the wall of the house. The old man passed him the bottle and motioned for him to have a drink. The alcohol coursed through Jake's veins like lightening and he felt his pain and exhaustion begin to soften into something more diffuse and insensate. As he lifted the bottle to his mouth for a second slug, he saw the silhouettes of three women, the young girl, and the prancing little foxy making their way down the drive towards the house, etched like stencils against the setting sun.

"Here comes trouble with a capital 'T', said Granpaw, winking at Jake and slapping his thigh.

Jake noticed that the women and the girl were like cardboard cutout dolls, virtually identical, just different ages and sizes. They all shared the same halo of dishevelled golden hair, and the long lean limbs of women of the land.

The old man watched Jake watch the womenfolk walking towards them. "Well, well, my, my, you appear to be dumbstruck, young man!" he said. "Didn't I tell you that all the wimin' in the Skulls family were right bloody good lookers? But the fun ain't started yet, sonny boy. When they see how bad those wounds a' yours need doctorin' and how sore you need cleanin' up, they're gonna fuss and fight over ya like groupies at a rock concert!"

Granpaw guffawed loudly again, fit to burst a person's ears, until another paroxysm of coughing overtook him. "That little Madge is the feistiest of them all, though — wouldn't surprise me if she got her claws into you good and proper!"

"Much appreciate the help, sir," Jake said. "As I said, I'll make it up to you."

Being looked after and fought over by a brood of good-looking country women was beginning to sound quite attractive. Jake had a feeling he would soon forget all about The Bird.

Under the Pōhutukawa Tree

Although I am Pākehā, I never knew my family or any other hapū or iwi, other than Ngā Puhi. Left for dead on the steep tangled slopes of Tama Hunga where Ngati Whātua attacked our small group of European settlers travelling overland, I would have perished there — deep in the undergrowth of the forest wild where I fell from my mother's arms as she fled, screaming, from her attackers — were it not for Old Marama who found me later that fateful day while grubbing for huhu under the rotting bark of ancient, fallen trees.

I did not learn the significance of these events, nor did I understand how they were to play a part in my future, until I was much older. Moreover, from whence my own people had come, bound for where, who they were, and how many were close family — these were mysteries I would never discover, for I was but an infant when Marama rescued me. Had she not come across me where I lay in a shaft of moonlight, curled like a shining shell and wet with dew on a bed of fern fronds, I would have joined the others of my kind lying lifeless nearby, for it was the winter solstice — Matariki — the days were short and dark, the nights long and bitter, and the cold wet breath of death was ever close.

And so, my journey towards my destiny continued in the arms of my saviour as she hurried back towards the coast carrying the news of this latest Ngāti Whātua attack to her own people. Growing warm again, and dry, under the shelter of her whakatipu, I lay in a hammock created by a fold in her sealskin robe, as she picked her way down the steep bush-clad slopes I had traversed with my birth family only a few hours before. And it seemed to me as if one of the great trees of the forest had gathered me up into its branches, cleaving me to itself. Nestling against its strong trunk, its dense foliage folded around me, it was as if this strong, tall tree carried me out of that jungle of darkness and horror into the only future I would ever know.

When Marama reached the lowlands she made her way by the light of the moon to a jade river's edge where she pulled a small waka from the undergrowth. Stowing me in its hull, she allowed the outgoing current to propel us downstream to a natural harbour where the land met the sea. Here she beached the canoe at a small settlement where fires blazed and crackled in the dark and the great domed sky above shimmered with uncountable constellations.

Others of her kind came forward to greet us and help us ashore, their voices exchanging information in a strange tongue, formerly unknown to me. Soon Marama took her place around one of the fires with her whānau and nestled down to sleep with me swaddled close beside her. Thus, my life as a foundling began in this new land to which my own people had recently migrated. And unbeknownst to me, this place — where Marama lived with her hapū on the shores of the selfsame ocean from whence my own people had come — was to become my eternal home.

Because Marama was childless, the colour of my skin did not concern her; she knew only that I was human and alive, a wonder of sorts, a treasure. She had no milk for me, so other lactating mothers put me to their breasts, as if I was their own. As I grew, she nourished me with huhu sweetened with cabbage tree sap, pushing the grubs down my throat like tui feed their young, together with morsels of raw fish, and pipi and kina too, all first softened in her own mouth. When I began to teethe, she gave me strips of dried shark meat to chew on to ease the cutting. She carried these life-saving victuals in a sack of cured stingray skin which hung from her waistband, alongside the tools she used to prize molluscs from their shells and dig for root vegetables.

And so, in the arms of my kuia I grew into childhood, learning well the ways of Ngā Puhi.

Marama called me Atarau, meaning moonlight or moonbeam, for she herself had been named for the moon. And my name was tika; the love Marama gave me shone through me like her own light. Her whānau and hapū came to revere me as she did; for my skin that shone pale and iridescent like the inside of an oyster shell, for my white frothy hair that was like the spume that rode the waves, and for my olive-green eyes that glistened like precious, polished pounamu.

As time passed, I learned that Marama's people had lived in this land for many generations — Aotearoa, the land of the large volcanic islands, the land of the long white clouds.

During the temperate seasons of the year when the sun was strong and the days were long, we roamed the indented bays of our territory harvesting kai moana and sleeping under the shelter of the pōhutukawa trees which grew prolifically where the bush fringed the beach. We tamariki spent hours playing in the clear blue-green shallows of the inland harbour where three rivers flowing from the Tama Hunga Ranges converged before they flowed out to the ocean. The tepid tranquil waters of the estuary washed the grime and stiffness of winter from our bodies and our hair, its saltiness healing any sores or sickness that afflicted us. Huge rays glided silently past beneath us and schools of small darting fish nibbled at our fingers and toes causing us to squeal and squirm with delight.

At the time of the summer solstice, our young men paddled the deeper channels of the harbour spearing kapetā, the small spotted shark, and returned to shore with huge catches which the women gutted, filleted, and prepared for drying, stringing them out on manuka poles across the beach. The pervasive smell of shark meat drying in the sun guided our warriors home from regional scouting trips up and down the coast, and stayed with us through the long, unforgiving winters of our lives, when the dried meat sustained us, for often there was no other.

Each day, as the sun moved across the sky towards its zenith, Marama would call me away from the other little ones and take me into the shade of the bush, fearing the sun would take her moonbeam from her. There, under cover of the forest canopy, she'd bathe me in a creek to cool my pink-hot skin. Then we would gather food to take back to our family — pikopiko, pūhā, kōwhitiwhiti and kawakawa. Marama also taught me how to construct a shelter and build a fire, how to read the weather, and how to interpret the sights and sounds of the bush. And in that hush and gloom of green, the little faeries which lived on fields of velvety moss — tiny colourful native orchids — became my playmates, and the whistles and calls of birdsong my waiata.

In the evenings we would return to our hapū on the beach. After eating our shared meal and exchanging information about our day, we'd prepare for sleep by digging hollows in the warm sand to nestle into. As we lay there under the wheeling night sky, replete on a diet of kai moana and with firelight dancing in our eyes, our kaumātua — the old ones — would speak of the language of the stars and of all creation, until the lulling of the tide became our lullaby and the smoke curling from the manuka fires shaped our dreams.

But the long, sunny days of our summers always came to an end, rapidly fading into memory. When the great red star, Rehua, began to fade in the night sky as she moved northwards, the season of cool mists and gentle rains came down upon us, and the waters of the harbour grew colder and greyer. This was when we began to prepare to move to higher ground and the shelter of the bush, spending the shortening days repairing our raupō huts at our pā at Pukematekeo on the slopes of Tama Hunga, replenishing our beds of fern and bracken, laying in stocks of firewood and storing kūmara and taro in subterranean pits, reinforcing our palisades and other fortifications, and clearing undergrowth from the escape trenches so they would again be useable, if needed.

After we relocated to the pā for winter, the days grew rapidly shorter as Matariki drew near. And in the dark of the year when the cold, lingering grip of frost held the earth fast and a hoary chill came down upon the land, we huddled close together around the smoky fires in our shelters, drawing our kiwi feather cloaks tight, staying dry and warm and waiting out the weather. It was at this time of year that rain became the subject of my instruction, until I could read rain as well as I later learned to fly through space and time: the sound and feel of rain in all its ways of being: spitting, lashing, trickling, splashing, blinding, drizzling, pounding, pattering, battering.

Blue and green were thus the perennial colours of my childhood: the pāua shades of sea and sky, the greenstone gradations of bush and forest. And always, the ever-changing mystery of the blue-green riverine waterways that crisscrossed our territory, reflecting the colour and mood of the bush that grows dense and lush along their banks, collecting every drop of rain that falls and allowing it to drain, down, down, down to the nadir, to meet the ocean which welcomes it with open arms.

And as I matured, the long history of my people and the story of their origins became mine too, as did the names of their enemies. So, too, in time, the events surrounding the death of my own kin were shared with me.

In the year of my birth, 1821, Ngā Puhi from the north, including Marama's own hapū, had conquered Ngāti Whātua at Te Ikā a Ranganui under the leadership of Hongi Hika, and driven them and their sub tribes south. Henceforth, Ngā Puhi had come to dominate the land as far south as Tāmaki Makaurau, controlling access to the plentiful fishing grounds of Te Kawau Bay where our hapū lived, and occupying the offshore islands. But small groups of marauding Ngāti Whātua warriors continued to raid the area from hideouts and strongholds to the south and west, slaughtering the unwary for muskets and other supplies, while plotting their rebellion against Ngā Puhi's invasion of their territory.

This was how my birth family had come to perish. They had been settlers — missionaries perhaps, or gum diggers, or perhaps even escaped convicts from Botany Bay; we would never know as, save for myself, they had all perished. A seafaring vessel had probably beached them to the east, and it had been their sad misfortune to have been travelling overland at that time — perhaps to join others of their kind who had settled on the Kaipara — and to have crossed the path of a Ngāti Whātua war party.

But these random attacks by Ngāti Whātua diminished throughout my childhood as our Ngā Puhi warriors drove them further and further south, to the Hauraki Plains and the Waikato. And so, my tribe had entered a time of peace and plenty as I grew from babyhood to young adulthood under the shadow of Tama Hunga, on the shores of Te Kawau Bay.

In my thirteenth year, when I came of age, Marama gifted me a taonga she had taken from my dead mother's neck the night she had found me. She'd kept it safely all these years, wrapped in a parcel of flax she'd buried at the base of a pōhutukawa tree. Marama had often taken me to visit this tree which grew on the headland where the harbour met the open sea. Even though she had been my mother since infancy there had been no whenua to bury, so she had buried my mother's taonga instead.

Hard and cold to the touch, not carved from shell or bone or stone, and blindingly shiny with no correlation of colour in the natural world, it reminded me of my otherness, making me feel uneasy. But my people pressed around me, comforting me, saying their ancestors had sent me to them to bring them the power of the Pākehā, that the magic of the white man had held them safe these past many, many years since Marama had found me, and that I, Atarau, was tapairu for Marama — the first born female of a high ranking family. They said I should wear the taonga my birth mother had bequeathed me with great pride, and go forward to meet my destiny.

I did my hapū's bidding, but from the moment the object touched my skin and was fastened around my neck, foreboding became my constant companion.

I fell ill with a clammy fever and a dull pain gnawed at my insides, inducing an unknown weakness and weariness in my limbs. Soon I began to bleed from between my legs, as if the very life force was draining from me. I couldn't leave my pallet of bracken and lay there for days with Marama weeping over me, crying, "Mauri tu, mauri ora, mauri noho, mauri mate — When we stand up and strive the desire to live is strong, when we give up or lie down we are more prone to sickness and death". Her pleas did little to alleviate my symptoms as I drifted in a fitful stupor, my dreams populated by the whispers of my dead birth family. They were near, like wairua in the trees, calling to me endlessly, and I was lost, helpless, fear of the unknown darkening my world like an eclipse of the sun.

Soon, there came a day when the ghostlike voices of my ancestors were drowned out by the louder and more insistent shouts of my hapū as they ran backwards and forwards in a state of panic, preparing for an attack. The news had reached our shores that Ngāti Whātua was returning with massive reinforcements from the Plains and Waikato tribes to win their land back.

They came from the south and from the west, from the plains and from the sea, to reclaim their ancestral territory. Their paddles cut the water into huge swathes of foam as they travelled up the coastline in their large, decorated war canoes, and upon reaching our bay, they beached their waka taua and their warriors swarmed ashore, trampling the bush in every direction, spooking the birds, flushing them from the forest canopy to fly screaming into the air.

In my sickness and my confusion, I believed the attack had something to do with me.

The kairākau who hacked Marama to death exclaimed and gesticulated about the strange taonga that hung from my neck, as if they knew of me, had sought me out. Together with some other notable members of our hapū, they threw me into a waka and took us to their encampment at Bostaquet Bay on Te Kawau Island. After beating me unconscious they hung me from a stake they had planted in the sand while they built a great fire. At sunset, they cut me down and dismembered me, throwing parts of my body into the hangi with some of the other rangatira. "To kill the spirit of the white witch from the north; to quell her Pākehā magic," they said. "And to sweeten the meal."

When my spirit left my body I travelled to Cape Reinga, to the dwelling place of Hine Nui Te Pō, Gate Keeper of the Longest Night, seeking entrance to the spirit world, as all our people do when they die. She came to welcome me, her seaweed hair flowing in long maroon braids behind her, her red eyes glittering like pōhutukawa flowers, her sharp barracuda teeth green with slime, her nails growing long and twisted to the ends of the earth.

"Where do you come from?" she asked me.

I told her of my tribe's history, my life on the shores of Te Kawau Bay.

"And where are you going?" the Great Lady of the Crossing continued, testing me. "Where is the place of your ancestral origins?"

But to these questions I had no answers, for I had no known home, no knowledge of the origins of my ancestors.

"You must return to Te Kawau Bay until you discover where your true resting place is, child: the home of your blood ancestors," the Lady of the Dark and of the Light told me.

And so, having no choice, no direction home, I returned to the shores of Te Kawau, close to where my bones lie still, deep in the sand at Bostaquet Bay.

When I first returned to the area, only a remnant of my tribe remained and Ngāti Whātua dominated the region once more. My spirit returned to human form and I tried to live again as before, but many who sensed I was not of this world shunned me, so I wandered the land alone. Strange vessels came from the ocean, like floating meeting houses, and pākehā came ashore to broker land deals with Ngāti Whātua. These newcomers trekked inland or sailed up river as far as they could, with horses, oxen, cows, sheep and goats. They felled huge swathes of forest and built wooden dwellings for themselves. While their women kept house, tended livestock, attempted to grow produce in the clearings and schooled their children, the men floated thousands of timber logs down the rivers to ships which carried them away, over the ocean.

Soon Māori began to live differently, covering their skin with western clothing and adopting Pākehā ways, no longer lords of their own domain. Illness spread among the tangata whenua and many died or were killed in the continuing land wars. Hapū were dissolved and our old way of life foregone, as men left their families to work for the Pākehā, in mining or forestry, or on roading and bridge building, and our women went into service in Pākehā homes or on their farms.

I was eventually taken into the employ of a colonist family who grew strange crops we had never seen before, and whose many children had tired their mother to the extent she was weak and needed help to manage her home and family. On Sundays, I accompanied them to a meeting house they called a church, high on a hill above the Mahu Rangi River. For the first time I saw and recognised the taonga my birth mother had left me; a cross like mine hung from the neck of the priest and many members of the congregation gathered there.

I dedicated myself to this religion believing that in this way I would gain knowledge of my own people. But when I asked the priest to help me trace my origins, he told me I was unclean.

He said that a heathen sinner who had lived among the savages would never be accepted into the Christian Kingdom of Heaven.

Many years passed, many changes came upon the land, and I, Atarau, was witness to them all. More and more Pākehā came from far away to settle our islands and Māori formed an alliance to attempt to repel the invaders, but after almost thirty years of the wars of dispossession, the Pākehā triumphed. A Pākehā government was established, under the auspices of the British Crown. Through all these years, I remained undying, yet fading from the eyes of the living, forever seeking the answer to my dilemma, trying to find the key to my destiny, searching for my way home.

But at every passing, Hine Nui Te Po would turn me away once more from the Gate to the Spirit World, sending me back, always, to Te Kawau Bay.

Eventually, when I had returned for perhaps the fifth or sixth passing to Cape Reinga, I became resigned to my situation, believing that I would live as a wairua — a ghost — for the rest of time. But the Lady of the Longest Night proved me wrong.

"You have done much travelling, Atarau," she said, "you have travelled long and far and to no avail. Through many incarnations, despite your earnest desire to reconnect with your own people, you have never been able to discover your ancestral homeland. Thus the time has come for you to forgo your quest, to reconcile yourself to your eternal fate.

"From this day forward, you will live forever as I do, as tipua — a being who lives in the place of the shape shifters, the place that exists between worlds, between the living and the dead. This is a special honour, Atarau, a mark of your unique destiny. I am granting you forthwith the magical powers of kai ure. You will be a guiding light in the darkness to humans who have left their birthplace behind and are forging a new life in Aotearoa. You will set them free from their traumatic memories, you will assuage their losses, you will gift them a new beginning, you will offer them ritual protection and blessing.

"Because your spirit has been in limbo for so many years, you have well learned the ways of flying, of how to travel through time and space," she said. "You will return to Te Kawau Bay as a great white mythical seabird to carry out your life's purpose. Your immortal task will be to fly swiftly to those in need and meet them in their dreams, to bring them comfort and hope."

When I returned to Te Kawau Bay, a mother and her three children often walked the headland beside the open sea where they stopped to rest under my pōhutukawa tree. They were immigrants from a distant land of struggle and strife and it took them a long time to settle in this place, particularly the eldest child who had left his heart behind in the country of his birth.

Thus, I began the work the Queen of the Night had charged me with, flying to this twelve-year-old boy in his dreams and inviting him to mount my back. I carried him across the harbour where he enjoyed swimming and fishing as I, too, had once done as a child. Turning back towards the land, I swooped up the Mahu Rangi River, soaring high above the streets of the settler town of Warkworth. Down below, people stopped to look up and wave at the boy, to welcome him to their land. He let out a sigh as he clung to the mantle above my great wings, and I felt his heart become lighter. We continued our flight down green valleys and up bush-clad gullies to the top of Mount Tama Hunga, where I came to rest on the mountain above the old fortified pā, Pukematekeo, where my people and I had spent all our winters when I was a child. The lad climbed from my back and stood beside me, taking in the great vista of land and ocean and sky that I had laid before him, accepting in this moment his fate, his destiny, as I had accepted mine.

When traversing this country, I often land on a high ridge to survey my territory. From this elevation, you can sight the sea but also look inland. Herons roost here in a row of beech trees bordering a vineyard that slopes away to the northwest, down into the lush, green Matakana Valley. In the distance, the densely forested sprawling torso, hunched shoulders and radar-crowned head of my dwelling place, Tama Hunga, rises to dominate the skyline. In the other direction, to the east, undulating pasture-covered hills fall away steeply through bush-tangled gullies down to the harbour where creeks and streams and rivers converge to meet the bay beyond.

Whenever I pause here, the scene before my eyes presents itself in different ways, depending on the time of year, or time of day. In spring, fresh viridescent leaves tap against each other in the salt-laden breeze sounding out the whisper of a new song. Along the shoreline, the carmine crowns of prolific pōhutukawa shade picnicking families and friends whose summer playground is shared alike by crake, bittern, shell duck, teal, and oystercatcher. Late summer gives way, suddenly, if grudgingly, to early morning mists and the quickening dark of autumn evenings, when the musty smell of ripe grapes hanging on the vines drifts sulphurous-like up the valley. And as the earth turns towards mid-winter — Matariki — the scent of wet clay underfoot and manuka wood smoke drifting in the air accost the senses while rain falls in sheets of wetness across the land.

If you are a rootless migrant far from home, and your waka beaches itself on these isles, step ashore and walk into your future. When you hear the keening of gulls along the shoreline, see the sudden swoop of a hawk as it falls like a thunderbolt to its kill, when you feel the dew-tinselled fan of a fern frond brushing across your cheek, and see herons flying high above you with awkward arching grace, their wings outstretched across the sky, when you return home after a winter walk, windblown and wet to the bone, to hug your cosy fire and draw your loved ones close, and when, on a clear, warm night, you venture outside to marvel at the stars and witness how the wayaway white moon illuminates the darkness, you can lay your burdens down. Your journey is over. You have reached your destination. You are in the right place. And when the landscapes and seascapes that confront you at every bend offer up so many subtle shades of blue and green no paint brush could ever capture and only the heart could hold, know that you will learn, as I did, to make this place your home.

On the headland where the motu meets the sea, a lone pōhutukawa stands, twisted and broken, bent and gnarled, just like me. This is the place you might meet me, watching, waiting, ready to set you free. All manner of creatures live off me. When summer comes, I crown myself in crimson glory. And when the moon is full, Marama still shines down on me.

Acknowledgements

This collection of short fiction has taken many years to come to fruition, during which time I have been much distracted by the stuff of life John Lennon famously referred to as "what happens while you're busy making other plans". Most of these stories were written in stolen moments, small blocks of time carved out of my busy life as a working solo mother juggling different sources of income.

One of my earliest stories, 'Jeannie, Jerome, the Publican and Pope John Paul Too', received a special mention by judge, Jane Westaway, in the BNZ Katherine Mansfield Competition. This small success encouraged me and led to me completing a master's degree in creative writing at Auckland University of Technology (AUT), for which I produced a collection of short stories in which characters reappear and themes reverberate across two hundred years of New Zealand history. The remit I challenged myself with was to explore the craft of short fiction and to treat apposite themes that had universal resonance but were also iconically "Kiwi". Those original stories have been extensively developed, and some have been individually published in various anthologies, journals and online platforms such as Fresh Ink, JAAM, Zoetrope, Flickr and literary e-zines. These and some of my more recent stories are collected here for the first time.

I'd like to express my deep appreciation to my lecturers at AUT, most notably John Cranna (course leader) and Stephanie Johnson (personal mentor), for their guidance and generosity in sharing their deep knowledge of the fictive craft. Also immensely helpful were individual workshops conducted during the course by a slew of other accomplished writers.

I'd also like to thank my cohort at AUT, many of whom have remained friends, for their support and encouragement in the initial stages of writing. I am now working on an epic historical novel which started life as a short story originally presented to this group for critique. When sitting hunched over my desk cursing backache, staring at black squiggles on a flickering screen and bleeding copiously all over the keyboard, I curse them for saying they felt this particular tale was worthy of novel treatment!

Grateful thanks to my students at Mahurangi College, Mahurangi Technical Institute, in various industry training settings, and more recently, at Bream Bay College and Te Rangi Aniwaniwa for allowing me to run a few of these stories by them as teaching materials in senior English classes. Their enthusiastic engagement and feedback is deeply appreciated.

Grateful thanks to the New Zealand Society of Authors for awarding me a manuscript assessment in 2019, and to my assessor, Chris Else, who provided extensive detailed and germane notes which greatly assisted me in developing these stories. I am indebted to his valuable and pertinent feedback.

Special thanks to prolific British short story writer, Brindley Hallam Dennis (aka Mike Smith), for his professional feedback on earlier drafts of the manuscript, and his warm encouragement. When Mike commented that reading *Transit Lounge* was "like being submerged in cold water, the shock of immersion swiftly followed by something profoundly absorbing that demands a slow-burn engagement", I felt I was getting close to achieving my purpose.

Special thanks also to author of historical fiction and award-winning New Zealand journalist, Saige England, for her insightful feedback on earlier drafts of the manuscript and her enthusiastic encouragement. I still glow like a Halloween pumpkin when I remember her saying I had the potential to be one of New Zealand's best short fiction writers.

Very grateful thanks to Mike Johnson and Leila Lees of Lasavia Publishing for believing there is a place for my work in the New Zealand canon and inviting me to join their fold, and to Mike for his generous editorial advice. Also to Rowan Sylva, assistant editor, for providing me with excellent editorial advice and manuscript curation, and to Daniela Gast, designer, for providing outstanding design assistance and creating an attractive publication I am immensely proud of. It is almost impossible to publish a collection of short stories unless you already have a well-established author profile. Thank you to the team at Lasavia for believing that my work is worthy of being available in print. I am forever in your debt.

I am also deeply indebted to Keith Morant (RIP), prolific artist, writer and poet, human rights advocate and humanitarian, who unexpectedly passed away earlier this year after a short illness. Keith generously gifted me an image of his artwork 'In the Midst of Life' for the cover of this book. I trust his memory will be well served by the use of this incredibly evocative piece which perfectly complements the contents of *Transit Lounge*.

Thank you to my dear sister-in-law, Isabbel Cooper, for being my soul sister and for always being there for me and our family. Thanks also to lifelong friends: Charles Mooney, for the use of your peaceful bach at Aramoana to work on the manuscript at a critical phase, and Claire Ellis, for your positive encouragement and feedback when I was on the verge of abandoning this project.

Lastly, my deepest gratitude goes to my close family whose support has been paramount in the production of this book. John Burns, my best friend and partner, is my sounding board for ideas, my first reader and my life support system. Thank you also to my children, Michael, Christine and Suzanne, now adults. You have always been there in the background, quietly supporting me in everything I do, while forging ahead with your own lives.

The encouragement of these close family members has got me through countless drafts, many rejections, and some difficult personal crises, health and otherwise. Needless to say, their love and support and their belief in my abilities mean the world to me.

In closing, I'd like to acknowledge my paternal and maternal grandmothers, Constance Purchase and Louise McCarthy, after whom I am named. Aside from making my life possible by bringing my parents into this world, these amazing women survived two world wars, faced many personal and other challenges, and did not have access to the education and opportunities many women born later in the twentieth century were fortunate enough to receive, myself included. It is to honour my grandmothers and the important role they played in my early life, as well as their contribution to my interest in the human condition and my sense of justice, that I use my initials as my nom-de-plume.

Thank you for reading. I trust I have left you with something of value that will stay with you always.

Jenny Purchase

JCL Purchase (aka Jenny Purchase) was born and raised in Zambia and educated in South Africa where she spent her early adulthood. In 1998, divorced and seeking a new direction in life, she immigrated to Aotearoa New Zealand with her three children. She is a senior secondary teacher of English and French by profession but has also taught an eclectic range of subjects in the adult education sector. Since gaining a master's degree in creative writing, she has published several short stories and worked as a producer on short film projects. She is currently writing a historical novel set in pre-apartheid South Africa and is collecting poetry, prose, and essays for an anthology on solo parenthood. She lives at Marsden Cove on the shores of the Whangārei Harbour with her partner, eleven bookcases, three pianos, a collection of guitars, a dog with googly eyes and two cats who detest each other. She gives thanks daily that her waka washed up on these shores.

www.ingramcontent.com/pod-product-compliance
Lightning Source LLC
Chambersburg PA
CBHW051144190726
48290CB00006B/1994